The Bounty
Hunting Sullivans

The Bounty
Hunting Sullivans

Richard M Beloin MD

Print information available on the last page.

Rev. date: 10/30/2020

To order additional copies of this book, contact:
Xlibris
844-714-8691
www.Xlibris.com
Orders@Xlibris.com
821996

CONTENTS

DEDICATION

I dedicate this book to my son Dennis who is a food producer and my daughter Lise who loves all animals.

CHAPTER 1

The Formative Years

Growing up in Central Texas was a good time for children during the 1870's. Such was the case for Bryce J Sullivan, born in 1871 in the small growing town of Abilene, located 150 miles south of Dallas and 150 miles east of Odessa. Bryce was the second born. His older sister by one year was Cindy-Sue and his younger sister, also by one year, was Anna-Mae. His dad was Jim Sullivan who worked the family gun shop with his dad, James Sullivan Sr. His mom was a stay at home mom caring for the three young Sullivans.

The daily routine of play with his sisters and the neighborhood kids came to a halt when it was time for Cindy-Sue to enter 1st grade. Because the senior Sullivan was in poor health, Jim and Sally decided to hold Cindy-Sue back one year, and jump

Anna-Mae a year earlier, thereby allowing all three kids to enter school at the same time. That decision allowed the entire family to leave their rural home at the same time, travel the two miles to town, leave off the kids at school and Jim and Sally would open up the shop by 7:30AM. The senior Sullivan would show up by 11AM and be heading home by 2PM. It was two weeks before Christmas that the senior Sullivan passed away from an intractable heart condition.

After the funeral and transferring the shop ownership to Jim and Sally, a new routine was established. Sally would be the front receiving customer agent and head salesman of all firearms. With Jim's help and several manuals, Sally knew her pistols, rifles, and shotguns. She then became a convincing salesperson that the public learned to trust. At 3PM when the kids walked to the shop from school, Sally and the girls would ride the buckboard back home to take care of household chores and preparing supper—keeping the trailing horse for dad and Bryce.

Bryce would stay with his dad and slowly learned the gun trade. Initially, Bryce was showed, at a young age, how to reload ammo. Not to shock the customers, Bryce had a secluded corner with a curtain to hide him as he reloaded ammo every day. Before long, he watched his dad disassemble a Colt Peacemaker and then reassemble it after repairing it. One day, he surprised his day by saying, "here, let me tear it down, and I'll put it back together after it's repaired." From that point, Bryce picked up all the tricks of the trade from cleaning guns, to performing action jobs, and eventually troubleshooting problems and repairing them. By 1885, Bryce was fourteen, and could handle any job in the shop, and would even take over his mom's job when she went home with the girls after school.

1885 was also a crucial time for his sisters. Cindy-Sue convinced the elderly leather worker, next door to the Sullivan's gun shop, to take on Anna-Mae and herself as apprentices in the leather trade, for six months without pay. The key argument was that they could both sew clothing and would work hard to help out the aging leather tradesman. It was only two months later that Adelbert Abbott admitted to Jim that the girls were not only talented gals quick to learn, but their presence in the shop was simply a life saver for his depressed state as a new widower. For the first time in months, he couldn't wait for school to be out so he could continue teaching the gals how to do their job in building saddlebags, pistol holsters, gun-belts, rifle scabbards, knife sheaths, protective chaps, and even leather vests. Every Saturday, the girls spent the entire day making products for Mr. Abbott to sell in the gun shop or several of the mercantiles.

Christmas of 1885 was another momentous occasion. It had always been a tradition for each of the family members to give one gift to each other family member. So, the "TREE" experience started with the girls. Each one received five boxes containing leather working tools, aprons, knives, punches, boxes of rivets and one envelope. The girls opened their envelope to each find $75 in US Currency and an individual employment contract from Adelbert Abbott promising a wage of 50 cents per school day for three hours from 3—6PM and $2 per day for Saturday and any day when there was no school, but without room and board—plus a big thank you for their help and brightening his days. Both girls spent the rest of Christmas Day ruining several handkerchiefs till their mom told them to take the buggy and go pick up Mr. Abbott for Christmas dinner.

Bryce had four packages under the tree. The first one, from his dad, threw Bryce for a loop. A brand-new Colt Peacemaker in 44-40 caliber with three boxes of ammo. The second was a state of the art reloader from the Ideal reloading company. Mom clarified the gift by saying that the reloading components were in the office. He was told to set up the reloader in the office, and half of the reloads went to the shop and the other half were his to shoot off for pleasure and training. The last two gifts from the girls were a gunbelt and a gunfighter holster for his Colt pistol.

The next two years till graduation was a routine that made each one feel like they were on solid ground, including Mr. Abbott. The routine was: wake up, ride to school and then the shop, changing of the guard after school, mom using the trail horse to go home, dad closing shop at 6PM and bringing the three kids home in the buckboard, supper, school work, shooting session, household chores, reloading and bedtime.

Bryce practiced his pistol shooting every evening after supper before nightfall. His dad taught him how to point and shoot, how to draw and fire his Colt with one hand, and even taught him the fine points of "quick draw." Later, he added fanning with point and shoot. This latter technique required changes made to the internal parts of the pistol to withstand the rigors of "fan shooting" which also included changing the hammer's shape to enable fanning.

With all these steps, Bryce would practice every day till he ran out of bullets or the arrival of darkness. After the practice session was over, he would go back to reloading or do schoolwork till bedtime.

***

Finally, graduation arrived in early June 1887. The ceremony was held at the local Methodist Church. In attendance were the parents and family of the graduates. It was a momentous occasion for the Sullivan family since all three kids were graduating together. The Sullivan's guest of honor was Mister Abbott and the town's lawman, Sheriff

Marlow. The required attendees were all the students in the school which numbered almost 100. The ceremony was simple. A short speech from the headmaster and the diplomas' handing-out. Bryce was suspicious why his dad had invited Sheriff Marlow to their table. *Little did he know that the sheriff was looking to mentor an apprentice who had potential as a future local lawman. Plus, he also was not aware that his dad had given the sheriff permission to make the offer. Also, it would be years for him to realize that there was an unknown girl in the seventh grade that he did not associate with since the High School 8th-10th grades were separated from the lower grades 1—7. This gal was a gorgeous youngster, tall, slim, in early development, with unusual short blond hair, and bright green eyes—the daughter of a successful "pig farmer." Bryce did not know her, but this gal certainly knew of him—as strong as any teenage crush could be.*

For the next two years, Bryce continued working at the gun shop as well as practicing his shooting. Sheriff Marlow started doing 5PM afternoon rounds while including Bryce before the family returned home by 6PM. The sheriff always had a subject to cover as they walked the Main Street boardwalk of their town—a town with a population of a thousand people in 1887.

Jim Sullivan knew this visiting with the sheriff could mold Bryce's destiny, and as much as he missed Bryce in the shop, he knew that his future would be living by the gun. Since this was inevitable, he hoped that working with a honorable lawman would instill safety, security and a respectable work ethic.

***

CHAPTER 2

The Early Years

A few days later, Sheriff Marlow came to see Bryce while at work in the gun shop. "Say Bryce, I hear thru the grapevine that you're quite fast with your Colt. What do you say we have a friendly competition of you against me in your dad's range behind the shop?" "Sure." "Great, then set up six 8-inch tin cans at 20 yards."

With everything set to go, the sheriff added, "it's not only important to be fast, but you need to hit your target, or you will be the loser in a gunfight if you only end up shooting air." With both shooters ready, Jim agreed to give the start order and to stop the competition as soon as one shooter hits all three cans. To clarify, he would yell "now' and "stop."

After a random delay, Jim yells "now." Sheriff Marlow draws and shoots the first tin can and as he was pulling the hammer for his second shot, the "stop" order was clearly heard. Meanwhile, during the sheriff's first shot, everyone heard a "BA-ba-BANG." The triple sound was faster than a Gatling gun and actually sounded like the echo of a single shot. However, everyone could see the three of Bryce's cans in midair.

"Sweet mercy! How is that possible?"

Jim responded, "because of speed fanning with a properly altered firearm, thousands of rounds down range, and years of dedicated practice."

"Can you teach some pistol, as well as rifle and shotgun, shooting techniques?" "Yes sir."

"Well here is my problem. When you were born the town had a population of 500. Today, eighteen years later, it is up to almost 3,000. I need three deputies and the council has approved their salaries and benefits. I can teach them as much as I can from my experiences, but I need someone to teach them how to handle guns. I also need someone who can have my back as I go against more aggressive opponents in our growing city. The railroad stockyards, although good business for the town, have brought in some unsavory characters that have no respect for the law."

"I see, how does this affect me?"

"It will, only if you agree to be my head deputy."

Bryce looked at his dad, looking for some guidance. "Your mom and I knew this day would come when we gave you your first Colt and Ideal reloader. This decision is yours to make. It's a fork in the road and only you can choose which path to take. We'll accept your decision as the road to the beginning of your destiny."

Bryce took a moment and with a smile said, "thank you sheriff, I'll take the job."

"Great, here are your benefits without housing allowance:

- $55 a month plus two meals a day at any local diner.
- You work five days a week and two 'overnight duty' in the jail. No one takes Saturday or Saturday night off.
- 100% medical if hurt or shot on job.
- Your salary will continue indefinitely if you become temporarily disabled and at 50%

if permanently disable—both from a work-related injury or a non-related illness.

- $2,000 work-related life insurance to your beneficiaries.
- Unlimited ammunition.
- 100% livery housing for your horse.
- You provide your guns, horse and tack.
- If on a manhunt, the sheriff will provide vittles and other needs. If you are hunting solo, the council will reimburse your expenses.
- If you arrest and jail an outlaw with a reward on his head. The bounty money is yours to keep."

"You start tomorrow at 8AM with the swearing-in ceremony and signing of official documents."

***

The first three days on the job was very slow. Sheriff Marlow hired two other greenhorn deputies, Dwight Abrams and Dexter Burke, and spent those three days with their indoctrination. Bryce spent those three days walking the boardwalks but there were no fist fights, robberies, domestic assaults, petty thefts, shootings or even cheating card players. So, he spent his days showing merchants and patrons that there was a new lawman on the prowl.

The third day, Bryce started his firearms training at the local public range just on the outskirts of town. Both Abrams and Burke had a long road to firearm precision but were both in their 20's and eager to learn. The interesting part of each day was the one-hour class Sheriff Marlow held every morning. Each day brought a new topic of material they needed to know. Bryce had the Wednesday and Saturday nightshift this week as well as the weekend duty with Thursday and Friday off.

Wednesday night, while on his 6PM rounds, he found the front door to Albright's Mercantile unlocked. Bryce walked in, in total darkness with his pistol drawn. Suddenly, a man bumped into him and his burlap bag fell to the floor. "Hold it right there, mister. You're under arrest for robbery." After some commotion with snoopers, Azra Albright was summoned. As he walked in, he said, "Eustache Backus, what is the meaning of this?"

"Well Mr. Albright, we ran out of venison and eggs three days ago and my kids were so hungry that I had to come and get something for them to eat."

"By breaking in!"

"Oh no, I would never do that. I picked your lock with this long neck fine screwdriver."

"So, you were going to steal these vittles and leave?"

"Oh no, I would never do that. I left a receipt on your desk."

Bryce walks over to the desk and picks up a paper. After reading it he says, "better read this Mr. Albright."

Azra picks up the paper and reads out loud. "IOU 10 pounds of bacon, 10 pounds of dried beans, 5 pounds of oatmeal, 5 pounds of flour and a tin of baking powder. Signed—Imogene Backus."

"Eustache, why didn't you come and see me today?

"Stupid pride, I was hoping to shoot some venison, or the chickens would start laying again. But after three days, I had no choice, even if I was carrying a credit of $62."

"Eustache, listen to me. I WILL FEED YOUR FAMILY ANYTIME, AND I DON'T CARE

IF YOUR CREDIT GETS TO A THOUSAND DOLLARS. So, hell with your pride, we'll work it out. Now add four half gallons of canned beef stew, some fresh vegetables, some sugar, some butter, and some candy for the kids."

Bryce was listening to all this and was very impressed with Mr. Albright. As he was woolgathering, he saw a good size bag of homemade sugar cookies for four bits. Bryce pulls the 50 cents from his pocket and hands it to Mr. Albright. The merchant simply smiled and accepted the funds. The bag of cookies went straight in Eustache's burlap bag. Once Eustache left the store, Azra said, "that was a thoughtful thing to do for his kids." "Really, not very significant compared to what you are doing for the family. Something tells me he's not the only homesteader getting your help, hey?" "Shush, about that." *Bryce thought—one of these days I will be able to financially help these struggling homesteaders.*

***

With his two days off, Bryce was a bit lost since he hadn't had a workday off in years. To fill in the time, he decided to get his black gelding and take a ride out of town to meet some of the ranchers. being a city boy, he had spent very little time on the roads leading to Abilene. Today, he headed out west. He stopped to see the first cattle rancher by the name of Sawyer Skinner. After social introductions were completed, Bryce was directed to the next westerly homestead, a pig farm owned by Waldo Adkins.

Arriving at the homestead, Bryce was sitting in his saddle next to the barn, completely surprised not to smell the usual odor of a piggery. As he sat there trying to decide if he should step down, suddenly the barn door opened and there stood a young woman with a full cap to cover her hair, rubber boots to her knees, work gloves too big for her hands, and a barn jacket that hid her female attributes. The young gal was totally flabbergasted. Bryce saw her embarrassment and spoke first.

"Are you Alie Adkins that I went to school with?" "Yes, and that's Allie with two l's. I was four years behind you, so we never got to associate. But I was at your graduation. I see you are now Deputy Sheriff Bryce Sullivan. Good for you. Unfortunately, I'm just a pig farmer."

"Whoa, hold on. I have two points to make. For just being a pig farming worker, you're a beauty to behold. Secondly, never berate or minimize your worth as a pig farmer. Like any profession, growing our food supply is a very honorable profession."

"Well I don't know about the beauty part in my work attire, but I appreciate your comments on our business. Would you like to meet my parents and get a tour of the barn?" "Yes Ma'am. I'd be happy to."

After introductions were done, Allie gave Bryce a quick tour of the different stalls and its tenants. Bryce was amazed how clean the animals and stalls were. Especially surprised was the fresh smell in the barn. After the tour, Bryce thanked them and as Allie walked him to his horse, she naturally took her head cap off and her golden short hair fell over her ears. As Bryce stepped onto his horse, he said, "thanks for the tour, I hope we get to meet again in town." "Well, at age 15, my parents don't let me out of their sight, but maybe when we deliver a pork carcass or get supplies from Albright's Mercantile, we could talk again."

The remainder of the day, he continued heading west and met all the ranchers and homesteaders for the next 10 miles, getting back home by nightfall. On Friday, after a long shooting practice, he rode north of town for another 10 miles and introduced himself to the locals. Saturday was back to work. His backup deputy during the day was Dwight and Dexter went on duty at 6PM. The day was rowdy at the saloons but nothing too disruptive. At 10PM, a messenger was sent by Sam Belknap, bartender at the "Wet Your Whistle Saloon."

"Sheriff, there's a man holding a gun on three card cheats and is gonna shoot em." "Ok, we'll be over. Dexter, take the shotgun with you and load it with OO Buckshot." As they arrived at the saloon's batwing doors, Bryce pulled out three bullets and replaced them with his special reloads. They then stepped in and walked to the table where a man was standing and pointing his pistol at the three card players. "Ok mister. Put the gun away and get a drink at the bar on me. I'll take over from here but tell me what happened." "Be glad to. The three cowboys arrived today and asked for a fourth player. I obliged. They appeared to be more than lucky, but when one fella showed four queens, I got up and pulled a gun on them—I was holding a legal queen in my hand."

"Ok boys pull up your sleeves." No one was responding so Dexter smashed the butt of his shotgun on one of the players left hand. "Aaaah, you broke my hand." "The Deputy said to pull up your sleeves, now do it." Instead, the three card cheats stood up and went for their guns. Bryce responded, drew his pistol, and fired three times.

To all the patrons surprise the three card cheats' shirts had a two- inch hole and the shirts were on fire. The cowpunchers were busy tearing their shirts off since the fires were spreading. The raw 2-inch spot on their chests was burning so much that they were pouring their beers to cool the burn. One had a fancy steel contraption on his arm that held a series of well-chosen cards.

Finally, Sam the bartender said, "what did you shoot them with. They got shot in the chest but don't have any bullet holes?"

"My special load of extra gunpowder to start a fire, and capped with cream of wheat and table salt.

It makes a hole in the shirt, starts the shirt afire, and burns the skin like all blazes."

"Now, put your guns on the table and turn around so my deputy can put the manacles on. And don't try anything because the next three bullets are real, and I'll use them if necessary."

The next morning, Sheriff Marlow found three cowboys in the cells, their chest burn plastered with a white salve. He had heard the whole story at Bessie's Diner. "Ok Bryce, your pistol is a lethal weapon. Now tell me why you shot them with black powder, cream of wheat and table salt. Are you for real?"

"I knew these cowboys would draw their guns, but I couldn't kill them since they weren't hardened outlaws. They were just too big for their britches, and needed to be brought down a notch. I wouldn't have done it if they were outlaws."

"Yes, you saved their lives, but now, the whole town knows you carry cream of wheat/salt in your Colt. Now, how many men will draw on you and you'll have to kill them. Remember, as a lawman, if an opponent goes for his gun, IT'S KILL OR BE KILLED. And cream of wheat/salt won't cut it. So never do it again, and let's hope that people forget about the event."

The next weeks were peaceful. Dwight and Dexter were getting comfortable with the rifle and shotgun. Pistol proficiency would take years, so Sheriff Marlow had the two coach shotguns cut down to just ahead of the fore-end grip, and had two backpack holsters made by Abbott's Leatherworks. Carrying a pistol was for every-day use and show. Both Dwight and Dexter were very capable 100-yard shooters with their rifles.

For the next month, all four lawmen were busy serving processes for Judge Wilfred Bull. They covered overdue town taxes, bank forfeitures, divorce announcement, and court appearances. For the most part, except for one, these were non-violent assignments. On one occasion, Bryce was with Dwight and served a court ordered appearance for a Fleming Brockman—to answer to neighbors' complaints that he regularly beats his wife in a malicious way.

Arriving at the Brockman ranch, Bryce knocked at the front door. "Yeah, who are you and what do you want?" "I'm Deputy Sheriff Bryce Sullivan and this is Deputy Sheriff Dwight Abrams. We were sent here by Judge Bull. You are hereby ordered to appear in three days before Judge Bull to answer to charges of cruel and abusive treatment to your wife, Eleanora Brockman. Here are the official papers. If you don't show up, we'll be back to arrest you and throw you in jail." DEPUTY, HELP ME, PLEASE.

"Who is asking for help?"

"That's the wife, she's sick in the head. Ignore her."

"Not likely, she's asking for help, so stand aside."

"Get out, or I'll throw you out." As he took a swing at Bryce but missed. Bryce came back and snapped a sap at Brockman's forehead. The man fell to the ground like a rock in a pond. Bryce said, "Dwight put the manacles on Brockman's wrists and ankles and tie him to a porch post."

Walking in the wife's bedroom, Bryce saw a scene that would never leave his mind. The lady was covered with bruises over her face, head, chest, abdomen, and legs. She was now not responding, and it was clear that both her forearms were broken and at an unnatural angle. Worse than this, she was clearly starving to death. Bryce walked out and asked Dwight to go in the carriage house and get a buckboard to transport the lady to the City Hospital. With a mattress added to the buckboard Bryce headed to the hospital, and Dwight lead a screaming Brockman draped over a ranch horse with his manacled wrists and ankles tied together under the horse with a piece of rope—just like a harvested game.

Arriving at the receiving area of the City Hospital, Doc Newcomb was first to receive them. "Who is this, Deputy, and what happened?"

"This is Eleanora Brockman and she's been beaten to near death by her brainless husband, Fleming, who is now in jail." "Very good, let's bring her into my examining room and I'll be back to give you my findings."

An hour later, Doc Newcomb came to talk to Bryce. "Deputy, Mrs. Brockman has swelling of the brain, her blood count is low, and she's lost a lot of blood presumed from internal bleeding, both her arms are broken, and she is near death from long term starvation. We can give her some medicine to shrink her swollen brain and we can feed her intravenously as well as thru a feeding tube. If she lives, it will be a long hospital stay."

"Do whatever needs to be done, if the town or county refuses to pay your bill, I will guarantee full payment out of my savings account."

"We will take care of her as best we can, and I would have treated her even if there was no pay involved."

And so was the first case where a benefactor fund could be used to help people in need. This case ended up with Fleming Brockman spending a month in the local jail, paying all the hospital bills and giving his wife a $5,000 divorce settlement. Eleanora survived intact, and moved to Dallas to live with her daughter.

After several months of peaceful living in a friendly town, things changed on a sunny Monday morning. The First National Bank was robbed of $25,000 and a teller was killed.

**

During the daily class given by Sheriff Marlow, a man came running into the office, "Sheriff, the First National Bank has been robbed." The four lawmen were on a dead run only two blocks away and arrived at the bank when the outlaws had already left. Goddard Abernathy, the President, was holding a towel to his bleeding forehead laceration but was able to relate the events. "Four men arrived, when three came in with pistols drawn, they demanded the tellers empty their tills of the cash. When I was ordered to open the vault, I refused. The gang leader pistol whipped me, but I still refused. In response, the gang leader then pistol-whipped Ansel Atwater to death, and I had to give in before he attacked another of my employees. They took only paper currency and emptied the vault. We are ruined since the parent company only reimburses 25% of our losses." Meanwhile Doc Newcomb arrived and was directed to check on Ansel.

"We didn't hear any shooting; do you mean to say that they accomplished this robbery without firing a shot?" "Yes, the bank had just opened and there were no customers to threaten. Consequently, they only pistol whipped me and Ansel." Doc Newcomb came to check on Goddard and announced that Ansel had died from a severe depressed skull fracture. President Abernathy's wound was cared for and Doc Newcomb left. It became clear that Goddard Abernathy was beside himself when he said, "Ansel is dead because I resisted opening the vault, it's all my fault, and I eventually opened the vault anyways."

Sheriff Marlow looked at his deputies and said, "get your horses and rifles. We're going to run this gang down—it's four of them against the four of us, and we want them bad. We'll stop at the office and get their wanted posters since the bank staff can identify them before we leave. I wouldn't be surprised that they're wanted dead or alive."

At a full gallop, the Abilene lawmen took off heading west. After three miles, the horses had to slow down. Sheriff Marlow told Bryce, "take the lead and, on clear straightaways, push hard. When you get to a bend in the road, stop and sneak a look around the bend to see if an ambush is awaiting us. Our horses are fresh, and we have to push them before we get to the Trent town line. That is the limit of our 25- mile jurisdiction."

Bryce turns around in the saddle and says, "what do you mean our 25-mile jurisdiction limit?"

"What I mean is that if we don't catch up with this gang by the Trent town line, then we have to hold back and return to town. These outlaws then become the responsibility of the US Marshals stationed in New Braunsfeld, under the judicial control of District Judge Hobart." Bryce was stunned, but this was not the time to discuss the issue. His pressing goal was to get his lawmen onto these outlaws before they got away. Realizing their horses could not maintain a power trot for 25 miles without getting wasted, the lawmen stopped to rest and water the animals anytime a water source was found. After hours on the trail, the four riders were seen some four miles ahead of them. Bryce felt encouraged till he saw a sign, "Trent town line."

Sheriff Marlow ordered the posse to stop. "That's it boys, we are done. Let's rest the horses and then we'll walk them into town to get some grub for us and the horses."

"Sheriff, this is wrong, the outlaws are within reach and we're just going to say, 'you win, we're out of mileage, so you win the game.' It is not a game; a man lost his life, and the lost money means catastrophe to a lot of good folks. Hell, a dog is free to go wherever he wants, but sheriffs can only go to a 25-mile limit. This is bull---t." Bryce removes his badge and exchanges it for the four wanted posters. "I quit, from now on, I'm a bounty hunter. I can go wherever I want, and I have no boundaries. I will return with the stolen money and all four bank robbers—dead or alive."

***

Bryce rode into Trent to water his horse, Blackie, at the town trough. He went into a mercantile and bought some beef jerky for himself, some oats for Blackie, and refilled his water canteen at the town well/hand pump. Then he got back on the trail and continued to follow the four outlaw tracks. He knew, because of two reasons, that the gang would not be going far to set up camp for the night— their horses were spent, and they knew the Abilene sheriff would not chase them past Trent. So, he took his time until he smelled camp smoke and knew that the showdown was near.

He ground tethered Blackie near a brook and fresh grass and reviewed the posters. The head outlaw was Vern Bartow wanted for rape, murder, robbery, and torture with a reward of $2,000. The other three were relative unknown sycophants whose rewards were $500 each. Bryce then took off with his coach shotgun and his Win 73 and walked toward the outlaw camp.

The outlaws were drinking and celebrating their newly acquired fortunes. They weren't watching their backtrail. Bryce saw the chance to sneak behind boulders and trees to get close enough for shotgun range. Within a half hour, he was within 25 yards of camp. With his rifle he took aim at one of the standing outlaws and fired. The shot took part of his shooting hand off. As soon as the shot rang out, Bryce was standing up and yelling, "put your hands up, you are all under arrest for bank robbery and murder. You animals are done." The apparent leader, presumed to be Bartow, yells back, "you're not taking me in, you punk kid." As the last word was said, Bartow went for his gun. Bryce's shot blew the pistol out of Bartow's hand.

Bryce quickly walked into camp and had one of the sycophants apply manacles to each outlaw's ankles, as well as securing each their wrists with manacles to an individual tree. Once the outlaws were secured, he cleaned and bandaged the outlaw who had lost part of his hand. Then their boots were checked for knives and derringers as well as their beltlines for mini pistols. The petty cash in their pockets totaled $182 which he pocketed. He then searched the saddlebags and found the stolen $25,000 plus another $431 which he also pocketed. His last acquisition included the four pistols and four rifles plus plenty of 44-40 ammo. To finish housekeeping, he went to get Blackie and he took the saddles off all five horses. As he was collecting the food in the outlaws' saddlebags, he realized he would inherit the cooking utensils, food, and would also be able to sell the guns, gunbelts, scabbards, saddlebags, saddles, tack, and horses. In addition, a possible bank reward for returning the money, and of course the wanted poster's bounty rewards.

Bryce then chose canned beans, bacon and coffee for his supper. Stoking up the fire, he added the grate, put the water to boil, and food to cook. He was about to start eating when the outlaws started complaining they needed to go to the bushes, another was thirsty and or hungry. Bryce got up, looked at Bartow and said, "I don't give a rat's behind about you or your wishes and urges. You are 'dead to me.' So be quiet or I will muzzle you, and if that fails, I'll bust up your face with a rock. It will be my way till I get you back to Marlow's jail in Abilene—not your way, heh."

Supper was delicious followed by a good night's rest in his bedroll with a winter coat for comfort. The outlaws shivered all night, had to relieve themselves in their britches and turned out to be more docile and resigned to their fate by morning.

After a breakfast of coffee, bacon and biscuits, Bryce went thru the routine of loading the four outlaws. It was a ritual of changing the manacles, so their hands were in front, to hold onto the saddle horn. Bryce helped each one to sit on the saddle and then lock an ankle manacle to a stirrup. Each one was warned that if they fell off the horse, that they would suffer a painful death as the horse's hoofs would trample over their bodies.

A long day later, they arrived in Abilene. Sheriff Marlow gladly took the outlaws to a bathing trough to clean them up and then threw them in jail. Bryce went to the bank to return the money, but before he let it be known that he had retrieved the stolen loot, he asked if there was a reward for returning the $25,000. President Abernathy said, "yes, the parent company in Dallas posted a 10% reward for the return of $25,000—no questions asked. Bryce smiled and said, "that is a rip off since they were in hock for 25% which in my book came to $6,250. But I'll take the $2,500 since it is better than nothing. Here is your stolen loot, and I'll start an account in my name."

Over the next week he gathered his earnings. $3,500 in bounty rewards, $600 in petty pocket cash, $2,500 in bank rewards, $380 in horses/saddles/scabbards/tack/saddlebags, $80 in pistols, $120 in rifles, plus food, cooking utensils and six boxes of ammo. So, he deposited $6,500 in the bank and pocketed over $600.

***

Meanwhile, Sheriff Marlow informed Jim Sullivan that Bryce had resigned as deputy sheriff and was going the bounty hunting route. Jim and Sally were not surprised and decided to prepare for a family discussion on the matter by sending a telegram off to Jim's brother in Dallas. To their satisfaction an answer came back within the hour that Joe would be in Abilene by 6PM supper time, and that he was looking forward to Sally's meatloaf and mashed potatoes.

That same afternoon Bryce went to see Eunice Atwater. Her home was a small house close to the community school and a short walk to the railroad office where she worked as the manager's secretary. "Hello, Ma'am, may I talk to you about your recent loss?" "Yes, please come in. I know you were the deputy who gave up his job to bring my husband's killers to justice."

After meeting the three Atwater kids and doing the usual pleasantries till the kids were excused, Bryce got to the point. "I'm here to find out how you're going to support yourselves. I know it's bold of me to ask, but I can because I'm willing to help you."

"I have $300 in the bank; the bank is giving me my husband's life insurance of $1,500 and the bank is marking our $500 mortgage balance as paid in full. I have a good job working for the railroad yard manager where I make $1.25 per day as bookkeeper and accountant. My kids can walk to school and my oldest can take care of the younger ones after school till I get home. The only difference is that the kids lost their dad, and I lost my husband. We will now live on my single income. It may be tight, but we'll manage." "Yes, I agree, you can survive. But don't you want more?" "Yes, like anyone would, but I cannot afford to make a change at my age of 44 with three kids to support."

"Approaching the 20th century, there is a dire need for private accountants and bookkeepers. If you are willing, I will finance you free of charge, to build an extension office to your home and open a private office to provide accounting and bookkeeping services. That way, you won't just be surviving, but you'll be able to get ahead."

"Why would you do this, you don't know me?"

"I only know that you are a victim of a violent crime and I want to help you. Take this bank draft and better yourself and guarantee your children's future. In addition, if you ever feel threaten and you need my help, tell my father at the gun shop and he will locate me. I will return no matter where I am in this vast west." Eunice started crying as Bryce took his exit to give her some privacy.

Bryce's next stop was the bank to set up a new joint account with Azra Albright. Arriving at the Mercantile, Azra greeted him and introduced his wife, Erna. "What can I do for you son?" "Accept this account in our name and pay off Eustache Backus's account. Then arrange for new clothes for the entire family, a good supply of vittles and plenty of ammo so he can hunt."

"Whoa, this is no 50-cent bag of cookies, this will run you almost a hundred dollars." "Sir, just look at the account's balance." "This can't be right, it says $1,500." "And you can spend it where it is needed. Pay off the credit accounts of those settlers who need the help, but keep it anonymous. When you need more, if I am not in town, tell my father at the gun shop. He will send me a telegram, and I'll do a bank transfer to this account from wherever I am."

Azra was totally shocked, he looked at his wife who gave him the nod of approval and said, "we'll keep a journal of the recipients and the dollar amounts donated" "Just make sure that the recipients don't feel ashamed in receiving help, it is fairness and good fortune, not charity."

Afterwards, Bryce went to see his parents. He informed them that he had decided to follow the bounty hunting trail for a few years. He could not stand seeing outlaws getting away because of lawmen's technicalities, and he wanted to build a Benefactor Fund to help people in need. The Sullivan's knew this discussion was forthcoming. Sally added, "as much as we hate to see you enter such a dangerous profession, we have a compromise that will help you and settle our own nerves. Your uncle will be at supper tonight for his traditional meatloaf meal, and he has an offer and a request you'll likely be comfortable with. Come early so we can visit with him before supper."

With a few hours to spend, he decided to go start stocking up on clothing. As he was about to enter the garment store, he saw the Adkins buggy go by and was headed to the City Hospital. Bryce walked over and found Allie sitting alone in the waiting room. "Hello, Allie with two l's. How are things going with your mom?" Bryce was set back to see Allie in tears and rephrased his question by saying, "is there anything I can do to help?"

"I'm afraid there is nothing anyone can do. Doc Newcomb believes mom has cancer of the bone marrow"—as the tears changed to uncontrollable crying. Bryce simply sat next to her, took her hand in his and gently held her hand till the tears dried up.

"Sorry to be blubbering all over you, but you're such a considerate person that it's easy to take advantage of you." "Hey, you can take advantage of me anytime." As this brought a smile to Allie, she added, "I'm told that you are leaving town to become a bounty hunter. Will you ever return to town?"

"This is a temporary destiny. I feel a strong pull to return one day and make this my permanent home."

"There is some charisma about you, and I believe that, despite the dangerous activities you face, that you will return to Abilene. As for myself, I have a difficult time ahead with my mom's illness and my father coping with it. Plus, we have a meat producing business to keep going. So, when you return, I'll still be here and hope to see you again. It's always so pleasant talking with you. So, good luck, stay safe and I hope to see you when you return."

"Since making contact with you, I feel a commitment and would like to say that during my time away, if you ever need protection because of any threat, then tell my father at the gun shop and he will contact me by telegram, and I will return to town by train as quick as I can."

They then shook hands and that is when they both felt something mystical that could not be explained at the time.

**

With time to spare, after collecting some clothing for his next caper, he stopped at the local blacksmith and after taking measurements he ordered a double body armor of hardened steel—the top portion for the chest and the lower portion for the belly.

Arriving at the family home at 5PM, Uncle Joe was already enjoying coffee with Jim and Sally. When Bryce entered, they hugged and after pleasantries, Joe laid out his story. "I have been a solo bounty hunter for twenty years and only in the past year have I had a partner; an Apache Indian called Red Sky."

"How on earth did you end up with such an individual—an Apache working with a white man is unheard of?"

"One day, two hombres I was chasing had captured Red Sky and were having fun torturing him by burning his feet and more. Well, I quickly dispatched the two outlaws, released Red Sky and treated his burns for four days while staying in camp. When it was time to go our separate ways, he followed me back to town and he's been with me ever since. It seems that since I saved his life, that he belongs to me till he saves my life. Well he has saved my life five times in the past three years and he's still with me, now as a partner in eliminating outlaws which has now become his perpetual revenge."

"Great story, now what is this proposal mom said you would discuss."

"After working the outlaw trail for almost 25 years, I've amassed $10,000 in savings. I'm now 47 years old and need to retire, but ten grand is not enough to live on. I have an arthritis condition that is eating away at my joints, liver, kidneys and heart. There is no treatment, and my life expectancy is +- 15 years with a lot of physical support and pain management. So, I have to stop going after these low-grade criminals that are not too dangerous for our twosome. I need to go after some serious outlaws, including gangs, with high bounties. In order to do this, I need a shootist with a very accurate fast draw, and that nephew is you."

"Whoa, this is a big thing. You want me to join you instead of going solo?"

"Yes, for one year. During this time, we should amass a small fortune. I propose we split it 45-45-10%. To make this legal, we both fill out our last will and testament. You name your parents your beneficiary, whereas, I will name your parents as beneficiary of my $10,000 old account, but any new income from this day forward will be yours if I die of violent or natural causes. Basically, I will share my life's experiences in trade for your shootist's prowess."

"Tell me how Red Sky saved your life and what are his useful attributes?"

"Like all Apaches, he's a superb tracker, great with hand to hand combat using a knife or war club, the best rifle shot at 100 yards I ever saw, and sleeps lightly at camp, or none at all if there is potential danger. But most of all, he is 100% reliable and trustworthy."

"Well, I'm no idiot, this is a win/win situation for both of us and I would be honored to work with you for the next year. Now mom and dad how did you convince Uncle Joe to make this offer, and what do you get out of this arrangement?"

Sally said, "our peace of mind knowing you have two experienced men at your back." His dad said, "to be upfront and truthful with you, I made this offer to Joe days ago. For taking you under his wings, after one year, I will build an extension to the gun shop to make an apartment for him— free of charge. He would have access to supplies and entertainment being in the center of town, and would have mom and I available for physical support as well as the City Hospital nearby. Finding housekeepers and or care givers in town should not be a problem."

Joe added, "heck, I might even find a good woman along the way and bring her back with me. Boy, wouldn't that be a laugh for an old bachelor!"

After a fantastic supper of mashed potatoes, broccoli, rolls and meatloaf, two of the dedicated dynamic Trio started making detailed plans for their future.

***

CHAPTER 3

The Trio at Work

The next day at dawn, Jim and Sally were up early preparing breakfast for the girls. Cindy Sue and Anna Mae had spent the evening working late at ·Abbott's shop putting out a large order of saddlebags to a gun shop in Dallas. They were eager to meet with Uncle Joe and knew they would be sending Bryce off today.

Finally, Uncle Joe got up and visited with the girls. With all the ruckus these two cackling hens were making, Bryce had no choice but to get up as well. All in all, a great visit was had and a pancake breakfast with corn syrup and coffee was enjoyed by all. When it came time to leave, Sally hands Bryce four dime novels written by Swanson, Harnell, Adams and McWain. Sally explained that, "these are four men who were successful bounty hunters who used individual unique techniques to capture outlaws. It will make great reading when spending hours on trains traveling between capers, and some of their methods may save your lives."

With goodbyes finished, Bryce and Uncle Joe headed for the livery where their horses were stabled. As they walked in the livery, they were greeted by a well-groomed black-haired Apache Indian dressed in standard cowboy clothes and wearing a specially holstered sawed-off shotgun at his side. "Nephew, I want you to meet Red, my Westernized local Indian. That thing on his hip is a new model single trigger with a tang safety and no external hammers. When the barrels are opened, the action cocks the hammers. Once the barrels are closed the gun is ready to fire. Red can then get two shots off to sound like one. He uses this firearm because he can't hit the broadside of a barn with a pistol."

After introductions were carried out, the Trio headed to the railroad yard with their three riding horses and one packhorse. "What did mom mean when she said we would need reading material to pass the time on our many train rides?"

"My hip arthritis kills me when I ride a horse more than five miles and besides, our capers can all be around Dallas, or far away locations in Texas with access by train. For work in Dallas, I use a buggy. For trail work, I have no choice and will use my well-padded saddled horse,"

The train ride to Dallas took an average of five hours to cover 150 miles. During the trip, there was ample time to describe their first caper. "In the outskirts of the city is a small neighborhood where a famous outlaw lives. This animal is called Quentin Poole, aka The Torturer, and his sidekick is Alvarado Lozada, aka Lozo."

"These two have committed every immoral and inhumane crime known to civilized man and have plagued the Mexican side of the Laredo area for years. Now they are hiding in Dallas, from the Mexican Police, under different names. They have killed several bounty hunters who have tried to capture them—all in self-defense. There is no lawman who can arrest them since they have not committed any crimes in the US. The bounty of $5,000 for Poole and $2,000 for Lozada have already been paid to the US Western Union, and payment of the bounty only needs certification by any US lawman. We're going to get them, dead or alive, and start our new bank accounts."

During the trip to Dallas, Bryce and Uncle Joe each read one of the four books. Several times, the readers broke out in laughter and each reader said they would buy some of their jungle warfare accessories. Arriving at the Dallas railyard, the Trio headed to Marshal Balinger's office. "I'm back Marshal, and this is my nephew, Bryce Sullivan. We're going after Poole and Lozada today."

"Well, be careful, yesterday Poole went against three bounty hunters, and with Lozo on a rooftop, they were able to put all three hunters down. Again, a fair fight. The city council wants this street bloodshed to stop, so I hope you can do it. Just watch out for Lozo on a rooftop with a rifle. You'll find them at the Blue Moon bar as usual."

Leaving their horses at Buster's Livery, Bryce said, "This is how we are going to do this. Uncle Joe, you wear this body armor under your shirt and britches. Stand to my right with your body turned so that your left shoulder is pointing at Poole. You'll be standing at port arms with your coach shotgun and he'll have to shoot you first, but your armor will deflect the bullet. Red you need to be on a rooftop with the sun at your back and as soon as Lozo shows his face, shoot him. I will be the one to shoot Poole, but being a kid, he won't think I'm a threat to him. I'll be playing with his head before the shooting starts, just play along."

Uncle Joe walked in the saloon and called Poole out in front of all the patrons. Pointing his shotgun at Poole, he said, "be out in the street in a half hour, or I'll shoot you now and be done with it. What will it be?" "I'll be outside in a few minutes."

Shortly thereafter, Bryce and Uncle Joe were in the street with the sun to their backs. Poole came out and was looking for his shades because of the 3PM sun in his face.

Bryce started, "so they call you the Torturer, heh? Must be the great deeds you've done in your life. Better put some shades on because this time you have the sun in your face. Does Lozo have shades or is he even on his rooftop yet. Think you are going to shoot my Uncle first with the shotgun. Not a good move, since I can kill you before you get your first shot off. Think I'm just a smart-ass kid trying to make a name for myself, well I will make a name for myself when I shoot the pistol out of your hand. So, go for it NOW."

Poole got spooked and jumped the gun, drew and pointed his pistol at Joe. As a shot rang out, the gun came flying out of Poole's hand along with Poole's thumb and the tip of his third and fourth finger. Poole screamed Aahrhh and grabbed his mashed hand. Within a second, a rifle shot was heard, as everyone in the street saw Lozo fall out of the rooftop to land with a loud thump on the street's boardwalk.

Uncle Joe walked up to Poole, slapped the manacles on his wrist, pulled the belly gun out of his back belt, sat him on the ground and removed both boots to see if a derringer or knife were in the boots. Then Uncle Joe said, "you're going to jail where Marshal Balinger will hold you till the Mexican Government authorizes extradition. Hopefully they'll give you some of what you gave them over the years, hah!"

That evening, they took two second floor rooms in the King Hotel, had a nice hot meal and went to bed early. Red shared a room with Uncle Joe and slept on his bedroll on the floor. Joe handed Bryce a wooden wedge to place under the door for security and then handed him three rat traps to put on the windowsill to surprise any intruders using a ladder to the second floor. Bryce laughed as he showed Uncle Joe his two double-tin-cans, one for the door's upper edge and the other for the top of the lower window frame.

The next morning after a full breakfast in Sam's Diner, the Trio went to the marshal's office. Marshal Balinger handed them the two vouchers totaling $7,000. They then headed to the bank and each started an account in the 1st National Bank since there was also a branch in Abilene. Uncle Joe and Bryce had decided to split all bounties in three ways evenly but Red refused. He was happy with his 10% which would cover his retirement needs in the reservation. "Ok, Red. But if you ever need more money in the future, I will gladly give it to you." "Hey, that's the same as 'money in the bank' boss!"

***

That day, the Trio went to a range and practiced shooting all their firearms. Afterwards, Joe went to see a gunsmith and had two coach shotguns sawed down to the fore-end tip, while Bryce went to see a leather-smith and had him make two backpacks to hold sawed-off shotguns. During the afternoon, each man was on his own. By evening the shotguns and holsters were ready, and the Trio gathered at Sam's Diner for supper. *No one knew that Joe had spent the afternoon with the housekeeping lady at the King Hotel where the Trio was staying.*

While waiting to place their order, Marshal Balinger walked in and sat at the Trio's table. When the waitress came to take their order, Marshal Balinger delayed things by saying, "Grace, bring us a pot of coffee, and we need time for a business meeting before ordering." With coffee, the marshal started, "just got a telegram from Ken Hodge, sheriff in Texarkana. The Merchants Bank just got robbed of $22,000 and that included a payroll deposit of $5,000 for several city businesses. The posse split up into six groups to follow six separate tracks out of town. To everyone's surprise, all six tracks returned to town. To be blunt, these bold outlaws are living in Sheriff Hodge's town and he has no idea who they are."

Uncle Joe spoke up, "that means they are planning to rob more of the local banks, and be arrogant enough to hide in plain sight."

"Correct, and of course, because of your reputation, Sheriff Hodge is requesting your detective ability to identify this gang and catch them in the act of robbing their next bank."

Uncle Joe looked at the marshal and said, "you don't happen to know when the next train leaves for Texarkana, by any chance, hey?"

"Why yes, it leaves at 11PM and it's the overnight express. It will arrive by 6AM at the latest. Just in time for breakfast with Sheriff Hodge. I'll telegraph him to meet you at the railroad platform. Have a nice supper and let me know how it went when you get back to town!"

Bryce waited for the marshal to leave when he asked, "well Uncle, what is this about your detective reputation?" "Let's eat first, then I'll tell you about this and the new way of robbing banks, over a beer at my local hangout, Mulligan's Saloon."

"I made this my hangout because they keep their beer on ice, that's the advantage of an ice factory in the city—and I like my cold beer. Now this is the 1890's and outlaws don't rob banks like they did ten years ago. They don't travel for weeks on horseback to get to the next sizable bank worth robbing. They travel by train, with their horses and gear in the stock cars. Once in town, the horses are stabled in the local liveries and the outlaws take rooms in the hotels. Two man per room and per hotel to keep a low profile and avoid the 'gang' appearance."

"They spend their days where men gather. During the day, it is usually at some business such as a diner, a blacksmith, a mercantile, a hardware store, a livery, a park or the ever-popular boardwalk on Main Street sitting on rocking chairs under the porch roofs' shade. In the evening it's in saloons. Again, two men at a time in a location, and never seen talking with the other gang members."

"They listen and talk to the locals about where the money is, where people work, which banks are the busiest, which banks handle payrolls, and so on. It's amazing how people talk when they are given free drinks. Eventually, the gang members meet and share the intelligence they individually gathered. The gang leader makes a decision of which location to hit and when to make it happen."

"Once the outlaws escape the posse, they then decide to move on, by train, to another large community and restart the intelligence gathering process. The only alternative approach, is to take advantage of the previously gathered information, hide in town and hit another financial institution. These are modern 'repeaters,' and these are the gangs we will be going after during the next year. And that is why we have been asked to assist Sheriff Hodge."

After a few more beers, the Trio went to their room at the King Hotel to pack their belongings. Bryce had plenty of time, so he sat down and wrote a letter to Allie Adkins;

"Dear Allie with two l's,

Thought I would touch base with you. We were able to captureQuentin Poole, the Torturer..alive Uncle Joe has a ....secret girlfriend

Heading to stop bank robbers..........in Texarkana
How is your mother.................................doing
How are you doing......................…..are you OK

Always, Bryce with a 'y.'"

"If you decide to write, send letter addressed to me at the King Hotel in Dallas, Tx. And add a note in the bottom left corner, "HOLD for B. Sullivan."

***

The train ride to Texarkana was an easy way to travel for most. Bryce was reading the McWain book under the kerosene lamp till 3AM when he finally succumbed to the clickety-clack of the wheels hitting the rail splices. The Trio slept thru several stops for coal and water, and were finally awakened by the conductor announcing their arrival in Texarkana by 7:30AM. Stepping on the platform was Sheriff Hodge holding a sign saying "Sullivan."

"Good morning sheriff, this is my new member, my nephew Bryce Sullivan and of course you know Red Sky." "Nice to meet you, let's head to Ginny's Diner for breakfast and a briefing on the goings on." Over ham and eggs, toast and coffee, Sheriff Hodge began. "We have no idea who the robbers are, but we know they are all in town. We have a large clientele of out-of-towners and there is no way we can identify them. All we know is that the first bank they hit had just received a payroll deposit of $5,000, so we suspect that their next hit will be the bank receiving the next 5,000 payroll deposit which will be in three days. So, with my two deputies we'll be at the Cattlemen's Bank on payroll receiving day, until the payroll is paid out. What I'm asking you is to try to figure out if another bank is the target and be there to protect them until this gang is caught. Better still, if you can figure who the outlaws are, then arrest them before they hit again."

"That's a tall order to accomplish in three days or less. Heck we don't even know if these goons have a bounty on their heads or whether there is a reward for their capture?"

"I'm certain they are wanted men, but it doesn't matter since the Banking Association has posted a $2,000 reward for their capture and the Merchants Bank is offering $2,200 reward for the return of the stolen money—that's 10% of the $22,000 stolen. Plus, if there are any pre-existing bounty rewards, they are yours as well."

"Very well, we'll start working on this right away. Please bring us a map of the town with locations where the banks are located, and we'll take it from there."

After breakfast they registered in the Grand Texan Hotel and left their horses in the livery nearest to the railroad. By 11AM the Trio had gone to a tonsorial shop and had enjoyed a shave, a bath, and a haircut. Bryce asked Red how come he was taking part in these white man activities. "Well, while I live with the white man, I want to look like him, so along with the dress, I am more accepted as a partner to you and your uncle."

That afternoon, each of the Trio went their separate ways to gather ideas on the recent bank robbery. They agreed to meet again at the same diner at 6PM to share their findings. Joe was first to arrive and ordered a pot of coffee. When the others arrived, Red went first.

"I listened along many boardwalk gatherings. There were two well healed outsiders who were asking a lot of questions and leading the locals on the subject. Basically, they were way too interested in finding out what the sheriff knew about the robbery. These same two men moved along the boardwalk and repeated their same questions over and over again. I committed their faces to memory, stopped at the sheriff's office and found these two posters—wanted for murder and bank robbery in the Laredo area. They are known as part of the Parker Gang."

Uncle Joe was next to speak, "I wasn't having any luck at the mercantiles and hardware stores. So, I decided to go check out the pile of wanted posters in the sheriff's office. Then I came up to Red holding the two posters of the men he just described. I then took over and went thru at least 100 old posters looking for more Parker gang members. It eventually paid off when I found the poster of Cleatus Parker wanted for murder and bank robbery in Oklahoma City. I also found a third poster of a gang member, but the last two escaped me and must be recent additions in Texas. Of the four posters, their bounty came to $2,000 for Parker and $1,000 for each of the other three."

Then came Bryce's turn. "I spent my time visiting the eight banks in town. By presenting myself as a new customer with family money from Canada, I was able to discover the business practices of every bank. I eliminated the Merchants Bank since it had already been robbed. These seven other banks had their own specialty practices."

"Some banks had a high clientele of working people, a clientele of local merchants, a clientele of professionals, others specialized in real-estate transactions, while others specialized in payroll processing. The one question that I did not think the bank representatives would admit to, was the amount of money on hand to cover my high deposit of $30,000. I was shocked to find only two banks could cover my deposit when the only other bank that even came close was the Cattlemen's Bank at $20,000. The other four banks were only keeping $5,000 on hand."

"Now, of the two banks with a lot of cash on hand. The first is the Trader's Bank which handles real estate, but the vault is randomly set to open one hour per day. With the vault on a random basis without a manual override, this is not the bank to rob. The other bank is the 1ˢᵗ National Bank. This is unbelievably the parent bank that backs up branches in Dallas, Abilene and New Braunsfels. So, it has to carry the cash to support business in its branches. The vault is opened by the bank president and the head vice president using a separate key and dial combination. I firmly believe, the 1ˢᵗ National is our next victim."

"Well, let's have supper at Ginny's Diner and we have to come to a decision on how to approach this before daybreak tomorrow."

***

After a supper of T-Bone steaks, baked potatoes, whole kernel corn, coffee and a raspberry pie dessert, Uncle Joe presented the two options. "In the morning we walk into the 1ˢᵗ National Bank and take over protecting its workers and assets for the next week. This has to be done so no one knows we are present in the bank and when we abort the robbery, we must keep Parker alive since he may be the only one who knows where the money is hidden from the first heist."

"The second choice is to collect the four gang members we have posters on. This will wipe out the chance that the two newbies could rob the bank by themselves."

Red asked, "How does this get our hands on that stolen $22,000?"

Bryce answered, "Well, you see, we'll have to torture Cleatus Parker till he tells us where it's hidden. After reading Swanson's book, I now carry an awl for such a purpose. It yields results without any physical evidence of human torture."

Uncle Joe said, "I favor the second method as long as we capture Cleatus Parker first. Were we to start gathering the sycophants first, Parker might see what was happening and abscond with the money and the two other outlaws."

Red saw a problem. "In the morning we can't be looking for Cleatus and protect the 1st National Bank at the same time. The Sheriff and his deputies already said they were protecting the Cattlemen's Bank since it's getting a payroll this week."

Bryce answered, "assuming Cleatus Parker is a late riser, he is probably a late visitor of saloons, gambling houses, and whore houses. So, we go three different ways and scout the many bawdy houses during the late hours and let's hope the woodchuck comes out of his hole. Otherwise, we are baby-sitting the 1ˢᵗ National before opening time. So, let's go to work boys and every hour we make contact in front of Ginny's Diner. Good luck."

~~~~~~~~~~~~

Meanwhile, 150 miles away, Allie was opening Bryce's letter. She was shocked and pleased as her shaking hand was holding the two-page letter. She had never received her own personal letter, say nothing of one from a man who stirred her insides. As she read the words, she reflected on its significance, but any reason given for the letter was all acceptable to Allie at this point. She decided to write:

"Dear Bryce with a "y"

Shocked and please to receive your letter of current events.
Yes...I'm OK.
Mom...is dying.
Dad...with her 24/7.
Stressful times...............Doc worried about dad.

Business ....in hands of foreman.
Stay current...............write after present caper.
Will manage...................................stay safe.

Always, Allie with two l's"

~~~~~~~~~~~~

In a town of +-2,800 people, Texarkana had 14 sites of saloons, gambling casinos, and whore houses. The boys were rotating between them and meeting every hour. On the hour, at 11PM Bryce walked in the "Ace of Hearts" casino and spotted Cleatus Parker at the Faro table. To not look conspicuous, he ordered a beer and stayed standing at the bar where he could watch Parker thru the mirror behind the bar. Pretending to go to the privy, Bryce went back to Ginny's Diner and waited for Uncle Joe and Red.

"The gopher is out. He's at the 'Ace of Heart's Saloon' and there's a gun toting toady at his side. Well, we don't want the toady to know what we are doing with Parker. Let's do this, Uncle Joe and I will wait near the casino's privy and when he comes out, we sap him and knock him out. Red, you'll wait with a rented wagon with high sides and a tarp, about a block from the privy. Once he's loaded and covered up, we'll whisk him to the sheriff's office and make him talk."

Two hours later, Cleatus was full of beer and a bladder to match. The man ran outside and didn't even get to the privy as he pulled himself out of his unbuttoned fly, and let loose a full stream on the walkway. Bryce quietly snuck up behind him and sapped him hard in the back of the head. With his tally-wacker still hanging out, Uncle Joe and Bryce unceremoniously dragged him by his feet with his face and tally-wacker scraping the dirt trail. They threw the lifeless body in the wagon and off they went with their prize.

By the time they arrived at the sheriff's office, the deputy was about to lock the door. "Now who is this?" "This is the notorious killer Cleatus Parker. Throwing him in the cell, they removed his gun-belt, pulled his britches off, found a belly gun in his back, pulled his boots and found a derringer in one ankle holster. Now in his socks and union suit, Bryce asked him, "we want to know the names of your men and which hotel they're staying in, but most of all we want to know where your hid the money from the first heist at the Merchants Bank!"

"Hah, hah, hah, I'll dangle at the end of a rope before I tell you a damn thing. Besides, my 'second' will still hit the next target with extreme violence as retribution for my arrest hah, hah, hah."

"You scoundrel, you may think you're a dead man, but you're not dead yet. You're still able to feel pain." Without a warning, Bryce pushes Cleatus on the cot, straddles his chest and holds his knees on Cleatus' elbows. He forces his mouth open and shoves a pointed nail-like tool in Cleatus' bad molar. Cleatus' eyes crossed, and his hips heaved to give Bryce a bucking bull-ride. As Bryce started to jiggle the tool in all directions, Cleatus squealed, wet himself and moved his bowels. All this happened in a matter of seconds.

Watching all this was Red and Uncle Joe. Joe was holding onto the bars with white knuckles, grinding his teeth and pounding the floor with his boot. He was moaning to match Cleatus' squealing. At the same time Red exclaimed, "whippy old spirit grandfather, you thought you knew all the Apache tortures. I hope you can see this white boy ruin this white outlaw's day. Love it, just love it."

When Cleatus' squealing and screaming seemed to run out of steam, Bryce removed the tool and said, "wow, this is more than Swanson said so in his book. Now Cleatus, you have several rotten teeth that I can do this to for hours to come. You look pretty washed out to me, got anything to say before round two." "Shoot me, cause I'm no rat."

"Why you idiot, you may be short a brick for a load, but you can't be that stupid. If I kill you, I kill the goose that laid the golden eggs. Round two coming up. The awl goes in and this time, instead of squealing and screaming, Bryce hears gibberish, 'bewooodadabecaca' as he pulls the awl out. Uncle Joe was turning blue from holding his breath but managed to say, "I think our rodent is trying to speak."

"What's it going to be, round 3 or some answers?"

"No more, no more, you win. On the fourth-floor attic of the Wilson Hotel is a saddlebag hidden in an old rolltop desk. Can't miss it. My 'second' is Ron Marsh in room 20 of that hotel. I have two men in the Cassidy Hotel, Daryl Simpson and Dan Carr.

The other two are Simeon Walters and Cranston Riley in the Hampton Hotel. Now let me clean up and leave me to my misery."

By midnight, the Trio was rushing the doors at all three hotels. Uncle Joe was first to step in and point his sawed-off shotgun at the two outlaws. Not a single shot was fired, and all five outlaws were searched for hidden arms. They were then allowed to redress with their britches and shirts but without boots.

The next day, after a filling breakfast, they confiscated the outlaws' personal articles of value. They collected four boxes of 44-40 ammo, one box of 41 caliber ammo for a derringer, a set of binoculars, a nice silver watch with chain and wind up alarm clock, a compass, and extra canteens. These items were divided up and Bryce got the watch with the alarm clock. The Trio then confiscated the horses, tack, six pistols, six rifles and six saddlebags with scabbards. Everything sold at the liveries, gun shops, and mercantiles for $930 (six horses $360, twelve firearms $300, saddles/tack/saddlebags/scabbards/canteens $270). Not counting the petty cash of $698 out of the outlaws' pockets.

The second day, Sheriff Hodge had the settlement in his office. Present were representatives from the Banking Association and the Merchants Bank. The tally was: Banking Association $2,000, Merchants Bank 10% finders fee $2,200, Cleatus Parker bounty reward $2,000, other five outlaws $4,000, for a total of $10,200 plus the $930 the day before gave a grand total of $11,130.

With the job done and a bank robbery averted, the Trio decided to take the overnight express train back to Dallas. After boarding the train, Bryce asked why we were returning to Dallas, and where would our next caper be. Uncle Joe said, "the heavy bounties are usually from towns with populations over 1,000. As far as returning to Dallas, well it really is a good place for a hub since, in 1890, Dallas has a population of 67,000. Either we get a caper in Dallas from Marshal Balinger or one in another community like we just did in Texarkana. Besides, it's where my home and my hangout saloon are located in the King Hotel and Mulligen's Saloon." Bryce added, "and where there is a certain housekeeping lady friend, heh?"

***

By morning, the Trio returned to the King Hotel. Red, now aware of Joe's lady friend and the need for privacy, took his own room. Bryce and Uncle Joe picked up their mail from the receptionist. Walking upstairs to their rooms, Bryce noted that his letter was from Allie in Abilene. Setting his gear down he read the letter over twice. Realizing the letter had already been held five days, and with its content of such bad news, Bryce sat down and started to write a response.

"Dear Allie with two l's,

I commiserate......................with your situation
End of life...........................is a passage for all
My thoughts.............................are with you
Your dad.....................will need your strength
Bank robbery.....................................averted
Keeping King Hotel...........................our hub
Keep in touch..............................are you OK

Always, Bryce with a y."

***

CHAPTER 4

Finding Allie

At noon, Marshal Balinger was waiting for the Trio in their office, Sam's Diner. "It's about time you get here, the word from the railroad manager is that you've been here hours."

"Well we had errands to run, and if we continue doing business here, Sam is going to charge us rent. So, what's on your mind?"

"The telegraph line to lawmen has been buzzing since the massacre in Trinidad, Colorado. A well-known ruthless seven-member gang, led by Herman Kidder, burned a full block in town, acting as a diversion, while the remainder of the gang robbed the Trinidad Community Bank of a recent payroll deposit. These are psychopathic murderers, and a total of four local residents lost their lives in the fire as well as one teller in the bank. They made their escape because the town's people were busy fighting the fire to avoid losing the entire town, and a posse could not be organized in time. The only things that were certain were that it was the Kidder gang, that they stole $16,000, killed five innocent locals, and that they were heading south."

Uncle Joe interrupted the marshal to say, "this gang has burnt their bridge behind them. With such loss of money, buildings, and human lives, this gang can never return to Colorado and they can't even make residence in Texas. This gang is heading to Mexico."

Bryce added, "And what better place to be than Juarez, just across the line to El Paso. El Paso is a boomtown with a population of 3,000 and increasing by the hundreds each day. This conurbation zone takes advantage of the Mexican Free Trade agreement. So, these Americans can live in Mexico, come to the US for entertainment and nefarious business purposes, and the US lawmen cannot enter Mexico to arrest them—only bounty hunters dare enter the not so friendly Mexico to apprehend them at their own risk."

Red, usually a good listener, interjects, "what is this word conurbation, isn't that like an old 'private' word?" "no, and get your head out of the gutter, conurbation is an extended urban area merging the suburbs of two cities—El Paso and Juarez."

Uncle Joe came back, "I think Bryce has a good point. Do you know where the gang has been seen to buy train tickets or buy supplies for cross-country riding."

"Yes, they purchased train tickets in Amarillo two days ago. They were also seen in Sweetwater yesterday to get supplies."

Bryce knew what they were planning. "Sweetwater is only 30 miles from Colorado City. Then heading west another 40 miles is Big Springs. Thereafter, some 300 miles is El Paso. Now there are three small towns between Big Springs and El Paso that they can board a train heading west— Stanton, Midland and or Odessa."

Uncle Joe finally understood what Bryce was hinting at. "This gang needs more than $16,000 to live in Mexico. They are planning to rob a bank in both Colorado City and Big Springs before taking the train to El Paso." Bryce adds, "Colorado City has a population of 2,500 and Big Springs of 1,200. These are both cattle shipping centers where buyers pay cash for entire herds being shipped north to processing centers. This means that banks will be carrying large amounts of ready US currency to pay for the herds."

Marshal Balinger is listening to all this and finally asks, "Bryce, you seem to know distances between towns, populations, and even the major economies of each location. Heck, it sounds like you carry the entire Texas map in your head."

"You're right marshal, in school Texas geography was my hobby interest and I use to know all these Texas facts from borders to shores."

Uncle Joe adds, "while you were talking, I computed where this gang is possibly presently located. I think they may already be near Colorado City. With us being in Dallas, some 250 miles away, it's going to be a neck to neck race as to who gets there first. We'll leave right away by train and you should telegraph the law in Colorado City and prepare them for a diverting inferno as well as a bank robbery. One thing is for certain, if we don't apprehend them in Colorado City, we must do so before they reach Big Springs, or these animals will make it to Mexico."

And Red adds, "and if they make it to Mexico, we'll have one heck of a time to get them out."

Marshal Balinger asks, "are you committing to getting these bastards, even in Mexico?"

Joe answers, "Yes, we'll take on the responsibility." "Well that's why I offered it to you. You agreed to take on these dangerous outlaws without knowing the pay involved. That's honorable, anyways, the Community Bank is offering a 20% finder's fee (or $3,200), the merchants and city council leaders who lost businesses to the fire are offering a $3,000 reward for their capture dead or alive, the family members of the dead victims are offering $2,000 reward, and the old Colorado rewards on all seven outlaws comes to $6,000, also dead or alive. Plus, the usual value of horses, firearms, petty cash, and personal belongings."

"I realize that this comes to about $15,000 but that's the value placed by others, and that's what we are entitled to by law, if we survive the ordeal. Is this an excessive fee, knowing that one or more of us may get killed trying to stop evil men from spreading their mayhem to honest and innocent folks?"

Marshal Balinger smiled and said, "no, it is fair compensation. Be careful and stay safe. Don't hesitate to shoot first, because these animals won't give you a second chance since they are doomed if brought in alive. I'll also tell Marshal Blaine Burris that you are on your way to help either abort a catastrophe, or go on the trail to apprehend these outlaws."

***

The only train to Colorado City was thru Abilene, where the train would have a westerly connection to their destination. The layover was one hour, but was at 4:30AM. By the time they got back on route, stopped twice for coal and water, they finally arrived in Colorado City at 9:30AM. Once stepping on the platform, they could hear the fire engine bell on its way to a fire. The Trio quickly picked up their horses and headed towards the sound of the fire engine bell.

Before they got to the fire, people were gathering in front of the Cattlemen's Bank. Marshal Burris was trying to organize a posse out of a rag tale gang of misfits not working on putting out the fire, when Joe introduced himself and asked what happened. "We've been robbed a bankrupting amount of ranchers money totaling $20,000 which was in anticipation of the weekly auction tomorrow. To make it worse, two innocent customers were shot dead for no apparent reason, other than to instill fear in everyone's mind. They were the Kidder gang for sure."

While Uncle Joe was getting as much info as possible, Bryce and Red were checking out the hoof marks heading west of town. Red found an unusually large hoof mark and said, "a horse with a hoof that large must be 18 or 19 hands and can carry a 300-pound bear of a man. That's the tract we'll be following if we can verify that such a large man was involved in the heist."

While Joe confirmed that a huge man was holding the outlaw horses during the heist, Bryce and Red were picking up vittles to fill their saddlebags. Before long, the Trio was on the hunt. Their goal was to catch up with the gang after dark at their camp site, which would likely be 30 miles to the west and only ten miles to Big Springs.

The Kidder gang had a 45-minute lead and were pushing their horses to get away from a possible posse. Although, the fire would likely delay if not prevent a posse from organizing. In any event, the gang's plan was to push for thirty miles before setting up camp. That would mean a full day in the saddle to reach their goal before nightfall.

Meanwhile, the Trio's pace was more relaxed with Red keeping an eye on the tracks. Uncle Joe was appreciative of the slower pace because of his aching arthritic back. At midnight, the Trio finally smelled wood smoke. They stepped down, Uncle Joe had to walk off the back and leg pain, before they gathered to make plans.

Uncle Joe asked Bryce how we should proceed to overpower this bunch of miscreants—knowing fully that an outright gunfight was inevitable. Bryce turned to Red with this question.

"On moccasins, how close do you think we can get, assuming they are drunk, or sleeping, or both."

"The ground cover is lush greenery without dry needles or leaves. I think we can get close enough to kick them in the ass."

"Wow, then get us within eight yards and our sawed-off shotguns will take care of the problem."

***

Literally creeping along, Red chose where to put his feet and avoid any twigs that could snap. At 50 yards, Red collapsed to the ground. An outlaw got up to go to the bushes and when he returned, he threw several pieces of wood on the fire to deal with the chilly night. The Trio waited a good fifteen minutes for the outlaw to resume snoring and the creeping resumed, this time keeping a low bent over profile in case an outlaw was awake. Before the Trio realized it, they had reached their 8- yard destination. Bryce could not believe how stupid outlaws could be. Anyone who had just robbed a bank, and were holding thousands of dollars, should at least have one if not two guards throughout the night.

Getting the nod of readiness from Red to his left and Bryce to his right, Uncle Joe yells out, "WAKE

UP, YOU DIRTBAGS. You're done, put your hands up and stand up. If you go for a gun, we're going to turn you into swiss cheese. We're holding three sawed-off shotguns on you and we mean to use them."

Uncle Joe hadn't spoken his last word when an outlaw shot at them thru his bedroll as the bullet hit Red in the right shoulder and knocked him to the ground. Before hitting the ground, he pulled his trigger twice and nearly decapitated the shooter with direct hits to his face. This started a cavalcade of blind shots coming at them. Joe and Bryce let go both barrels of #3 Buckshot with each shot devastating the outlaws with 20 pellets of lethal lead. The result was a group of men moaning and some who were in the final throws of escaping life.

Uncle Joe rushed into the center of camp as Bryce stayed back with his pistol drawn and watching for someone to point a gun at Uncle Joe. Joe finally called Bryce in to apply three manacles to surviving outlaws. Afterwards, Bryce rushed to check out Red. He had a clear entrance wound to his shoulder, but no exit would. That meant that the bullet was likely impacted in bone and would need surgical exploration to extract it. At the same time the wound tract would also need to be explored for detritus that could cause infection. So, after pouring carbolic acid in the wound to sterilize it, he then dressed the wound with a pressure dressing to prevent blood loss.

The three surviving outlaws were laced with pellets from head to toes. Although these were not fatal wounds, they certainly had taken the fight our of them. Among the living was Kidder himself. The outlaws were then manacled to a tree and their body and boots searched for other firearms. Afterwards, the camp was searched and the $20,000 was found in Kidder's saddlebags. The pockets of living and dead outlaws revealed $791 which they divided and pocketed.

With the money recovered and the outlaws no longer a threat, the Trio went about preparing a nice breakfast of beans, bangers, hoe cakes and coffee. Afterwards, Bryce and Joe loaded the four dead outlaws to their horses' saddles. The living outlaws were loaded to their horses and both ankles were manacled to the stirrups. Then Joe said, "Bryce, you and Red head out for Colorado City. You can make the 30 miles easily by noon and the sooner the doc takes care of Red's wound, the lesser the chance of an infection. I'll be alright with these goons since, unless their horse breaks a leg or dies of a heart attack, they are in the saddle for the duration of the trip. And by the way, bring the $20,000 and the outlaws' firearms back with you. I'll be arriving just before dark and we can meet at the marshal's office."

By noon, the money was back in the bank, and Red was under ether anesthesia getting surgery at the local hospital. As a surprise, Uncle Joe pulled in with his live and dead shipment by 4PM. Marshal Burris decided that the local doc would be called in to extract the pellets without anesthesia—of course.

Red's surgery went well and was discharged the next morning. The Trio then got together for a late breakfast at Susie's Diner. After eating their fill, Uncle Joe asked if everyone felt like heading back to Dallas. Red was ready to return home to Dallas and Uncle Joe was willing to escort him back. Bryce hesitated. "I'll join you as far as Abilene, but I will stop there for a few days to visit my parents and a special young woman who is going thru a stressful time."

The Trio divided the $15,000 and started bank accounts in Colorado City. It was safer to do this than carry thousands of dollars in this violent land. Bank transfers were arranged, and the Trio sent their money to their individual accounts at the 1st National in Abilene.

During the train ride to Abilene, Bryce wondered how his encounter with Allie would go. Uncle Joe realized that Bryce was very pensive and decided to say something.

"Hey nephew, I can see that you are bothered with something. I suspect it's a woman. I will only say two things. As a bounty hunter you must have a clear head at all times. Secondly, if you have to clearly make a commitment to someone who cares for you, then do it and get it past you. Only then can you return to Dallas and continue our year's journey safely."

"I agree, when and if I return, I won't have any encumbrances and I will have a clear head."

***

Going their different ways in Abilene, Bryce got his horse and rode to his parent's gun shop. "Well lord be, this is a pleasant surprise, what brings you to town? We expected you at the end of your year's mission, but this is a welcomed premature event. We know you didn't stop in Abilene to visit us, so what are you doing here."

"Well, we were returning to Dallas from a bank robbery in Colorado City when I decided to hold up in town for a few days. Before I embarked in bounty hunting with Uncle Joe, I made the acquaintance of an old forgotten school classmate. We've been writing and I'm aware that her mom is terminal. I thought I would stop and try to give her some moral support."

Jim started, "son, first of all her mom died ten days ago. We went to her funeral and had a long talk with Allie. This is some sharp and pleasant young lady, and if I was you, I'd try to make her more than an acquaintance." Sally took over, "now the real sad news is that her dad died yesterday. Doc Newcomb said that he died of a broken heart. The funeral was this morning and we attended. Presently, there is a community dinner at the Adkins home put on by the Lutheran Church Ladies' Association. We could not attend that event since we had to open the gun shop. After dinner there will be an open house for visiting with friends, neighbors, and church members." Jim added, "this is a good time to extend your sympathies to Allie in a public setting, and maybe you can get some private time with her and. . . . .*Jim and Sally looked at each other as they realized that Bryce had not heard all their comments, since the front door bell rang and the door closed as Jim was still talking without an audience.*

Arriving at the Adkins home, Bryce tied his horse to the railing, stepped on the porch, and with the front door open, he stepped inside the parlor where the men had gathered. Azra Albright spotted him and came over to welcome him with a handshake (noticed by Eustache Backus). Azra said, "what brings you here today?" "I was hoping to extend my sympathies to Allie and possibly have a word with her in private."

Azra could see more in his answer and said, "step into the office and I will tell Allie she has a drop-in visitor she needs to greet. When she enters,

I'll stand at the door to give you some private time with her."

Bryce was leaning on the large office desk as the door opened and Allie rushed in. Bryce saw Allie, tall, slim with golden blonde short hair and dressed in a lovely black dress; as well as exuding the appearance of youth, beauty and newly acquired shapeliness. As she slammed the door shut, her eyes made contact with the last person on earth she ever expected to see. Then it happened, they both started walking toward each other, without recollection, and fell into each other's arms. Allie whimpered but quickly mumbled the words, "God, how I've missed you." Bryce looked into her eyes and said, "with me, it's been more of a 'longing' since I left town." The inevitable happened, their lips touched, locked, and froze in an inexplicable passion.

When the mood settled down, Allie said she had much to share with him and asked that he join her for breakfast in the AM. Today was a day reserved for the neighbors and friends. As they came out of the office, for all to see, Allie said, "Bryce, I'll leave you with the men for now. I suspect you know most of these men." As Allie excused herself to return to the kitchen with the ladies, Bryce walked around and made small talk with several of the men to include: Sheriff Marlow, Doc Newcomb, Zeke Ashworth (blacksmith), Rudy Tate (hardware), Frank Riley (livery), Nate Zimmer (feed and grain), Sawyer Skinner (neighbor east of Adkins), and several other town's people.

Bryce carried on several talks with all these men but three of the subjects were recorded into Bryce's memory banks. Eustache Backus had serially planted 150 acres of corn and the early planting was approaching maturity. Tate's Hardware had received a new horse drawn double row corn chopper and a four-row corn planter. Nate Zimmer explained why the cost of feed and grain had gone up 25% in the past month and was expected to stay that way indefinitely. Later, it was clear that Allie would be occupied with the guests, so Bryce decided to return home to visit with his parents and get a home cooked meal.

***

Bryce was up early to make coffee and was off by 7:30AM to the Adkins residence. Arriving, he stepped to the porch and was about to knock when the door opened, and a beautiful young woman grabbed his hand and pulled him in the house. As the door closed, they found themselves sharing another passionate kiss. Out of necessity, the two moved over to the kitchen stove where the bacon was ready to start cooking. It quickly became comfortable working together as they cooked bacon, eggs, home fries, toasted home-made bread over plenty of coffee. After a full meal, cleaning up the dishes, and continuing sipping coffee, the two were finally able to talk.

Allie began, "dad never got over losing mom and after the funeral he gave up. He refused to eat and wouldn't leave his chair. He never went back in their bedroom. He insisted on showing me the books and discussed how to run the pork business. Other than seeing where the money went for expenses, I knew how the business was run from day to day. He gave me his will and showed me his bank account with a balance of $5,000. Being the only child and no other relatives on earth, I inherited the business, the house, the 640 acres and the barn. Yes, I inherited an expense free piggery."

"Now, what do you plan to do with it?"

"I plan to operate the business. Actually, I have no choice at this time. I'm 17 years old and have no training, other than homemaking and a tenth-grade education. I know how to raise pigs for pork meat at a profit. Do you think this is wrong of me?"

"Heck no, it takes a strong-willed woman to embark on a business venture—at any age. I am proud to see you accept the challenge, and I'm even willing to help you. Now, what do you see as an immediate business problem that has to be dealt with?"

"The price of feed is going up 25% and that's going to cut in the business profits. I need to find a source of feed that is affordable. Right now, we use pig mash, pellets, and vegetables out of our gardens. I know the answer is to grow our own food to include corn, soybeans, sugar beets, and others. But for now, this is a major change and use of my 640 acres which I cannot undertake by myself."

"I agree, but I may have the solution to this problem. We'll work on that tomorrow. Anything else that needs our immediate attention?"

"Yes, Mr. Abernathy at the 1st National Bank quickly mentioned a problem in passing. At seventeen, it appears I am not legal to inherit a business and a bank account. Nor am I legal in conducting business transactions or hire employees. All this will change at age eighteen, but for now I have a problem. He asked that I go see him today to learn about a solution."

"Great, I figured there might be a solution. Let's hope the solution is not too costly or stressful. Let's head out to the bank and find out the facts. On our way back, we'll go see a homesteader about a corn crop."

Goddard Abernathy greeted them and said, "Please come in. I just want to start by thanking you again, Bryce, for returning that stolen money when we were robbed. And thank you Allie for addressing the legal issue at hand. I've mentioned this problem to Judge Bull and apparently there is a legal solution."

"Does it involve an adult backing up Allie financially? If it does, I'm ready to do so."

"Actually no, not completely. Allie needs to be emancipated. It's a complex legal entity that will be explained by Judge Bull, who is expecting you today."

Walking toward the courthouse, Allie says, "I remember reading about this in civics class, and as I recall, it involves my exact situation."

"Humm, I must have been sleeping that day, or I missed school because this is all new to me." *Allie thought, or you were busy staring at Mary Jo with the long red hair and big boobs.*

Arriving at the courthouse, the judge's secretary escorted them into the judge's chambers. "How may I help you folks?"

"My name is Allie Adkins, and this is Bryce Sullivan. I am a seventeen-year-old woman who has inherited a pig farm, 640 acres, a bank account of $5,000 and I can't do any business because I am not of legal age. I'm requesting to be emancipated so I can be free to take over my parents' life-long business of raising pork meat."

"Well, that is a very concise and clear request. From what I hear, you are certainly capable of carrying on the business. And who is the adult sponsoring you?"

"I am your honor, Bryce Sullivan, son of Jim and Sally Sullivan and resident of this town."

"I know who you are, and thank you for the honorable work you and your uncle are doing. Now as sponsor, are you willing to be Allie's guarantor in case she cannot pay her bills during the next year?"

"Yes sir, without a doubt."

"In that case, can you post a $5,000 bond at the 1st National Bank as I am told this amount matches the Adkins' bank account. These funds would only be used if the Adkins' funds are used up for whatever purpose."

"Allie adds, "Bryce are you sure? That's a lot of money to hold on escrow?"

"Allie, that's a small amount compared to my bank account balance, and I've been sure of this for some time."

"Yes, your honor. Money is not an issue."

"Very well, then allow me to fill out this Declaration of Emancipation." After completion, the judge signed his name, as did Allie and Bryce, and the county seal was added to the document.

"Now, you need to bring this document to the town clerk, property tax office, the bank, and every business in town that you intend to do business with and carry a line of credit. Otherwise, good luck and I suspect that one day, I will be signing your marriage license!" Bryce and Allie left holding hands with a smile on their faces.

After visiting the town clerk, Allie left with a deed in her name. Allie was able to set up her own line of credit at the hardware store, mercantile, and the feed store. In addition, Allie left a $500 deposit at the feed store to guarantee regular deliveries of piglet mash and hog pellets. With the bond posted at the 1st National Bank, the couple retired to Veronicas Diner for dinner before Bryce's plans for the afternoon.

***

After dinner, Bryce and Allie rode their horses west past Allie's home to the next neighbor,

Eustache and Imogene Backus. After greetings were done, Bryce took the lead, "we see that you have a large 150-acre corn field serially planted in six row sections. How do you plan to sell your crop?"

"Well, initially I had planned to chop it up and sell it to ranchers as supplemental feed. But with the end of the drought, there is plenty of grass and hay to support their herd. I had anticipated this and so I planted sweet corn. Now, I had to cancel the corn chopper and I'll sell my ears of corn by the baker's dozen at the farmer's market and the many mercantiles in town. It's not the most profitable method, and it is the most labor intensive, but I have no other choice."

"I think there may be an alternative choice. Allie needs a cheaper feed for her growing pigs and hogs. Let me propose this: I'll buy the corn chopper at Tate's Hardware; you harvest enough rows each day to fill the wagon I spotted coming into your homestead. You bring the chopped corn to Allie's farm, unload the wagon in wheelbarrows and feed the entire stock. This lightens the load for the farm workers. Afterwards, finish your 8-hour day by helping Allie and her foreman. In return, Allie will pay you $3 per day for your corn silage and your time. Also, you keep replacing the harvested corn with regular new plantings of 'feed' corn, and the seed will be free."

"Oh Mr. Sullivan, this is an incredible offer, but I feel bad in taking your offer since I feel I'm taking advantage of you and Allie. I know I was born at night, but it wasn't last night. I know it was you who added that bag of sugar cookies for my kids, and I know that it was you who paid my credit bill, gave me $1500 to buy work horses, plow and harrows, and a corn seeder to plant this field." Allie interrupted him and said, "Mr. Backus, Bryce did this out of his care for others. What we are proposing is a business deal, and frankly I need the feed and the help, now that my dad is gone."

"Well then, you have a deal and I look forward to working with your foreman, Alva Bassett, is a good man. After shaking hands on the deal, Bryce and Allie returned to the farm.

***

Allie went to work preparing supper of boiled potatoes, pork chops, apple sauce, mashed rutabagas and coffee. While she was at work, Bryce asked if she had plans for future change. "Yes, I have plans but for now I have to get use to my new responsibilities."

"Out of curiosity, and just thinking out loud, what would you change right now if you could."

"Naw, you don't really want to know!"

"Yes, I'm interested, now come on, spit it out!"

"Well since you insist, I would go out and purchase two one-year old boars with colored hides. I would buy a purebred 'Duroc' boar which is red in color and a purebred 'Hampshire' which is black in color, and I would dive in crossbreeding them with my purebred white pigs—the 'Yorkshire' and the 'Landrace.'"

"Wow, that is one heck of a mouthful, and I guess I asked for it. Now, I've heard about crossbreeding cattle as a new way of improving on the animal's growth and yield, as well as the meat flavor and quality. Is this the same thing?"

"Yes. Crossbreeding is a planned approach to mating pigs with different genetic backgrounds.

This results in 'Heterosis' or 'Hybrid Vigor' where the new offspring have advantages over the parent purebreds by inheriting the best of both breeds. Actually, the crossbreeds yield pigs with several advantages to include: growing faster on less feed by absorbing more nutrition from the feed, reproductive efficiency and ease of farrowing, improved animal cleanliness, and a more docile personality. The biggest effect is on the meat. There is more meat on crossbreed carcasses than purebreds and, more lean meat, more bacon, more tender meat, and more flavor. And that is what the butcher and the customers want."

"I'm curious, what specific traits are you mixing with all four different purebreeds?"

"Our white 'Landrace' (droopy ears) are long bodied hogs that are heavy milkers and farrow large piglets. The long bodies promote large hams and tenderloins. Our other white 'Yorkshire" (erect ears) are known for lean meat and low back fat. This is a very durable and healthy line of hogs. It is a good producer of bacon and in general, it is one of the most popular meat hogs in the area."

"Now the new breeds for crossbreeding. The 'Duroc' (droopy ears) adds the trait of fast growing and higher total body weight at marketing maturity—and that means more income for the producers. These hogs also emphasize the new lean meat much lower in meat fat and lard. The hogs have a much longer longevity and docile nature. The red color imparts a reassurance to the butcher of tender and tasty meat."

"Not to forget the 'Hampshire' (erect ears), is the black hide hog. The cross piglets often have large black and white stripes instead of being grey. The advantageous traits match the 'Duroc'. The sows have good mothering and nursing qualities with long reproductive years. Its lean meat, with low backfat, produces quality carcasses with a high total body weight."

"Another way of explaining crossbreeding is to say that it is the opposite of inbreeding from the same litter or from the female's father, That way, it tends to avoid small litters, stillborns, failing to thrive and runt piglets from the devastating result of mixing recessive genes."

"Wow, I have a lot to learn. This is a new world for me!"

"In that case, let me get you something." Walking back from her office, she hands Bryce two books. Bryce reads the titles, "Raising Commercial Hogs for Meat" and "The Science of Crossbreeding Hogs."

"Yes, these will be helpful as starters. There is no doubt that, being involved with you, I want to know the business."

"I especially like 'the involved with you portion,'" as she takes his hand, and they embrace with a passionate kiss. While Allie was putting the finishing touches to their supper, Bryce asked, "how much do these one-year old Duroc and Hampshire boars sell for?"

"A lot more than their value in meat, or $300 each."

"How many sows do you have for breeding?"

"I have ten older sows in different stages of nursing, but I have fifty purebred white gilts that are 10 months old and ready for breeding. This is what I would use the new boars for. I would pen a boar with ten gilts and in three weeks, all ten would have mated and be pregnant."

"What guarantees do these sellers provide with the boars' sale."

"These are reputable growers from Austin. They guarantee high pregnancy rates, a good size healthy litter, or they replace the hog."

"Sounds like this is another win-win situation. Assuming this crossbreeding program starts soon, how long before you can expect your first farrowing?"

"Sow's gestation is 3 months, 3 weeks and 3 days."

"In that case, as he's writing a $1200 bank draft, tomorrow you can order two each of Durocs and Hampshires. Handing her the bank draft, he adds, "it pleases me to be part of this business improvement plan." "As it does with me!"

After a great supper and cleaning up the dishes, Bryce started a coal fire in the parlor stove, and the two sat on the sofa holding hands in silence. Allie finally spoke, "we've had an extremely full day from getting emancipated, to finding an affordable feed supply, to obtaining some extra help for our foreman, and to agree in ordering some crossbreeding hogs for our new business enterprise" ...."whoa, did you say 'our' foreman and 'our' new business enterprise?"

"Was I being presumptive?"

"Presumptive is good, now let me show you how I really feel."

The kissing started and expanded to sharing their tongues with an open mouth. Eventually, both their hands started roaming. Bryce was caressing Allie's breasts as Allie was unbuttoning her blouse and her chemise. Before either realized it, Allie was nude from the waist up and Bryce was kissing her nipples. Allie was sweating and started moaning. There was no need for asking any permission as Allie shed her skirt and panty underwear. It was the only time that Bryce said, "I want to pleasure you, will you let me?"

In answer, Allie guided his hand to her private area. Allie's moaning and gyrating increased to a sudden body stiffening followed by uncontrollable body spasms and resolving in a short period of near unconsciousness. Somewhat concerned, Bryce asked, "are you OK Allie?"

Still trying to catch her breath, Allie said, "for a moment, I thought I was going to lose my mind, then a pleasurable relief arrived. I think you just stole my soul. Now I want to steel yours."

Allie turned to Bryce and started fondling him. In short order, Bryce felt uncontrollable contractions and came to his nirvana. After a period of afterglow, both of them were cuddling in each other's arms as Bryce said, "we just shared some beautiful intimacy and I feel that we made a commitment to each other. How do you feel about that?"

"Yes, yes and yes. I will wait for you till the end of time. I don't know what love is, but what I feel now is more powerful than that word." "And I feel the same way." After an hour passed, the two retired to Allie's bedroom and shared her bed. The two never redressed and slept in their nude embrace all night. By morning, they quickly dressed, used the privy and performed their morning ablutions before they started preparing their first replenishing breakfast.

After breakfast, Bryce brought up the last issue he wanted to discuss. "Allie, you are a beautiful available woman with money. There will be suitors or violent men to take advantage of you. Would you start wearing a firearm every day whether you are on the farm or in town doing business?"

"My father taught me how to shoot a rifle, shotgun and Colt pistol. I'm very accurate with all three, but the Colt pistol is too heavy for me to wear all the time."

"I see. Well, as much as I hate to say this, but I need to take the noon train back to Dallas to finish my year's commitment with Red and Uncle Joe. Before we leave for town, would you introduce me to your foreman. Then we'll go to my parent's gun shop and resolve the firearm issue."

Stepping in the barn, Allie said, "Alva, I'd like you to meet Bryce Sullivan, the man I have committed to." After introductions and pleasantries were made, Bryce told Alva that Eustache Backus would be bringing a wagonload of corn silage every day and then would help out with daily chores. Allie asked, "are you going to need more help with my father's passing?"

"Yes, your father was the key man during butchering. I will need some help with this job. May I suggest that my brother Alec, who just retired from the post office, has been doing private butchering as a side income, would likely be interested in working for you."

Allie never hesitated, "Yes, hire him either part time as needed, or so many days routinely each week. We'll work out his pay later."

Arriving in town, Bryce and Allie went to the telegraph office to send off an order and payment for the four purebred hogs. Afterwards, they went to his parent's gun shop. "Mom and dad, you know Allie but what you don't know is that this is your future daughter in law, as he placed his arm around Allie's waist. There is no official announcement, but we have committed to each other. Now, I'll be leaving to finish my commitment with Uncle Joe, and we need to arm her with a pistol she can wear all day."

Jim took out a Webley Bulldog with a hip holster and several boxes of ammo. He said, "this is a five shot pistol that is double action and you can shoot it without pulling back the hammer. It fires a powerful American made rimfire 44 caliber cartridge that is a perfect self-defense ammo. Take it out back and try it at short range targets."

After a fairly long shooting session, they came back inside the gun shop. Bryce said, "this is the perfect pistol for Allie." As they were leaving, Sally said, "Allie, I know you're a regular church goer, so after the Sunday service, would you join us for our family dinner so we can get to know each other. I know you know our daughters since you went to school with them." "I would love that, thank you Mrs. Sullivan."

"Mrs. Sullivan was my mother-in-law, please call us Sally and Jim or mom and dad."

"I will also feel relieved knowing you are making contact with Allie at least once a week."

Riding to the train yard, Bryce purchased a ticket to Dallas with a tag for his horse in the stock car. Before boarding, Bryce simply took Allie in his arms and said, "I love you Allie Adkins with two l's. I'll be back soon between capers since I won't be able to stay away for six months without having you in my arms."

"I'll be here waiting for you. I love you so much. Be safe and yes, I'm really OK."

***

CHAPTER 5

Have Job will Rail-Travel

The train ride started off as a sad situation. Bryce had found the woman he wanted to be with. All attractions were back in Abilene, but here he was heading 150 miles from where he wanted to be. He finally rationalized that he had a commitment to see thru with Uncle Joe and at the same time, he would be building his bank account—assuming he could stay alive dealing with these heartless killers from day to day.

To pass the time, he opened one of the books Allie had given him. Since he knew something about crossbreeding, he decided to refine his knowledge and read the book called, "The Science of Crossbreeding Hogs." This was a 50-page booklet and, to his surprise, there was little to add since he was already convinced that this was the wave of the future. There was no doubt that to compete with other producers, crossbreeding was the first thing to achieve.

The one thing he learned and studied in detail was the method of breeding animals and the rebreeding of their litters to continue mixing the purebred genes. The combination of mixing four purebred lines offered innumerable combinations with the ultimate production of a litter of piglets with all four purebred genetic lines. He now understood what Allie meant by the term "planned mating" to achieve a hybrid combination of beneficial traits.

When he checked out the second book, this one was a thick 300- page textbook called, "Raising Commercial Hogs for meat." He quickly realized that this book should have been called, "Everything you could ever want to know about raising pigs." The text had a preface that explained the names used in swine nomenclature.

- Gilt–a young female that has not farrowed its first litter.
- Sow–a female that has farrowed at least one litter.
- Newborn pig–piglet

- Shoat-a weaned piglet.
- Barrow–a castrated male.
- Boar–an uncastrated male use for breeding.
- Hog–a pig weighing more than 120 pounds.

Next, he checked out the table of contents with its subdivisions.

1. Breeding. Ideal age/mating/heat cycles.
2. Farrowing. Time per piglet/per litter, assistance.
3. Care of newborn piglets. Heat requirements/ supplemental feed.
4. Castration. Ideal age/technique.
5. Feed choices. Creep feed/weaning diet/ growing pigs/mature hogs/nursing sows/ finishing feed.
6. Hog habits. Tail biting/rooting/cooling off/ cleanliness.
7. Pig diseases. Six common illnesses.
8. Health issues. Three common disorders.
9. How to grow pigs faster. Diet/supplements/ feed prep and amount.
10. Growing crops for feed. Basic corn/ soybeans/oats/barley/sorghum.

11. Slaughtering. Ideal weight/blood collecting/ skin scalding.
12. Meat cuts. Ham/loin/bacon/ribs/boned or boneless roasts/ground pork/chops/lard.
13. How to make. Bacon/blood sausage/salt pork/pork rinds/head cheese.
14. Economics of raising pigs as a "cash crop."

Bryce realized two things. Allie wanted him to acquire some basic facts so they can discuss things in the future and this book would serve this purpose. Secondly, he would have to learn each chapter and prepare a list of questions that needed clarification. This was a long-term project and he would know this textbook from cover to cover before he saw Allie again.

***

As the train was approaching the yard in Dallas, Bryce saw Marshal Balinger standing on the passenger platform along with Uncle Joe and Red. Bryce knew that something important was amiss. Stepping down, Uncle Joe came to greet Bryce, "welcome back nephew. We knew you were arriving on this train because the telegraph wire has been singing between Abilene, Dallas, and Wichita Falls to find you. There is an emergency situation in Wichita Falls. If we accept the job, we'll be taking this same train heading north in 2 hours. The yard crew needs that time to unload freight and add new freight heading north."

Marshal Balinger adds, "we have time to get you a hot meal, so let's step into your office and I'll fill you in on the emergency. Entering Sam's Diner, Marshal Balinger showed the waitress an uplifted hand with four fingers upright. The waitress nodded and walked back with a pot of coffee and four tin cups.

The marshal started, "Wichita Falls, population 2,000 is another cattle receiving center along the railroad line. The land around town was owned by the Vaughan family before the town developed. For the past ten years, Calhoun Vaughan, a real estate developer, has been selling lots and has become a rich man. Yet, despite the riches, he is the town's own philanthropist who has built the courthouse, the town clerk/tax collector office, sheriff's office, town hall, public park, and is the financial benefactor behind the 'overseer of the poor organization.'"

Uncle Joe says, "Nice background, but what is the point."

"Yesterday, Calhoun Vaughan's wife, Victoria, was kidnapped. Last night, a ransom note arrived with a ring finger and its wedding ring. The ransom request was for $100,000 to be paid in three days or the next body part would be the victim's external genitals. Included were the directions to the delivery site. There was one warning, if the law was involved, her body would be returned in six parts—dismembered, decapitated, and a disemboweled body. With a footnote, all done by Butch the Butcher with the victim alive."

"Sounds real, but how did this isolated event get to us, we're 150 miles from Wichita Falls?"

"Well, Mr. Vaughan's long-time friend is the local law, Sheriff Blevin. It was the sheriff who pointed out that even if the ransom was paid, that the kidnappers would certainly kill his wife anyways since she could identify her kidnappers. Out of desperation, he followed his friend's recommendation to seek outside help."

Bryce added, and why us?"

"Because the word is out on the lawmen's telegraph trail. You work behind the scenes but always get positive results. The reference is in regard to the capers in Abilene, Dallas, Texarkana, and Colorado City. Your job will be to deliver the ransom money and hopefully capture the 'pickup' man. You'll have to take any measure to make him talk and give up the hideout where they are keeping Victoria Vaughan. If you are successful in getting the information, your duty is to save Missus Vaughan's life at whatever cost to the outlaws. Your pay has not been established but I'm certain that if you are successful, Mister. Vaughan will be very generous."

Uncle Joe looked at Red and Bryce and got two nods. "We'll take the job and, after we have supper, we'll be on the train to Wichita Falls." Uncle Joe and Bryce heard Red mussitating, "let's hope this is not our 'last supper.'" Uncle Joe added, "we'll get there by morning and will have plenty of time to get the ransom money to the deposit site by noon."

Marshal Balinger left and the Trio ordered supper. Bryce tells the waitress, as she came to take their orders, "it would be wise if you not mention wine, bread and fresh fish as the supper special. My Indian friend is rather superstitious of such a menu."

***

The train ride was mesmerizing with the lanterns out; and Uncle Joe and Red slept all night. Bryce was in a corner with his own kerosene lantern. *He was tackling Chapter 1—Breeding. (taking notes) Age: Gilts start having an estrus cycle at six months, it recurs every 21 days and lasts 12 to 36 hours. The best age to start breeding them is 10 months. Each Sow can have two litters per year and each litter varies from six to twelve piglets.*

Mating: Some boars can mate daily, but the yield in litters is best if the boars mate every other day or more. The mating process is a bit different from other animals. The boar's penis locks in the cervix and ejaculation lasts five minutes or more. Breeding is best done by pen breeding where a boar is with ten sows/gilts and in three weeks the females will all have been inseminated. In selective breeding, supervised mating is frequently practiced.

**Heat:** _Workers need to watch for signs of "Heat." A female is in heat every 21 days. The signs of heat are: Restlessness, not eating, vulva swollen, stands still if worker touches the animals side mimicking being held for mating. Missing a heat cycle delays farrowing by three weeks._

Although the chapter contained many more facts, the essence of the chapter on breeding was in his notes. After two hours of reading, Bryce turned off the lamp and slept the remainder of the trip.

Arriving in Wichita Falls, the Trio hit the nearest diner for coffee and breakfast of steak and eggs. They had a meeting with Calhoun Vaughan at 8AM. Stepping on the porch of the massive mansion on Vaughan Street, the Trio was escorted to Mister Vaughan's office where a lawman was sitting next to Vaughan's desk.

Bryce noted that Vaughan's appearance was a mess. "Please, have a seat. I know I look disheveled, but I have lost the only thing in life that matters to me. I must have my loving wife back at all costs, for without her, I no longer wish to live. I am willing to pay ten times the asking ransom price, but they only asked for $100,000. Sheriff Blevin feels that the asking ransom price will not prevent these kidnappers from killing my wife. So, the short of it, you are my only hope to save my wife."

Sheriff Blevin then takes over, "did Marshal Balinger explain what may be needed to find the kidnappers hideout where Victoria will be located?"

Uncle Joe answered, "yes, we know. Although it is not usually our style to torture, we all accept the fact that this is an exception, and it is the lives of the outlaws versus the innocent victim's life. We will do what is necessary."

Vaughan came back, "do whatever is necessary to bring back my wife and I'll take complete responsibility for your actions. Here is the ransom fee and good luck. Please God, allow them to succeed."

The Trio needed to make plans before making the drop. Bryce read the delivery instructions. "Travel on horseback, some five miles north of town. On the right of the road, a large oak tree will have a red bandana attached to a limb at eye level. Turn right at that tree and follow three more red bandanas on trees. On the third bandana, leave the bag of money on the ground, step back, and leave the area. You will be watched till you are out of sight. If you return and try to follow the pickup man, then the watchman with a rifle will shoot you dead."

Uncle Joe and Bryce reread the directions several times trying to find a way to get their hands on the pickup man. The watchman was the variable that ruined any plan. Red then took the directions, read them himself only once and said, "I know what needs to be done."

"Really, well then you'd better tell us, oh wise Indian."

"That's right, this requires Indian work. I will dress in standard Indian garb, rent a pinto horse, wear a long-haired wig and add face mudding to look very old. I will ride past the first red bandana, very slow to look like a sick old Indian. Once I'm past safely out of sight, I will dump the disguise and head for the woods. Once I find the trail the pickup man used to reach the drop off site, I will follow it to his horse. If there are two horses, then he does have a watchman with a rifle. If there is one horse, then he is alone. I predict that there will only be one horse since the Butcher is a coward and won't want to stay anywhere without protection from his toadies. If there is a watchman, I will dispatch him first. Then I will be hiding, waiting for the pickup man to get his horse. I will then attack him and when you hear the horrible scream of terror, you can then join me for the party."

Bryce and Uncle Joe looked at each other, shrugged their shoulders, and Uncle Joe added, "sounds like a plan. Since I appear the least threatening, I'll make the drop."

Bryce added, "and what about me, what am I chopped liver. What do I do?"

"You can help this crazy Indian torture the dude, and then we'll rely on you as the shootist during the rescue."

**

The Trio was on their mission. Red looked like an old Indian who had died in the saddle. Bryce and Uncle Joe stayed two hundred yards behind the first red bandana. An hour later, they figured that Red was in position. Uncle Joe took the money, rode his horse to the first bandana, did a right hand turn and rode to the third bandana, dropped the money bag on the ground and headed back towards Bryce.

The pickup man waited 15 minutes before picking up the money bag and then slowly walked to his horse while looking in the bag. Suddenly, an Indian's painted face appeared before his eyes, having just fallen out of the tree above his horse. Pickup man startled as Red swiped his knife and sliced off the outlaws left ear. The outlaw let a scream of terror that made the pine branches wave in the air.

Meanwhile, Uncle Joe and Bryce jumped at the terrifying sound made from a human being. "Yep, Red has just scared the crap out of that poor unsuspecting soul. I wonder what part of his body has been amputated and what is next. We'd better get up there before there is nothing left for us to torture, heh?"

Getting close to where Red and the outlaw were located, there was, a second howl. As they arrived, the outlaw was tied to a tree with manacles around his wrists and Red was reapplying a paste to the bleeding ear stump, as the outlaw was screaming at the top of his lungs. "What's the paste for, Red?"

"It's an old Indian recipe to stop bleeding, but it burns like a red-hot poker. We don't want him to die from blood loss!"

Uncle Joe then said, "well Mister, I'd say your goose is cooked. We want to know how many men The Butcher has and where his hideout is located. You tell us these two things, and we'll even let you go after you lead us to his hideout, of course."

"I have a counteroffer. I'll give you the $100,000 and you let me go."

"No, can't do that because The Butcher will start whacking off the lady's female attributes and then send her body back in six pieces. Not a good idea. No, you tell us what we want to know, or we'll make you tell us."

"F---You!"

"Oh, now we are dealing with the DF Disease. Well Bryce has a cure for that."

Bryce walks up to the ear stump, looks in and says, "so that's what the inside of the ear looks like." Without warning, he pulls out his awl and sticks it in the cute little membrane. Pickup man's eyes start jerking violently in the direction of the awl and without warning has an explosive vomiting episode.

When Bryce jerks the awl, the outlaw retches again and again and again.

Uncle Joe came back, "well, that was fun. Got any words for us yet."

"Kill me, but I won't talk."

"Hey buddy, there are things worse than death. OK Red, It's your turn this time. Make it something worse than death, hey."

Red stepped up to the outlaw, pushed his head against the tree and placed his thumb in the corner of his right eye, growls, and a sucking sound was heard followed by a loud POP. To Uncle Joe and Bryce, who had no idea what Red was up to, they cringed as they saw the eyeball come flying out of pickup man's eye socket. The outlaw was screaming and hopping around like a chicken without a head as Red was picking up the eyeball and attaching it to a string along with the earlobe, making a neckless for himself.

Uncle Joe looked somewhat shaken up as he said, "well that was a new one on me. Popped out kind of nice didn't it. Unless you have something to say, Bryce you're next."

Pickup man was still screaming and spitting at Uncle Joe. Bryce took out his dull jackknife, picked it open, opened pickup man's fly, pulled out his tally-wacker, pulled the skin off the shaft, and started sawing off a perfect donut to add to Red's necklace. Pickup man went silent as he was looking, with one eye, to see if he had any tool left.

Pickup man was now pushing air thru his front teeth like the mad animal he was becoming. When Uncle Joe asked if he was ready to talk, pickup man started to growl like a rabid dog. Uncle Joe finally began to think that there was no way he was going to break down. As final effort, he said to Red that it was his turn and that a definitive maneuver was needed.

"I was going to cut off his complete tally-wacker, but that would make him bleed to death, and we can't have that. So instead, I'm going to cut off one leg at the knee. Without hesitating, he shoved his knife in the knee joint and started cutting when suddenly pickup man yelled, "Stop, you win. I can go to my grave with one ear, one eye and no foreskin, but I cannot climb the gallows, like a man, without both legs. If you promise to let me loose, I will take you to The Butcher and Missus Vaughan."

Uncle Joe said, "once we have Missus Vaughan alive and free, I promise you'll be a free man." Bryce thought, how strange that a man believed he was not whole without both legs?

***

The outlaw's wrists were manacled, a rope tied to the saddle horn, one ankle manacled to the stirrup, and his mouth was gagged with a bandana. With everyone following, he led the caravan north along the road for another five miles. At a huge monolithic and obsidian rock, the pickup man turned and entered a large stream with a rocky bottom. They rode north in the stream till they came to a blowdown covering half of the stream. Turning west again, the horses were traveling on a well beaten path. About a mile later, pick up man stopped. Bryce, put his pistol to his face, removed the gag and allowed him to softly speak. "About 500 yards around that bend, you'll be able to see a rustic log cabin seasonally used by hunters. The Butcher is in there with two men and Missus

Vaughan. He is expecting me about this time today. When I don't show up, he will work out his alternate plan. Now in your case, you have a choice of hiding along the trail to ambush him as he comes looking for me today or tomorrow morning, or you can sneak to the cabin tonight and rush the door after they all fall asleep likely from alcohol stupor."

The Trio dismounted, and considered their options. Uncle Joe thought it over and said, "the problem with setting up an ambush is that there will likely be two riders coming at us. With one gunshot heard, whoever is guarding Missus Vaughan will likely kill her on the spot. No, I don't like it, I prefer we rush the cabin's door assuming we can creep over there without alerting any of those three outlaws." Red added, "we can appear at that front door like ghosts—look at the ground cover of moss and green grasses." "Then it's settled, we'll set up a cold camp, walk the horses away from camp, and take out the cheese, crackers and cold beans for supper."

Bryce helped pickup man down from his horse and manacles, brought him to the bushes for some relief, and as he returned to camp, Uncle

Joe handed him a plate of cheese, crackers, beans with a tin cup of cold water from a nearby spring. After supper, Red took a cloth and cleaned the amputated ear stump as well as the enucleated socket. The men waited till about midnight, and then secured pickup man with wrist manacles around a tree. As they were leaving for the cabin, pickup man said, "I hope you can get the best of the Butcher because he's a hard one to put down. If you fail, then the lady and me will be tortured to death, so good luck." Uncle Joe then gagged him out of precaution and then the Trio started their slow trek on moccasins.

Arriving at the cabin, Red placed a saddle blanket on the porch floor to minimize creaky boards. Bryce took out a small can of gun oil and squirted the external hinges to prevent unwanted squeaking. Uncle Joe picked up a 2-inch round piece of oak firewood. It was understood that the Butcher was Uncle Joe's target. As the unlocked door opened, Missus Vaughan was seen awake and fortunately tied to a rocking chair away from the three outlaws—away from the likely shooting. The Butcher was on the center cot and the two other toadies were each side of him. Bryce placed his index finger to his lips as Missus Vaughan nodded in agreement.

Uncle Joe walked right up to the Butcher and swung the oak stick to the outlaw's genitals. The Butcher sat up with a howl, as Uncle Joe tapped the round oak stick to his forehead and laid him out unconscious. The noise woke the two toadies and one went for his gun on the nightstand. Red lifted his sawed-off shotgun and let go one barrel. The outlaw rolled off the cot and ended up in the far corner of the cabin. The other toady sprang up in his cot, but when he realized that he was unarmed, simply put his hands up.

Meanwhile, The Butcher was groaning and becoming alert. Finally, he realized that someone was standing over him. Without thinking about it, he put his hand on his pistol grip and the oak stick came down on his nose and mouth, again knocking him out. This time, Uncle Joe took his gun-belt off and manacled his wrists and ankles. They did the same to the other toady as Red walked to the victim, took out his knife, and cut the ropes holding her in the chair. Red said, "you're free now Ma'am, would you like some cold water or go to the privy?" Missus Vaughan started to cry as Red just placed his hand on her shoulder as a measure of comfort. "Thank you, please call me Victoria, and yes, the privy sounds good."

After pulling out the dead toady, Bryce asked where that awful smell of a dead animal came from. Uncle Joe said, "It's the Butcher, I bet he has never bathed. Let's drag him to the water trough, strip his clothes off and scrub him with a horse brush and lye soap. Then we can leave him in Sheriff Blevin's jail."

The Trio went to work, as soon as the Butcher hit the water he woke up, but with his wrists manacled in his back, he was like a beached whale out of water. Once clean, they managed to put a clean pair of britches on him and then secured him to a horse along with the other captured toady. The dead one was tied to a saddle and everyone, including Victoria Vaughan, was brought to their cold camp. It was now predawn and a firepit was dug. A complete breakfast was prepared for the Trio, pickup man, and Victoria, to include bacon, home fries, beans, biscuits, bangers and plenty of coffee.

During their meal, the Butcher yelled out that they were hungry too. Uncle Joe stepped over to the tree that secured the outlaws, with that round oak limb-wood, and said, "you are some lunatic. You cut off that lady's ring finger and were about to send her external genitals, and you demand service from me. Uncle Joe could not restrain himself as he swung the piece of limb-wood and crashed it on the Butcher's left knee cap. Despite the loud screaming, howling and thrashing about, the Butcher managed to hear, "the next time you open your mouth, you'll lose the right knee cap. Oh. and by the way, your nose is kind of flattened to the side. Here, let me straighten it so you can breathe thru your nose." "No, no, nooh." As Uncle Joe grabs the nose and straightens it out rather slowly. Again, the Butcher was singing another tune—a bit off key, as he tried to pull himself away from Uncle Joe.

After the Butcher's delightful attitude adjustment. Uncle Joe steps up to the pickup man who was now free of manacles and finishing his breakfast. "Well, you lived up to your promise of bringing us to the kidnappers. We kept the Butcher far enough from camp and he hasn't seen you. You're now a free man. Here is one of their unloaded pistols and rifles. They both need 44-40 ammo. Let me suggest, you need to get out of Texas. Although, we're letting you go free, I suspect that you may have bounties on your head in Texas. Head north, and Burkburnett Texas is a small town just a few miles north of here where you'll be able to get ammo and vittles for the road. Lawton, Oklahoma is 50 miles north of here where you can get proper medical attention. I'm giving you $500 to get you started somewhere else, preferably Oklahoma. So, good luck. Oh, in case we ever meet again, what is your name?"

"It's Tate Thompson, aka 'double T.'"

***

The Trio arrived at Wichita Falls that afternoon. Their first stop was the Vaughan home. Stepping down, Victoria was swept up by her husband who was shaking and crying out of control. It was minutes before Calhoun could find personal control to speak. "Gentlemen, you have given me my life back. How do I repay the three of you?

Bryce spoke, "Well we usually find our pay out of the bounty rewards offered. So, here is your ransom bag of money we reclaimed from the outlaws. Red steps up and gives the $100,000 back to Missus

Vaughan. Victoria whispers in her husband's ear and after a moment, he nodded a clear yes. Victoria stepped up to the Trio and said, "my husband and I are very grateful for risking your lives to save me, in return, we would like to offer you this bag of money as the utmost token of our appreciation."

Uncle Joe was shaking his head in the negative. "Oh Ma'am, we cannot accept this. Our fee is rarely over $10,000 and more commonly in the $5,000 range. It would not be right."

Calhoun added, "in our hearts, since it sounds fair, then it is right. Please accept this graciously and may your families benefit from it in the future. Thank you. Also, don't forget how it is such a small world, and if I can ever do something for you, please don't hesitate to ask."

Meanwhile, Sheriff Blevin was making arrangements to escort the two outlaws to jail and have the undertaker dispose of the dead outlaw. The sheriff failed to ask what had happened to the fourth outlaw, since he presumed, he had been given the incorrect intelligence from the wire.

***

That evening, the Trio enjoyed a visit at a tonsorial shop to get a haircut, shave and bath. Changing in clean clothes, they went to the bank to deposit the $100,000. They then arranged a bank transfers to their 1st National Bank in Abilene. After a full supper at their railroad hotel, they went downtown to have a few beers. It was Sheriff Blevin who came barging in Georgie's Saloon holding the usual telegram's yellow paper in his hand.

"Sorry for the intrusion, but Marshal Balinger has marked this urgent for immediate delivery. Bryce accepted the paper and read.

Two bank robberies in past week STOP

Only vault money taken after execution of tellers STOP

Suspect inside job—but no gang members identified STOP

Need to stop employee executions and bank robberies STOP

Having meeting with Dallas Banking Association in AM STOP

Can you attend STOP from Marshal Balinger, Dallas, Texas.

Uncle Joe looked at Bryce and Red. Getting the nod of approval, Sheriff Blevin took the positive response to the telegraph office, while the Trio headed to the ticket office to get passage to Dallas on the Overnight Express—which was becoming their standard mode of transportation from job to job during the overnight hours.

***

CHAPTER 6

On the Rail Again

Waiting for the Midnight Express to arrive, the Trio got into a discussion. Bryce started, "it appears that all our jobs are accessed thru the railroad lines. We haven't used our horses to track outlaws very much. Actually, we have our horses follow in the stock cars, then pay the livery fees to care for them, in case we might need them. Is this pattern going to continue?"

Uncle Joe was prepared for this question. "Times have changed and the state of Texas with its railroad service promotes this new outlaw mode of operation. Outlaws no longer spend days and weeks riding between small cities. The communities with populations of 500 or more inhabitants have the money in banks to maintain services. In other words, outlaws don't waste time going thru towns with less than 500 people to get to large towns or cities—and they use the railroad to get there. Cities are commonly located 100 to 175 miles in this expansive state. By rail at 30 to 40 mph, you can get anywhere overnight or the same day."

Red was listening to all this and was doing the math. "At today's rate of three cents per mile, our140-mile trip will cost us $4.20 each. We'll do this distance in an average of 4 hours. Now compare this to the pre railroad era. This 140-mile trip would take four days on horseback. Now, taking into consideration that a cowboy makes a dollar a day plus found, he would lose his wages of $4.00 to be on the trail for four days. Seems like a no brainer to me, heh?"

Uncle Joe added, "time saved may equal the working man's day wages, but less saddle time saves the pain in my back and my ass. So, let's stay with the times and travel by rail to our next jobs, OK."

The Express train arrived on time and loaded with freight from Colorado. Sitting in the passenger car under a kerosene lamp, Bryce opened his textbook on pigs. *Chapter 2 thru 4 were short and seemed related, so Bryce started to read—farrowing, care of newborn piglets and castration. Again taking notes, the birthing process rarely needed assistance. The normal birthing time averaged out to be 15 minutes per piglet and a litter of 10 piglets (the average number) would take over two hours. Occasionally, a piglet would need traction to negotiate the birthing canal, so watching the event was crucial.*

A newborn piglet would weigh 3 pounds, and require 85°F for 3 days to maintain body temperature and then 80°F for a week before being exposed to barn temperatures. During nursing weeks, piglets would often need to be supplemented with "creep feed" which was a "gruel" of 50-50 milk starter powder and water. Newborns would be weaned at 4 weeks when they weighed 10 pounds.

Castration was performed at 14 days of age, when the piglets still had colostrum protection from the mother, to minimize the chances for infection. The technique involved pulling the testicle out of the sac thru a small incision. The procedure was necessary to sell meat without the awful "pork taint" meat taste cause by male hormones.

Next, Bryce read a booklet on "ear tagging" pigs when crossbreeding lines. Putting down the booklet and manual, Bryce decided to write Allie a letter:

"Miss you...all the time.
Successful kidnaping caper..........saved the victim.
Paid with a windfall......................for our future.
Heading to Dallas.................for bank robberies.
Are Duroc and Hampshire hogs............breeding.
How is business doing..........how are new workers.
When have time/order pig ear tags......see PS below.
I will come soon..............are you OK—Love you.

PS—enclosed is a booklet on why ear tagging is so important in identifying crossbred offspring— generation by generations."

Bryce placed the booklet and his letter in an envelope, addressed it, and then turned off the lamp to get some shut eye.

When Bryce woke up, he knew that the solution to the banking robberies had been revealed in his dreams. Arriving early, Bryce went to the nearest newspaper to order a dozen special ink printing stamps. While his order was being prepared, he posted his letter to Allie and then joined his team at Sam's Diner—their office.

Marshal Balinger joined them for breakfast. "What's the story marshal? How come you have had two successful robberies?" "Because of a new method of operation. They wear face masks, and flash large hunting knives and pistols. To get the bank president to open the safe, they kill a teller or innocent customer by cutting their throat open. There is no shooting, and everyone is tied up and gagged before leaving the bank with a closed sign on the locked door. The last robbery took an hour for my office to be notified. By then the tracks could not be followed because the six outlaws all took a different street out of the city."

"That's important knowledge to know, let's have breakfast and then please join us at the Banking Association meeting."

The meeting started at 9AM promptly. Present were the presidents of all twelve financial institutions: three community banks, two credit unions, four national chains, two Cattlemen's banks and one 'quick cashing' outfit. A spokesman had been named to start the conversation, President

Colbert Algier of the 1st National Bank (ironically, the Trio's bank in Dallas).

"We are getting nervous that any bank may be next to be robbed. These outlaws are treacherous killers and why they only take vault money is not clear to us. Without knowing who the outlaws are and where they hide, we are at a loss to stop them. That is why we sent for you since you have a reputation of finding a way to abort robberies and catch the culprits. To make it your worthwhile, the ten banks that have not been robbed, are putting up a $10,000 reward to stop the robberies and bring an end to these murderers."

Uncle Joe said, "we can do this job, but it will require one more bank robbery and some work on your part. During this last robbery, there is no point in refusing to open the vault, since after the outlaws kill someone, any of you will have no choice but to comply. If your employees know you will comply, then they will not refuse to come to work. Otherwise, you'll be closing your doors down—and that is stupid. Now my nephew, Bryce, will explain what you have to do."

"Have you ever wondered why the outlaws are only taking vault money and not bothering with the teller's business change?" With shrugging shoulders and negative head shakes, Bryce continued. "This is a new gunshot free 'snatch and go quickly' method of taking the big bills in the vault, usually amounting to +-$5,000, and not bothering with the coin change, and $1--$5 bills at the teller's window. Now, in order for us to find who these outlaws are, we need to catch them trying to pay for goods or services with marked money. Yes, the key to us catching this gang is marked bills."

President Algier asks, "how do we do this, write down the serial numbers of every US currency note we have in the vault?

"If we were dealing with money laundering of large amounts of cash, that would be the method for catching the outlaws. But no, we want to catch the little guy trying to pass off a $10 or $20 bill to pay for services. Then when they are identified, we will persuade them to identify their gang or follow them to their outlaw camp."

"Sounds simple, but how do we mark these bills."

"With this stamp and ink blotter prepared by the newspaper printing shop. This imparts a round 3/8-inch ink circle to each stamped bill on the top left corner. Yes, you and only you must mark the bills and none of your employees must know what you have done. Until we have a robbery, you must keep the tellers' cash tray monies separate from the marked bills. This will require that you must keep some unmarked large bills on your body in case of a large cash withdrawal." President Algier got the nod of approval from his members and the process of acquiring one or more outlaws had started.

***

Two days later, at the slow banking time of 2PM, the Merchants Bank was quietly robbed, and no one was hurt or killed. The thieves left with a pile of US currency that amounted to $5,000, which was again the standard backup cash in most banks. The difference was that these were all $10 and $20 bills. The bank president had pilfered all bills $50 and up and was hiding them in his locked office desk.

The Trio then set up a plan to catch their prey. The three members visited every saloon, gambling hall and bordello in the city. The person in charge or the bartender was shown a sample of $10 or $20 bills with a marked black circle stamped in the upper left corner. If such a bill was used, reporting it immediately to the King Hotel receptionist would be rewarded with a $100 bill.

It was two more days before the plan paid off. One evening around 11PM, a messenger arrived at the King Hotel with a marked $10 bill. The messenger said it came from a gambling table at the "Watering Hole Saloon, and the bartender had sent him on the errand. Bryce took the marked bill, gave the messenger a good $10 bill in return. The Trio then headed out to confront the owner of the marked bill.

Red stepped inside the bar, handed the bartender $110 to replace the marked bill and pay his reward. The bartender made the cash disappear and simply said, "table 7 in left corner by outside door to privy."

Red committed all three faces to memory and relayed the message. The Trio waited outside the rear of the saloon hidden in the bushes, but within visibility of the privy. Within an hour, the beer was doing its thing and one outlaw stepped outside heading to the privy. Bryce stepped up to the privy's door and when the outlaw stepped out, he was sapped in the forehead and crumbled to the ground not even realizing who or what hit him. They dragged the outlaw into the trees and waited to see what his two buddies would do. Within 15 minutes, the two other outlaws came outside looking for their friend.

"Damn, I don't know what happened to Toby, but I don't like it. I think we'd better hightail it back to camp and tell the boss what happened."

Red had anticipated this move and was ready. His horse was tied in front of the saloon with the other patron horses. After the two outlaws took off, Red was on their trail. Meanwhile, Uncle Joe and Bryce brought the unconscious outlaw to the marshal's office. After slapping him into consciousness, Bryce offered to make him talk. Without any warning, Bryce sat on the outlaw's chest with his knees holding down the man's arms. When the awl hit home, the outlaw's eyes crossed, his head jerked back, and his legs started flailing in all directions. The deputy marshal who was watching this had to sit down to avoid passing out. Uncle Joe added, "deputy, this is making an outlaw talk without leaving any signs of physical torture."

After the nerve was destroyed, Bryce took the awl out and showed it to the outlaw. Uncle Joe took the good guy approach and said, "now son, there is no need for you to experience that trauma again. Were you to turn state's evidence and give us the name of your gang's members, we could speak on your behalf at your trial and likely save you from hanging. Otherwise, Bryce will continue till you run out of rotten teeth, and then it won't be pretty because we will make you talk."

"No stop, I'm doomed either way, but I don't want to hang. The gang leader is named Freeman Banning and the other five men are also wanted dead or alive. Their names are............................ We are all from San Antonio where we are wanted for murder and bank robbery. Our camp is four miles cross-country north of the city—just below a high rock cliff which you cannot miss."

"There's only one other thing I need to know, who is the man who cut those innocent victims' throats?"

"That was 'Wolf Man' or Edgar Wolfe from the names I gave you. You can't miss him. He has long white hair to his neck, full bushy black eyebrows, a full-face white beard that comes to a point on his chin. Makes him look like a mad dog with those small green beady eyes—a real fright."

At the same time, Red arrived at the marshal's office. "I followed those two to their camp and listened to them explain how they had lost their partner. The boss man was not happy and told them that they were breaking camp after sunup, and getting out of the area with their loot. They were going to hide in Indian Territory till things cooled off."

"Hell, we can be at the campsite by 1AM and have plenty of time to set up some jungle warfare to really make their day, huh?"

***

The Trio was carrying their bags of jungle paraphernalia as close as 100 yards. Red explained that drinking whiskey allowed a man to fall in a deep sleep for several hours, and since it was 1AM, it was time to start setting up their plan. Uncle Joe took out five rat traps and said, "a man always sleeps with his pistol nearby. Go get them for me and leave a rat trap in its place, in case someone wakes up unexpectedly. While they were gone, Uncle Joe took 5 cartridges apart to get 5 bullet tips. With the pistols in hand, he removed the cylinder, shoved a bullet tip deep in the pistol's barrel, and replaced the loaded cylinder. The pistols went back to their owners. Meanwhile Bryce went to help Red set up a spring-loaded reactive snare, on the trail to the bushes. Tripping on the snare would lift a man up into a tree by his feet.

To finish the setups, the loaded rat traps were attached to all pistol grips, a double stick of dynamite was attached to a wire which passed over the fire pit, by pulling the wire across the fire, the dynamite fuses would light up. The wire was then attached to 100 yards of cord for the Trio to pull from afar. Wolf Man had a rope with a slip knot attached to one leg and the other end tied to a horse's neck. All the horses' reins were released from the picket line and ready to pull off if the horses were frightened. One of the outlaw's left boot was booby trapped with a 2-inch nail pushed thru the sole, just ahead of the heel. Another man had a loaded shotgun laying next to him. A string was attached to the trigger, the hammer pulled back and the other end of the cord tied to his hand. Any motion of that hand would fire the shotgun and likely take some toes off the outlaw. The last thing the Trio did was to lay out several bear traps around the camp—just in case something went wrong with the plan.

With things set, the Trio moved back 100 yards with a cord tied to the dynamite's fire-proofed wire. Bryce knew that if he pulled the cord five feet, that the dynamite would be dragged in the pit of hot red coals. While waiting for the show to start, Red asked, "why did you insist we put that nail in the left boot?" "Because a white man always puts on his right boot first. In a hurry, he won't check for critters in his boots, especially when the first boot went on without issues."

Bryce had one question, "why did you choose Wolfe Man to be dragged to his certain death, since that spooked horse won't stop till he gets a mile away from the dynamite boom?"

"Because, he was the throat cutting murderer, and a quick death on the gallows was not retribution for the lost innocent lives. He needs to meet his maker with a face of 'pain and fright'—that will be justice."

***

An hour later, the Trio saw a man stand up, stretch, and start walking to the bushes barefoot. How he missed the bear traps was a total surprise, but he did not miss the snare. The Trio clearly heard a loud swish and a screech that sounded like a swooping eagle. Once dangling head down, the prey started screaming, "get me the hell down, is this your idea of a joke? Thanks to you I'm not only pissed off, but pissed on. One of his buddies yelled back, "let me put by boots on and I'll cut you down." The right boot went on, followed by the left with a howl from hell. "Take my boot off, there's a critter in my boot and it bit me bad." The boss, Freeman Banning, suspected something else and went for his gun as the Trio heard a loud "SNAP" followed by ouch, damn it, what the hell, this is a rat trap, we're under attack, wake up boys!"

That was the cue Bryce was waiting for. Bryce pulled the cord five feet, jumped behind a boulder with Red and Uncle Joe, and waited. Within 30 seconds the explosion sent every piece of red coals into the air. Fire was everywhere in camp. The horses all scattered, and Wolfe Man streaked thru camp on his way to hell with his mouth wide open in a state of perpetual horror. Since most of the outlaws appeared unconscious, the Trio rushed their camp with shotguns at the ready.

In camp, the Trio was busy putting out fires, especially the clothing fires of unconscious outlaws. The first to regain consciousness was the boss himself. Drawing his pistol and pointing it at Bryce, Uncle Joe said, "uh, I wouldn't pull the trigger, that pistol has been booby trapped." "Yeah right, that's a perfect line for someone about to die." The Trio immediately dropped to the ground as Banning pulled the trigger. The blast was bright red, steel shrapnel flying in every direction, and a stub left where Banning's hand use to be.

Banning was staring at his bleeding stump in total shock. Red stepped up and tied a pigging string in a tourniquet, saying, "best to stop the bleeding if we want to get him to trial, heh!"

While the Trio was applying manacles, one outlaw managed to sneak away, but never made it past the first bear trap. The snap even gave Bryce some goose bumps. When they released the trap, the outlaw collapsed when he saw his foot dangling from a broken bone. With all the traps set off, the fires doused, the upside down hanging outlaw brought down, then every manacled outlaw was secured to trees, Uncle Joe asked Bryce and Red to go retrieve the horses and whatever was left to Wolf Man's body. "At least bring the head, which we need to collect the bounty reward."

While the boys were gone, Uncle Joe started checking saddlebags and other belongings. First, he collected the other four pistols, and pushed out the lead plug out of the barrels. Then he collected the rifles and shotguns and last he started collecting US currency. Every saddlebag had thousands of dollars and one had all the marked bills with the black circle in the top left corner. The total came to $17,148. He separated the excess of $2,148, which he would divide equally as petty cash, and kept the $15,000 as returnable funds to the three robbed banks.

When the boys returned, they had all the horses plus a half body to include two arms, parts of a chest, and a head. The other body parts were not found. After making a full breakfast and catching a nap, the Trio loaded their sickly outlaws securely onto their horses, and headed for Dallas.

Two days later, Marshal Balinger gave the Trio their financial settlement. First was the $10,000 reward offered by the Banking Association, then the bounty rewards of $4,500. Part of the settlement was the fact, that the two banks who had murdered victims, settled with family members for $5,000 each—thereby avoiding a civil suit. The outlaw horses, pistols, rifles, saddles and tack came up to the usual $125 per outlaw for all their gear—in this case $750. Plus, the unmentioned petty cash. All funds were deposited in the 1st National Bank with bank transfers to the Abilene branch.

***

During those two days, Bryce got a long letter from Allie, read several more chapters of Allie's textbook and found an interesting marketing book for future business expansion. Of course, he started with Allie's letter:

Dear Bryce,

Miss you	beyond belief.
A couple in love	needs to be together.
A windfall not necessary	together, we'll make our fortune.
Crossbreeding in progress	60 females now pregnant.
Eustache and Alec	perfect Trio with Alva...
Ear tagging	great idea.
Boars, sows, gilts and barrows	tagged.
Next tagging	first crossbred litter.
Want and need	to be with you—but I'm OK.

Love, Allie PS There is a big meat packer/distributor in Abilene who wants to buy the farm. I refused a generous offer. Herschel Ayers not accepting my refusal. This is our future and I'm not selling. RSVP.

Bryce posted a short reply the same day:"

Dear Allie,

Agree	don't sell out.
Need to be with you	drive, uncontrollable.
Will arrive at	first lull in jobs.

PS. The enclosed booklet is on commercial refrigeration in 1890 Texas. See what you think. Love you, always, Bryce

The same day, Bryce decided to read a few more chapters of Allie's textbook. *Chapter 5 was on feed choices and Chapter 6 was on hog habits. Again, he kept notes as he read along.*

Pig feed depends on the age and needs of different pigs. Nursing piglets need "creep feed" supplements already mentioned. There is a mash for weaning piglets that is mixed with water to make a gruel that stimulates the apatite more than dry mash. The growing pigs need as much feed as they can tolerate. The nursing sows need extra vitamins, minerals and protein to produce enough milk— usually ten or more pounds of super-pellets a day. Boars need to have their weight managed by their diet, since a boar over 400 pounds can injure a 200-pound gilt. Growing pigs need anywhere from 2 to 5 pounds of grain a day, considering they go to market around 6 months, that means hundreds of pounds monthly to get them to a finishing diet for the last three weeks. The average pig grain/feed contains wheat, corn, barley, oats and sorghum. The finishing diet is similar, but it also contains, soybeans, vitamins, minerals and amino acids.

Garden vegetables are an excellent supplement to any pig's diet. Popular ones are: beets, carrots, cabbage, turnip, corn and corn stalks, potatoes, pumpkins, squash, and cucumbers. These are usually fed raw and ground up with the plants and roots. For poor feeders, boiling the vegetables and feeding them whole will stimulate a pig's apatite.

Hog habits was an interesting chapter. Hogs root because it is natural and a way to search for food. A spent garden is usually fenced off to let selected pigs roam and root. The rooted dirt is upended and ready for harrowing and seeding. Hogs like to prod with their noses as a method of communication. Pigs are very clean, and in their pens, they always poop in the same spot—their toilet. The average 250-pound hog puts out at least 10 pounds of manure a day.

Pigs don't sweat and in 80+ degrees, need to be cooled off with cold water in special cooling vats.

Tail docking is necessary since pigs like to chew the tails off young pigs—tasting blood increases aggressiveness. Unlike cows, pigs don't regurgitate their food and chew their cud. Piglets who bite a sow have their needle teeth snipped off. Boars that become aggressive have their tusks cut off with bolt cutters.

Before he knew it, Bryce managed to zip thru Chapters 7 and 8. Chapter 7 was about the common pig diseases: exudative dermatitis with greasy skin, coccidiosis parasites in suckling pigs, respiratory infections such as influenza (swine flu), dysentery diarrhea, mastitis, and Parvovirus that affects reproductivity. Chapter 8 discussed the common every-day health problems include constipation, respiratory illnesses, and arthritis in older hogs. Since there was no mention of treatment or management, Bryce would discuss it with Allie.

Getting tired of reading, Bryce went for a walk. Dallas, with its population of 65,000 people, also had a wealth of businesses and specialty stores. One such establishment was the Dallas Book Store and Coffee Shop. Bryce had been in this store before and had purchased the booklet on ear tagging pigs and the latest booklet on food refrigeration. Bryce walked in and was greeted at the door. "Welcome to our store, we can order any book for you, but with our large inventory, we invite you to pick up any book to peruse or totally read it over our 10-cent homemade donut and unlimited coffee."

Bryce knew where the business marketing section was located and walked right to it. He looked at hundreds of books that were not applicable to raising animals for meat. Then suddenly he found a winner, "Bingo, this is what may change our future." "Commercial Canning to Preserve Food." Enclosed in the list of 'food' was vegetables, fruits, beans, soups, stews, and of course Meat.

Bryce took the book to the coffee shop, paid his 10 cents and sat down with a donut and a fresh cup of coffee. Two hours later, 7 donuts and many cups of coffee, Bryce finished the book. The author's note at the end of the book mentioned that his factory in Wichita Falls, Texas manufactured tin cans and commercial canners to match the tin can size. Wichita Falls certainly rang a bell and Bryce heard himself talking out loud, "who in blazes is this author?" As he closed the book back to the cover he saw the author's name at the bottom of the cover, "Commerrcial.........Food." By Calhoun and Victoria Vaughan.

Bryce's eyebrows went up and a smile came across his face. He remembered Calhoun's exact words, "Thank you. Also don't forget how it is such a small world, and if I can ever do something for you, please don't hesitate to ask."

Bryce got up, paid his donut tab, and purchased four copies of the book—one to send to Allie, one for him to reread, and two on reserve. The next time he read it, he would take notes to discuss with Allie.

***

The next morning while getting their breakfast in their office, Sam's Diner, Bryce mentioned to Uncle Joe that if there was a lull in jobs, he would like to take a week off and go visit Allie. Uncle Joe thought a minute and said, "If we don't hear of a job by noon, go ahead and take the 1PM train to home, you'll be there by 6PM." The Trio continued with their breakfast when Marshal Balinger entered the diner and tripped on the threshold. Paddling air, he managed to right himself as the entire diner patrons had whistles, guffaws and applause at his managing not to clean the floor with his face.

Bryce saw the marshal and said, "oh no, there goes my visit to Abilene down the drain." Red was laughing out loud and Uncle Joe said, "slow down marshal. You're going to break a leg or your neck."

"Sorry, but this is somewhat of an emergency. Something terrible is happening in Longview. There have been five murders of middle age women who work or live in the city—with one abomination occurring each month. The local marshal has not been able to catch the culprit and the city council hired the Pinkerton Agency for the past three months. Two weeks ago, was the fifth murder and yesterday the Pinkerton Agency was fired for lack of progress—they admitted they didn't have a single clue or suspect to follow up on."

Uncle Joe interrupted him and said, "why us, we're bounty hunters, not detectives or local lawmen. Why don't they call the US Marshal Service?"

"The entire Marshal Service is on assignment between Lubbock and Amarillo dealing with a range war between cattlemen and sheep farmers.

They are up to 20 deaths and the war is still out of control. So, Longview is not high on their list of priorities."

"But, there are many private detective agencies in Texas"........! "Yes, but they want your team."

"Why?"

"Your track record and you don't charge if you don't deliver."

"Like I said, we're bounty hunters, how do we get paid to find some sick lunatic killer—a nobody without a bounty on his head."

"You don't need a bounty, the merchants along with the city council are putting up an unadvertised reward of $12,000. It's unadvertised to avoid an onrush of gun crazy misfits shooting up the innocent men in the city for just walking the streets after dark."

Uncle Joe finally said, "well, it's up to my team. How do you vote Red?" "I'll be glad to help out, but I'm not the inquisitive type and will need to follow your lead." "And what about you Bryce?"

"I admit that I have some idea of where to start and I can follow leads even when they are vague and subtle. But that means no vacation with Allie. So, it's up to you to break the tie."

"Well I see several advantages to try this caper. First, I feel we can solve this and prevent future deaths. Secondly, it will be a feather in our cap, which will boost our reputation, and add a new MO to our services. Thirdly, the pay is adequate. So, whether we succeed or not, after the caper terminates, I guarantee you a ten-day holiday—no if's, and's, or but's! So, marshal, when is the next train to Longview?"

"In two hours. When you get there, I'll wire the local lawman, Marshal Warren. He'll meet you at the depot and will add to the information I gave you. Good luck and stay safe."

Meanwhile in Abilene, Allie and Alva were doing weekly rounds in town, picking up supplies, paying up credit accounts and collecting fees for the carcasses left with the butchers. Coming out of Albright's Mercantile, Herschel Ayers was facing her on the boardwalk. Next to him were three apparent gunfighters with quickdraw holsters, arrogant swaggers and malicious looking faces. Herschel spoke first.

"Miss Adkins, I will double my offer to buy your farm—that's $10,000. It will take you ten years to clear such a profit. Now be smart and take my offer while it's on the table only today." "Mister Ayers, I'm not selling for two reasons. First, my future husband and I want to grow this business into a major enterprise for the future of our family. Secondly, if I sell to you, you will have a monopoly. I know you have bought out all the pig farmers' pork meat production within a twenty-mile radius. That will give you control of pork prices in Abilene, and for the good of the community, I cannot allow this to happen. Good day, and do not come back with another offer. The answer will still be no."

***

CHAPTER 7

The Detective Trio

For once, the train ride was in daylight. Station stops were quick to allow disembarking passengers and adding new ones. The coal/water stops were every 40 miles, and the entire 125-mile trip took 5 hours. Bryce decided to work on a few more chapters of Allie's textbook. *Chapter 9 was about how to grow pigs faster. The answer was to make the grain appealing by mixing it with water. Feeding pens allow competition for food, and this promotes more eating. Increase the amount of food offered as the pigs increase in size. Adding vitamins and minerals are always a plus. The basic diet should be low in fiber and high in fat and protein. Adding sorghum improves the taste of grain and is part of the finishing diet.*

Chapter 10 was an introduction to raising your own crops to feed these animals. This cuts down the amount of purchased grain which can cut down on profits. The chapter included how to raise, corn, soybeans, oats, barley, wheat, sorghum and sugar beets. These crops provided a mixture of natural grains high in carbohydrates, fat and protein. Also grown for feed were vegetable gardens with emphasis on squash, carrots, beets, cucumbers, pumpkins, turnips, cabbage and potatoes. These, along with sugar beets, were ground up along with the entire plant and its roots.

Bryce realized that raising crops required fertile land with a good water source, work horses, agricultural equipment and storage facilities to keep the grains dry and fresh. The often by product of straw and stems was useful as bedding—which pigs required. This would be a secondary business enterprise to control costs and would require a financial outlay of funds.

For the remainder of the trip he started working out a plan on how to proceed, what to ask, and catch the clues that fly over people's heads. Bryce needed more information and was eager to speak to

Marshal Warren. As the train approached the depot, Marshal Warren was standing on the platform with a worried look on his face.

Uncle Joe was first to shake the marshal's hand. After introductions were completed, Marshal Warren asked that they follow him to his office after they gathered their horses.

Uncle Joe started the discussion by saying, "we hope you know more than Marshal Balinger, which wasn't much." "I'll tell you what I know then you can ask questions. This town is in an uproar. People are scared to death, women won't leave their house without an escort, several business wives have been murdered to include Mrs. Butman of Butman's Mercantile and Mrs. Babcock of Babcock's Hardware. The other three were city residents. All victims are in their early 40's. Most were abducted when they went out to the privy. They were never seen again till their bodies were found in the ditch just outside of town."

"Were the victims autopsied?"

"Yes, according to our local surgeon doctor, the victims were killed with a massive blow to the head as caused by a sledgehammer. The five victims had been eviscerated with a saw/knife combo from neck to crotch. All organs from windpipe to colon were gone. The one finding, that all five victims had and was kept quiet, if you can follow my meaning, was the fact that they were all sodomized instead of being raped thru the usual passage. All evidence indicated that the sodomy and evisceration occurred after death."

Bryce interjected, "yes, I follow your meaning. However, this appears more than just necrophilia. Sodomizing a dead person reflects shame, humiliation and punishment for the victim. This is a real sick and sadistic animal that has no cure. He does not belong to the human race and has to be eliminated as evil as he is."

Red was listening carefully, and when Bryce went silent, he softly asks Uncle Joe, "what is sodomize and necrophilia?" "I believe that is having anal relations with a dead person!" "PEE... EW, only white men think of doing such things."

Marshal Warren paused and asked, "If the dead victim has already been punished and humiliated, why eviscerate them and remove all their internal organs?"

"I don't know, yet. And, have you found the organs yet?"

"No, not a single trace or even a blood trail."

Uncle Joe appeared frustrated and said, "where on earth do we start?"

Red, who never says anything, adds, "start with his elders who have known him since a child!"

Bryce's eyebrows lifted up as he says, "that's it, who best to know this man than a teacher who saw him grow up over the years. Assuming this man is in his 30's, who would have been the town teacher some 20-25 years ago?"

"Why, that would have been Maude Meacham and she is in her 70's. She lives at Millie's Boarding House for elderly women who need housing, homemaking, or physical assistance."

"Before we start with Miss Meacham, is there any other information we should know?"

"Yes, three things. The murders occur on the 25th day of each month and the local doc thinks this relates to either a moon cycle, a monthly menstrual cycle, or some other symbolic date from the past. The other thing, the unadvertised reward has been increased to $25,000. Apparently, a philanthropist from Wichita Falls has increased the reward because of a past gratitude in saving a loved one, and strangely enough the higher reward was posted the same day we sent you a telegram requesting your help. Could this be of significance?"

"No idea, well we are off to see Miss Meacham. We'll see you again once we have some news or a lead to follow."

"Wait, there is the matter of the third thing. In order for you to carry some clout and get some answers, the council wants you three to be deputy city marshals. So, raise your right hand and repeat after me...................I will." The three bounty hunters left the marshal's office wearing a city marshal's badge, as Uncle Joe kept mussitating how a badge would make them look like nontraditional bounty hunters.

Finally walking up to Millie's Boarding House, Uncle Joe easily convinced Millie to grant them an interview with Maude Meacham. The Trio was invited to a private parlor to wait for Miss Meacham. "Well hello gentlemen, my oh my, three lawmen at my disposal. What on earth can I do for you officers?"

Uncle Joe did the initial introductions, "we have been asked by the city council to investigate the deaths of five local middle age ladies."

"Yes, I knew all five as my students. Great women, what a loss!" Bryce took over, "we believe the murderer may be between the ages of 30-40 and might have been in your school during the time those five ladies attended. Of particular interest would be a young man who was a loner, generally not popular, avoided by girls, often ridiculed and most important showing some paranoid ideation—with or without anger."

"Well, I knew my students and I can think of several young men during the years when these five victims were in different classes. But I can only think of three that showed paranoid ideation. These are Josh Baldwin, Chet Beardsley, and Silas Binder."

"Can you tell us about each of these young men?

"Certainly, but don't I need a warrant or something?"

"No Ma'am. But this is so important, that we can come back with a court order if that will make your more comfortable."

"Well, I guess at my age, it doesn't really matter, so here goes."

"Josh Baldwin was a shy fella that had very low self-esteem. He didn't ever participate in school sports, never made friends and girls made fun of him which led to several paranoid statements. Then one day, another shy gal made contact with him and overnight, this boy became a totally different individual. He went to work for her dad who owned a harness shop, eventually married, and now runs a very successful leather shop. I don't think he's your man, but I specifically recall an episode when Mrs. Butman and Mrs. Babcock were the gals who ridiculed Josh in public."

"Chet Beardsley was a boy with a low intelligence, difficulty learning, and seeming to just go with the flow without any goal in life. One day, a well-known 'active gal' became supposedly pregnant and accused him of rape. Without a defense in a case of 'he said she said,' he pled guilty and was sentenced to one year in Huntsville. Six months later this presumed pregnant gal left town with her boyfriend—obviously not pregnant. Chet's sentence was suddenly vacated and possibly expunged. I am told that he has worked for years at the Bar G Ranch as a wrangler and can still be found there. I mention him because the supposedly pregnant gal was a sister to one of the five victims."

"Silas Binder was a sad case. Once a month he would show up at school with bruises and other signs of being in a physical scrap. He was a quiet type, refused to explain the bruises, and clearly shunned the girls. His mother was a known dominatrix who was suspected of being the one physically abusing Silas. Strangely, this bruising was usually at the end of each month. It was postulated that his mother was having her monthly and had a violent personality change during this time. In any event, his mother suddenly died after falling down the stairs. After the funeral, Silas never returned to school. He apparently lived in his mother's house and lived on her life insurance benefit. He befriended one local man who worked at the Winchell Slaughterhouse and eventually, I heard Silas started working at the same slaughterhouse. I lost track of him after that."

"Wouldn't happen to know what his friend's name was?"

"Yes, Archie Kline."

"What association do you have with him and the five victims?"

"None like Josh and Chet. Yet, my gut feeling and knowing my students, I always felt that there was something strange the way his brain behaved. He was the only student, in 50 years of teaching, to frighten me with eyes that held a thousand words. I always felt that his mother's death would be the turning point in his life and that his personality could go either way."

"What was his mother's name? and do you know the date and year of the funeral, and the day she died if they were different."

"Her name was Lenora and the death date and funeral will be available at the town clerk's office."

"Thank you for your help."

***

The Trio's next stop was to ask the marshal to request a court order to obtain results of Lenora Binder's and the five victims' autopsies. Meanwhile the Trio went to visit Josh Baldwin at the leather shop.

After introducing themselves, Josh was asked if he could give his whereabouts on the evenings of the 25th for the past five months between the hours of dusk to dawn. His answer was that he was home with his wife. His wife was at his side and confirmed that he was with her all night. The Trio left feeling safe that this was not their man.

Traveling to the Bar G Ranch, the Trio met with the ranch foreman, Tom Wellman. Uncle Joe started the questioning, "does Chet Beardsley still work here, and if so, how long has he worked here."

"Chet is an icon at this ranch. I've been here ten years and he was here when I started working here. He is a whisperer and the wrangler for the entire remuda. He's well liked and highly respected."

"How often does he go to town?"

"Never."

"Oh come on, cowboys all go to town on Saturday night."

"Not Chet, I swear to God. He's a bit strange, I admit, but all horse whisperers are a bit off."

"Are you willing to swear that Chet was in the bunkhouse the nights of the 25th the last five months."

"Absolutely, and here he is. Ask him yourself."

"Hello Chet, when was the last time you went to town to buy your personal items."

"I only go to town at Christmas time to buy presents for the cowhands. When I need something, I give the money to the 'cookie' and he picks up what I need. This is my home with the cowhands and the horses, and I have no use for the saloons and girlies."

"Thank you for your time and have a nice day."

The Trio's next stop was the town clerk's office. "Lenora Binder died on the 25th of November some 17 years ago. Her funeral was held the same day, which was common in those days."

"What was the cause of death and was there an autopsy?"

"Broken neck, and yes there was an autopsy performed by our new doctor, Doc Samuels. I don't have the results and Doc Samuels may be able to help you with that."

"Can we have her last known address?"

"It is 41 Mountain Heights."

"Who presently are the current residents at that address?"

"Why her son, Silas, and he is still paying the property taxes.

"Thank you for your help."

The next stop was at the marshal's office to pick up the court order for the autopsy results. Arriving at Doc Samuels, the Trio waited their turn to see the doctor. The Trio explained their request and gave Doc Samuels the court order. Doc Samuels started. "Marshal Warren already told you the victims' major findings. What you don't know is that the last victim had strange red blood cells. They were smaller in size than regular red cells and likely caused by an iron deficiency anemia."

"We'll keep this information in mind, so you can tell the difference between human red cells compared to animals—say cattle?"

"Certainly."

"Any other findings?"

"Yes, I forgot to mention to the marshal that the victims all had one nipple removed."

"You mean like a trophy?"

"Yes. And that's it."

"Could we have the autopsy results on Lenora Binder, from 17 years ago.

"Can do, let me get the file. Lenora Binder died of a broken neck."

"We know that, were there any other physical findings."

"Well, with this court order, I will give you more information. There was a skull fracture in the back of the head, which could be the result of the fall itself, or the cause of the fall. This was disregarded by the investigating lawman. There was one other finding. The anus was widely dilated."

"Caused by?" "Your guess is as good as mine, heh?"

***

The Trio needed time to reflect on their findings. They went to the nearest saloon and all three men were sucking down their third beer. Finally, Uncle Jim said, "what do you think is going on here?"

"Seems to me that Silas Binder is a high suspect. Let's review the facts. He works in a slaughterhouse, he's a loner, the victims were eviscerated and all organs removed, the victims were all sodomized, his mother was likely sodomized, the victims all had their heads bashed in, his mother also had her head bashed in, the victims' organs have never been found which could easily be disposed of in a slaughterhouse."

Red then added, "if it quacks like a duck, it's likely not a chicken."

Uncle Joe adds, "Ok, so he's our number one suspect. What is our next move?"

"We need a court ordered warrant to search his home at 41 Mountain Heights (without the suspect being present), and we need to interview Mister Winchell at the slaughterhouse."

On their way to the slaughterhouse, the Trio stopped at the courthouse. In Judge Skinner's chambers, the Trio explained their suspicions about the suspect. The Judge agreed to the warrant, and as he was filling out the form, he adds, "you must have Marshal Warren present as a witness. If you take anything as evidence, it must be taken by the marshal."

Mister Winchell was in his office in the packing house. It was Bryce who took over the interview after the usual pleasantries. "Sir, we are investigating the recent murders and would like to ask you some questions."

"Well, I don't see how that would involve a slaughterhouse and meat packing business, but go ahead."

"Silas Binder works here, what actually is his job?"

"He's the first man on the assembly line and often helps the foreman on the last position."

"The first and last position on the assembly involve what kind or work?"

"The first position is when the animal is killed with a sledgehammer strike to the head, followed by cutting the throat to bleed the animal. The last position is when the internal organs are removed, and the carcass is split in two halves."

"What happens to the internal organs?"

"The tongue, heart and liver are saved for packing. The remaining organs are placed in a 50-gallon steel drum, and when a drum is full, it's shipped to the rendering plant that processes the offal for dog food."

"What happens to partially filled barrels?"

"We keep them overnight in the refrigerated section of the plant. We only get paid for full barrels."

"Thank you, please keep our meeting private and do not mention it to Silas Binder, under penalty of being arrested. Before we leave, could we speak to your foreman." "Archie Kline is the foreman, and his office is next door to mine. Follow me and I'll introduce you to him."

With introductions done, Bryce took the lead again. "We know you are friends with Silas Binder, but our investigation must be kept secret. What do you know about Silas relationship with his departed mother?"

"What was told to me was told in confidence, and I'm not going to repeat it."

"Very well. Red cuff him, bring him to jail and charge him with interfering with a murder investigation."

"Wait, did you say murder investigation?"

"Yes the five butchered housewives in your town."

"Very well, I'll tell you what I know. Lenora Binder abused Silas in many ways. During her monthly, she forced him to perform an unnatural sex act with her, and then beat him senseless with a two-inch cane. It took him years to settle down after her suspicious death."

"Has he had a change of personality in the past six months?"

"Yes, he claimed to have met this girl months ago, but suddenly she dropped him. Ever since them, he's been moody and by the end of each month he stopped coming to work. He claims that the killing of animals gets to him and by the end of the month he burns out. It takes him a week to come back to work."

"Thank you for your information. If Silas Binder is alerted of our meeting, we will come back and arrest you. So, keep it hush, hey!"

Leaving Winchell's, Uncle Joe said, "it's too late to go search Binder's house since the day shift will be out soon. We need a break, let's get some supper, take a hotel room and try to forget the sordid details this day has brought out."

The next day, after a full breakfast, the Trio was watching the house at 41 Mountain Heights. At 7:42AM, Silas Binder came out of his house, locked the front door, and stupidly placed the key over the doorsill. He then left on a run and was seen entering the slaughterhouse. Red was set under a tree for shade, and was to watch the street to make sure that the suspect did not return to his house unexpectedly. Bryce, Uncle Joe, and Marshal Warren picked up the key, unlocked the door, replaced the key on the doorsill and entered. Red was to perform an owl hoot sound if someone was approaching the house.

It was a small home with the usual kitchen, parlor and one bedroom downstairs. The slaughterhouse coveralls were not in the laundry area, so it was assumed that the clothing was supplied and laundered at work. At first glance, there seemed to be very little evidence worth gathering until Bryce saw something in the kitchen sink. "Look here marshal, between the drain and the bottom of the sink is a bright red ring of liquid red. I believe this is blood. We'll suck it up with an eyedropper, that I saw in the bedroom cabinet, and bring it to Doc Samuels for analysis."

Heading upstairs were two rooms and a walk-in closet. The closet was packed with old abandoned junk of no relevance to the case. The bedroom on the left was a guest room no longer used. It had a bed, mattress, chair and empty dresser—nothing of significance. The other room on the right remained to be checked out. As Uncle Joe grabbed the door handle, Bryce stopped him, pointed to a fine thread at the bottom of the door that was attached to the door and door frame with a clear salve—just to hold the thread in place. It was instantly clear to Uncle Joe and Marshal Warren that the thread was a security system—if the thread was not replaced, it would mean that someone had been in the room.

The thread was pulled aside as they entered the room. All three investigators froze in place. They had walked into some kind of shrine. A female mannequin was dressed in an old dusty dress and on a table was an old tin-type photo of a middle-aged woman labeled Lenora. The woman 's dress in the photograph was the same one as the one worn by the mannequin. Marshal Warren said, "my goodness, this is a shrine to his mother." Along several pieces of furniture was plenty of memorabilia especially the newspaper article about her sudden death. The funeral was sparsely attended by her son, the undertaker, Doc Samuels and the grave diggers.

Opening up a chifferobe wardrobe, Uncle Joe nearly collapsed. The internal drawers had been removed and red velvet shelves had been installed. Each of the six shelves had a female nipple in a jar of alcohol. Marshal Warren spoke first, "that is absolute proof that Silas Binder is our killer and these nipples can be matched to the five victims, but why are there six?"

"Because if you look carefully, one nipple is darker and more shriveled up. I suspect this one belonged to his mother."

Uncle Joe added, "it's a good thing Red is outside watching the street, if he had been with us, we would have gotten another 'PEE….EW.' about white men—etcetera."

"Well marshal, I agree with you that this is proof enough to hang the man, but isn't it also proof that the man is mentally ill and could be classed as a 'criminally insane' individual?"

"Could be, but that has to be decided by Judge Skinner."

"Ok, we'll do that today, for now take one jar of the newer specimens and we'll show it to Judge Skinner." Leaving the room, they left one window curtain slightly open and carefully replaced the thread across the door. When they left the house, they relocked the front door and replaced the key on the doorsill.

On their way to the courthouse, they stopped to see Doc Samuels. He took the blood sample, placed it under the microscope. After a short time, he looked up and said, "this is human red blood cells and they are small in size, called microcytes, and are definitely the result of iron deficiency anemia like the fifth victim. I should be able to prove that this blood sample in his kitchen sink was not the suspect's own."

"Thank you for your help, and we may need you to testify."

Their next stop was at the courthouse. The Trio met with Judge Skinner again, related Doc Samuel's findings, described the shrine to his mother and the macabre finding of six female nipples in the altered chifferobe wardrobe. When Judge Skinner was handed the alcohol bottle with its content, Judge Skinner simply said, "the Lord help us, we certainly have the killer, but what do we do with him. He may be mentally ill and criminally insane. What do you want of me?"

Would you call an emergency meeting to include us, Marshal Warren, the local prosecutor, Doc Samuels, and a public defendant attorney. This is for the purpose of obtaining a plea arrangement that would allow a court ordered mental evaluation in a state approved mental institution. If he is deemed criminally insane, then he can be committed to a mental institution till cured or for life if not curable."

"I will arrange this emergency proceeding and we'll meet in my chambers after our noon dinner at 1PM."

As the meeting began, Marshal Warren introduced the Trio and clarified that, since Bryce had the lead all along, would present the case. Bryce went thru the entire scenario from the time they met with Marshal Warren, Maude Meecham, Doc Samuels, Mister Winchell, and Archie Kline. Then Doc Samuels went thru the gory details of all the autopsies, and the blood sample found in the Binder kitchen.

Resting their presentation, the prosecutor, Craven Bullock, was first to speak. "The evidence is clear, he's a killer and he needs to be prosecuted to the fullest. Insane or not, he did it and he will hang. I suggest that we arrest him immediately and we will provide a quick trial to avoid a mob building up to lynch him."

The defense attorney, Benedict Beardsley, was next to speak, "I object to Mister Bullock's reasoning and proposed disposition. Our prosecutor is behind the times and is simply seeing a quick case to win for his record. I propose that we arrest him, and you can order a mental evaluation in the State Mental Hospital in Austin. If he is certified as criminally insane, he will spend the rest of his life in a mental institution.

"Your honor, I object"................. "On what grounds Craven, you know the law regarding mental illness. This is no longer the dark ages. Go ahead gentlemen, find Silas Binder and bring him in— alive please."

The Trio went straight to the slaughterhouse. Binder was not in the building and Archie Kline said, "this is the end of the month and he went home early saying that he couldn't kill another animal without some R & R."

The Trio looked at each other and Uncle Joe said, "oh no, this is the 24th of the month." All three men took off at a dead run to 41 Mountain Heights.

As dark came, the Trio spread out in three sites, the front door, the back door and high in a tree to watch the room with the chifferobe shrine, thru the partially open curtain left that way by Bryce. Binder was in his house having supper when he got up and headed upstairs. Seeing the thread still in place, he entered the special room. Bryce was in the tree and could easily follow Binder who visited the many tin-type photos of his mother. Then he started talking to the mannequin and slapped her in the face several times. He then moved to the chifferobe, opened both doors, and his eyes moved from the top shelf to the bottom one. Bryce could see that the man was obviously perturbed as he started looking around the tables for the missing bottle of nipples. Binder actually appeared frantic when the realism struck him that someone had taken one of his prized specimens.

Binder left the shrine room in a huff and went downstairs where he walked right into a closet. When he never came out, the Trio took the doorsill key, went inside, walked into the closet and saw a throw rug rolled up over a floor access door. Opening the door they all went into the cellar they had missed. The cellar floor was dirt, and a large pit was dug up. The contents were partially covered with lime and other powders to promote tissue decomposition. Red said, "so, this is where he is disposing of the human organs."

"Yes, and that is a human heart that didn't get covered with decomposing chemicals, move it aside, and we'll use it as evidence."

Looking around the cellar, an underground passage was found to the outside. "So, this is how he left the house unseen. He either saw one of us and decided to leave the city or he is going to replace the nipple an evening early. If he is escaping, there is no way we can stop him since he would have had a horse stabled close by and would have had a 'get out' survival pack ready to take with him."

Uncle Joe asked Bryce, "which avenue do you think he took?"

"This is a sick puppy who is not thinking straight, I'm certain he went to kill his sixth victim and replace his trophy."

"How do we catch him before he strikes again?"
"We bait him!"

***

Shortly thereafter, theTrio was standing in the Murdock Theatre. Bryce went to talk to a receptionist and all three men were escorted to the makeup room.

Uncle Joe shouts out, "are you nuts, you want me to wear a wig, wear a dress, carry a reticule and walk in high heels?" "Yes, and this lady will add makeup to your face."

"So, I'm the bait, heh?"

"Yes, and you can't wear your Colt. Here is a Bulldog you can place in your reticule for protection; and a sap to protect your womanhood from sex fiends." Red was dying to keep from laughing when Aunt Josephine came out fully disguised.

"Ok, smart one, what is the plan?"

"Binder will be impatient, and will want a quick candidate to desecrate. The only place to get a 'quickie' without reconnaissance is at a saloon that has waitresses and soiled doves—they all have to use the privy."

"No, I'm not posing for either jobs."

"I agree. I have made plans at Russel's Bar to use the back kitchen with a door to the outside privy. Every fifteen minutes or so, you'll walk into the privy to do your business. When you come out, Silas Binder will eventually be waiting for you as you open the door to leave. Just to deceive him, every time you go to the privy, wear a different apron or shawl to imitate the many waitresses working tonight. We need to be patient and we'll get him alive."

Two hours later, and many trips to the privy, Aunt Josephine was getting moody from the feet blisters trying to stay upright in high heels. On her current walk to the privy, Red who was hiding in the treeline behind the privy, noticed a shadow moving to the privy. Red followed and saw the man knock on the door and say, "please hurry, Ma'am, I need to go bad." As the door opened, Binder saw a man holding a woman's wig in his left hand. Binder knew he had been had, and out of self-preservation, raised the right hand-held sledgehammer over his head ready to cave in this trickster's skull. At that moment, Red's war club made contact with Binder's right elbow 'funny' bone and the sledgehammer fell to the ground. Uncle Joe responded to the shocked Binder with, "you're not getting my nipple, you pervert." The sap in Uncle Joe's right hand made contact with Binder's forehead as Binder dropped to the ground like a stone in standing water.

When Binder woke up, he found himself behind bars. Marshal Warren started asking him questions, but Binder only had one line, "I ain't talking without a lawyer present."

"You don't have to talk, just listen to Deputy Marshal Bryce Sullivan who will review the evidence against you." Bryce started from the beginning and was interrupted with, "that's all circumstantial evidence, my lawyer can fight that."

"Oh but it gets better. Doc Samuels can tie the last victim to the blood on your hand-held sledgehammer because of a documented blood disease. The intact heart in your cellar pit will be proven as human, four of the nipples can be matched to buried bodies, the fifth one in Marshal Warren's safe was taken out of your shrine room with three witnesses, and your pattern of missing work after the five murders will also be confirmed by Archie Kline. Hell, we even know you killed your own mother. You are some real puke, and you will hang for your deeds."

The jail went silent as the four lawmen stepped out of the cell room to let the animal digest the evidence against him. The lawmen were pouring a fresh cup of coffee when Binder yelled out, "is there a way I can negotiate a plea deal to avoid hanging?" "Plead guilty to all six killings, and we'll bring it to prosecutor Bullock, public defender Beardsley, and Judge Skinner. If everyone accepts the guilty confession, then it's up to the Judge to offer you a sentence."

The next day, all parties met in the courthouse trial room. The confession was accepted, and Judge Skinner handed down his ruling. "Silas Binder, you would hang by this confession or by being convicted in a trial. However, because it is suspected that you are mentally ill, I will order a 90-day evaluation in the State Mental Hospital in Austin. You will be evaluated and examined by six MD's who specialize in mental illnesses. It takes a vote of four doctors to certify you as criminally insane, for which you will spend the rest of your life in a locked down mental institution for your kind. If you are not found insane, you will be returned to this jurisdiction and will be put on trial for multiple heinous murders. Any questions?" "No your honor." The gavel came down with Judge Skinner's words, "case disposed."

The next day, three deputy marshals escorted Silas Binder to Austin by train in the special boxcar with a barred cell. That same day an article was placed in the local newspaper explaining the sequence of investigative findings and the judge's ruling. That way, there was no chance that the accused would end up lynched by a drunken mob while awaiting trial.

That same afternoon, the Community Bank handed over the $25,000 which was sent to Abilene in their individual 1st National Bank's accounts. After supper, Uncle Joe said to Bryce, "I'm a man of my word. Before we head back to Dallas and get another job, take off from here right away and you'll travel the 300 miles in some eleven hours. You can make it to Allie tomorrow afternoon. Then let us know your future plans in the next 10-14 days. Don't do anything I wouldn't do, but if you do, be prepared to accept the consequences, heh."

Bryce never hesitated, went to the hotel to pack, picked up his horse and headed to the railroad ticket counter. The 300-mile trip cost him $9 and $1 for his horse. Waiting an hour, the overnight express train started its journey. Bryce thought, *for no reason I suspect my bounty hunting days are coming to an end. I sense that this is now the beginning of my designated and permanent destiny—a business venture and a life with Allie.*

***

CHAPTER 8

Saving Allie

The late passenger train, called the red eye, started rolling at 9PM and the connection in Dallas had a three-hour layover. Arriving in Dallas at 3AM, the connection brought the travelers to 6AM. Bryce calculated that if there were no delays, he would arrive in Abilene at noon.

Planning his time for reading, he decided to read by lamp till he got sleepy, then would sleep till he got to the Dallas connection. In Dallas he would read in the comfort of the railroad station. He would then sleep again on route to Abilene. Realizing he had plenty of reading time, he decided to finish Allie's textbook on raising pigs, before his arrival in Abilene. He would need all this information to get answers from Allie or at least carry an informed discussion with her. Per routine, he started taking notes.

With four chapters to go, he started with Chapter 11—Slaughtering. Hogs grown for meat are best fed liberally in pens—or force fed as is commonly called. Yet, everyone knows you cannot force feed an animal. The idea is to keep food available, varied and with minimal requirements. The ideal weight of a hog ready for butchering is a 22-week hog weighing +-240 pounds now eating a minimum of six pounds or more of feed, grain or crops, plus six or more liters of water.

The animal is mercifully killed with a 22-caliber shot behind the ears and pointed at the brain. Once the animal is down, it is quickly hoisted up by the hind legs, and the throat is cut to bleed the animal. The blood is collected for specialty foods mentioned in Chapter 13. The animal is then lowered in a trough and boiling water is poured over the animal to scald the skin. The scalded skin allows the easy removal of hair, plus the softening of the skin for human mastication. The animal is then hoisted up and the hair is rinsed off and residual hairs are then removed with a razor.

The animal is then eviscerated, and the organs removed. The heart, liver and the hocks are collected for retailing (the hocks are used to make an old gravy recipe called ragu). The head is then removed behind the ears and the face muscles are collected for a specialty food. The last step is to split the carcass with a saw into two halves—each half weighing approximately 75-85 pounds each.

With proper refrigeration, the carcasses can hang anywhere from 7 to 14 days to improve meat tenderness. Then starts the art of preparing the cuts of meat. Chapter 12 describes the different cuts that can be retrieved from a side of pork. A 75-pound side generally includes: ham 12 lbs. loin 9 lbs. bacon 10 lbs. spareribs 2 lbs. roasts (shoulder, butt, back with bone) 19 lbs. lard 15 lbs. and trimmings/bones 8 lbs. These cuts separate the general distribution of a half carcass. The butcher then prepares individual cuts for retail use to include pork chops, ground pork, pork steak, and many others.

As he became sleepy, he put down the textbook and fell asleep to the clickety-clack of the iron wheels on the rail unions. He woke up when the conductor announced their arrival at Dallas for a

3-hour connection. After getting an egg sandwich and coffee, Bryce went back to his textbook and resumed taking notes.

Chapter 13 covered how to prepare specialty foods. The most common was blood pudding (aka blood sausage). The ingredients included: 1 quart of blood, 3 lbs. of ground pork, ¼ lb. of fat, 2 cups of chopped onions, ¼ cup of lard, 3 tablespoons of salt. And one tablespoon of pepper—cooked in the oven and served in 1-inch slices.

Other items included cured salt pork from the belly or sides, pork rinds from deep-fried skin, and head cheese. Contrary to popular belief, head cheese is not made from pig's brain. It's made from ground up facial muscle trimmings plus fat/lard and other ingredients to make a spread.

Bacon was made from the pork bellies. The process of making bacon involved curing the full thickness bellies in a solution of salt nitrates and sugar for 3-5 days. Then the cured bellies were smoked, for 2-4 hours, at 225-250 °F till the bacon internal temperature reached 150 °F. The sugar increased lactic acid which prevented hostile organisms from spoiling the meat.

The other popular breakfast meat was pork sausage, commonly called bangers, which consisted of ground pork, salt, pepper, thyme, brown sugar, sage, all spice and nutmeg—prepared in links or patties.

It was fitting, that the last chapter, covered the economics of raising pigs as a "cash crop." The basis of a profitable business is weighing the cost of feed versus the going rate for a 240 lb. live weight. If the average weight of consumed feed equals 5- 6 lbs. per day, then to reach 22 weeks and weigh 240 lbs. will require 700-900 pounds of feed.   T h a t makes it imperative that a hog cannot be purely fed purchased grain. The diet must be 99% plant based and include crops of corn, soybeans, oats, sorghum, barley, sugar beets and the multitude of garden vegetables and table scraps. Most city customers will not purchase pork products that are raised on animal internal organs from slaughterhouses. Fortunately, most cities have a processing plant that picks up animal internal organs and are converted with vegetables into dry dog and cat food.

As Bryce closed the textbook, he pondered about the next subjects of refrigeration and canning meat.

Bryce realized that these new modalities would bring the pork meat business in the 1900's. For now, he and Allie needed to make certain that crossbreeding would be a success as well as ear tagging for identification of profitable hog generations. The next step would be to establish a crop planting and harvesting system to feed the growing hogs. Along with this would be the expansion of the barns, a grain storage system, and a mechanized commercial slaughterhouse.

***

Bryce slept a few hours heading to Abilene, but for the last 3 hours he was too wound up to even enjoy the scenery. He was simply buying his time till he got to the railroad platform in town.

Arriving at noon, he skipped dinner, picked up his horse and headed out to the Adkins homestead.

Meanwhile at the Adkins home, Allie was busy in her office filling in her expense/profit ledger when she heard someone walk into her home without knocking. Allie stood up and was confronted with two rough looking men. The one carrying some papers finally spoke, "Mister

Ayers wants you to sign this bill of sale and I'll give you this check which was his last offer."

"I'm not selling, now get out!"

The other man stepped up and slapped Allie enough to nearly drop her to the floor. The miscreant then grabbed Allie's neck and started to squeeze her windpipe. Allie reacted, by drawing her Bulldog. The one trying to choke her saw the pistol come up and grabbed her other hand to prevent her from pulling back the pistol's hammer to shoot him. What he didn't realize was that the Bulldog was a double action pistol and did not require the hammer to be pulled back to fire. To the man's total surprise and shock, Allie shot him in the belly button. The man doubled up and crumpled to the floor. Allie was about to point her pistol at the other man when she felt a sharp pain in the back of her head, saw blue stars and then things went black.

Allie had not seen the third intruder who had entered thru the kitchen's back door. Realizing that the two men needed to get out, one man started to head for the front door as the other left Allie a personal message, he tore her blouse open, ripped her chemise, and pulled her britches down along with her underwear. He then left the bill of sale on her face and started for the front door. To his surprise he heard someone yell, "stop right there, bubba," as it was followed by a loud shotgun blast. To make it worse, another man was galloping hard and stopped next to the shotgun toting man.

Bryce said, "what is going on Eustache? I heard a gunshot as I was approaching the access road and now, I see you holding a smoking shotgun and a dead man on the ground. Where is Allie/"

"I don't know, I just got here with my daily load of chopped corn when I saw three horses tied to the railing. So I stopped to check on Miss Adkins when this dude ran from the house to his horse. When I yelled for him to stop, he pulled his Colt and I had no choice but the let him have one barrel of OO Buckshot and then you arrived."

"That means that there is another man inside. Go out back and watch the kitchen door to prevent anyone from escaping. I'll go in the front door."

Bryce was expecting the worse but prayed not to be too late. He stepped on the porch with his pistol drawn. The front door was ajar, and he simply pushed it open. The sight he saw would never leave him.

Allie was on the parlor floor, nude, unconscious or dead, with blood between her legs. Bryce wanted to rush in and check on her but realized that someone was waiting for him with deadly intent on his mind. Before stepping over the threshold, he happened to look at the space between the door and the door frame. There was a man behind the door, holding a pistol, with the hammer pulled back. Bryce recognized the murderous intent on his face, put the tip of his pistol's muzzle in the crack and pulled the trigger. The intruder caught the bullet in his left upper arm, and it traveled to his chest where it blew his heart open.

Bryce hurried to Allie's side. She was breathing and had a pulse. When he found an egg in the back of her head, he knew she had been knocked out. He quickly placed a towel between her legs, pulled up her britches, and closed her blouse as best as he could, then wrapped her in a blanket. Eustache had gone to the carriage house to get Allie's buggy with a long box in the back for delivering carcasses. Bryce placed a small cot mattress in the buggy and laid her on it. Bryce stayed with her as Alva was pushing the horses at a fast trot to the city hospital.

Driving to the Emergency Reception door, Doc Newcomb received them. "Hello Bryce, it's been a year, as he saw Allie in the buggy he said, "what happened to Allie?" Bryce related the story as he knew it while still holding the bill of sale he found on Allie's face. His last words to Doc Newcomb were, "she is bleeding from her private area and may have been raped."

"Well, let's bring her in to my examining table, I'll examine her and get back to you in the waiting room."

It was a long hour during which time Bryce did some soul searching. If he could get Allie back, he would never leave her alone again. It did not matter what condition she would be in, for he promised his creator, that he would take care of her medically if she had brain damage, and would be happy to raise her child if she became pregnant from the rape. He reminded his creator, that although they had not been spoken over the book at a church marriage, that they were already committed to each other for life.

Bryce was pulled out of his reverie by the waiting room doors popping open as Doc Newcomb started speaking. "Allie has had a common concussion and may have some mild brain swelling that will keep her unconscious for some time. There are some new medicines for brain swelling as you may remember when you brought in Eleanora Brockman in from a beating. Fortunately, Allie's brain swelling is likely much milder than Mrs. Brockman. She should respond in two days, but during the next two days, Allie will be in and out of consciousness and when is responsive, she will likely talk gibberish or make statements or requests that don't make sense. But in two days, she should be back to her normal self."

Bryce simply thanked the doctor and then said, "seeing she was attacked, I'll be staying at her side continuously till she comes home—if that's Ok with you."

"Certainly. As Doc Newcomb turned to leave, he added, "you didn't ask me about the bleeding in her private area."

"It doesn't matter, we'll be married within the week and we'll raise the child if she is pregnant."

"Well, that's nice to know. I know Allie and you'll be getting a hell of a wife. And by the way, the blood is from her monthly period. The trauma of the attack caused the clinical gushing of blood as a response. Allie was not raped, and I assure you she is still intact—if it matters, which I now doubt, heh."

***

After Allie had been hooked to the medicine and transferred to her hospital room. Bryce sat next to her and held her hand. Alva had been patiently waiting outside her hospital room when he entered. "May I enquire how the boss is, I'm very worried."

"The Doc claims she'll be back to normal in two days. Before you go back to the farm would you run a few errands for me since I don't want to leave Allie's side." "Certainly." "Stop by my parent's gun shop and tell them what has happened. Also stop and inform Sheriff Marlow of the attack on Allie, the shooting, and the three dead attackers. He'll want to investigate and bring the undertaker with him. Ask him to check with me when he is done. Until we return home, you are in charge of the entire homestead and farm. And tell Eustache that I'll thank him properly the next time I see him."

As Alva was leaving, he stopped and turned around to add, "may I add, Eustache has been a real keeper. He brings a fresh load of chopped corn every day at noon, feeds the hogs, and works all afternoon till 5PM. The man is a good and reliable worker and always has a smile on his face. He is very happy with his employment, as Alec and I are."

That same hour Jim and Sally arrived in a huff. After hugging their son, they asked to be filled in. After a long explanation, Sally said that she would bring his meals. Jim was worried that this guy Ayers would try something deadly, since his hired thugs never reported back, and his signed bill of sale was missing—what he didn't know was that his three messengers were dead.

Three hours later, Allie had not responded. Sheriff Marlow arrived to discuss the situation. Bryce gave him a detailed sequence of events. Sheriff Marlow then said, "if you want me to go see this Herschel Ayers, I will go and confront him. The evidence is circumstantial, and the bill of sale could have been forged. But I can plant the fear of God into him and make it clear that I would be following his activities from now on."

"No, please don't. That could push him to send more assassins to wipe out Allie before she awakens and can implicate him in this fiasco. It's best that he is kept in the dark. Let's bury the attackers and keep the entire event quiet and out of the newspapers. I will visit with him after Allie gets home, and I will place the fear of 'Sullivan' into his mind instead of the fear of God." "I'm willing to go along with that plan."

"Thanks, one last thing, when you tell the undertaker to bury the attackers, please give him this note." (the sealed envelope contained a specific request and two $100 bills).

Sally showed up at 6PM with a meatloaf sandwich and a bread pudding for dessert. Admitting that she could not find a way to bring hot coffee, he informed her that the hospital cook made coffee available 24 hours a day for family members who were sitting with their loved ones. After a short visit, Sally hugged her son and left till morning.

Doc Newcomb arrived at 7PM on his evening rounds. He took out his rubber hammer, pulled out the nail out of the handle and a brush hidden in the hammer head behind the rubber tip. He asked if she had showed some signs of responding. When Bryce said no, he proceeded to use those strange tools to check out her reflexes, muscular response to the nail and a few other reflexes. When he finished, he said, "good, everything is the same, I'll see her in the morning. I expect she will be in an out of consciousness some time during the night."

Allie's first response was at midnight. She squeezed Bryce's hand and opened her eyes. "Who are you?" "It's me Allie." Allie showed a faint smile, closed her eyes and went out. Two hours later, Allie woke up, saw Bryce and said, "is that really you, Bryce. I missed you so." "Yes, I love you so much," as Allie again went out.

Her next response did not make any sense. She was apparently awake and kept saying "water, water, water." Bryce called the night nurse in and she simply grabbed a toilet seat/pan and pushed Bryce out of the room to take care of business.

After the ordeal, Bryce resumed his vigil. The next time Allie woke up she was more oriented.

Bryce started by kissing her which seemed to brighten Allie's face. Allie was still a bit confused when she asked if they had been married yet. Bryce then took over the conversation as Allie was very attentive. "We'll get married as soon as you are discharged from the hospital. I will never leave you again. It took a lifetime to find you, and from now on, you're going to be tied to me at the hip."

Realizing that Allie was still alert, he got on his knees and said, "Allie Adkins, will you marry me and share your life with me?"

"Yes, I will marry you and spend the rest of our days together. I will be your friend, your partner, and your lover."

By morning, Allie was alert and mentally intact. She had a light breakfast and plenty of coffee. By 10 AM she was sitting in the chair and using the bedside commode. After a light noon dinner, Allie was taking long walks in the hospital hall. Doc Newcomb examined her, took her medicine away, and told her that she would likely be dischargeable by tomorrow morning.

That night they were enjoying private time as the door was closed to Allie's room. Although intimacy could not be fully achieved because of Allie's monthly, they both realized that this would be over with by the wedding day. They held each other, kissed passionately with some mild fondling. The affectionate demonstration was real despite its lack of fulfillment.

The next morning, Allie was discharged. Alva arrived with the buggy with his own horse trailing. He handed the reins to Bryce as he rode his horse back to the farm. Bryce stopped at the jeweler and purchase their wedding bands. Then they stopped at St. Mark's Methodist Church and arranged for a wedding in four days with Pastor Peabody. Their next stop was Becky's Diner for a quick lunch of coffee and a roast beef sandwich. After their meal they arranged for a reception noon dinner for the wedding guests. The next errand of the day was the local newspaper print shop to purchase some standard wedding invitations. Before they left town, they stopped at the telegraph office and sent a telegram to Dallas requesting that Uncle Joe and Red take the overnight train to Abilene. They were needed as bodyguards ASAP.

On their ride home, they agreed they would return for Allie to buy a wedding dress, for Bryce to buy a suit, and for reservations to be made at the Abilene General Hotel for the honeymoon suite. They also agreed on a guest list to include: Azra and Erna Albright, Alva and Alec Bassett, Eustache and Imogene Backus, Doc and Missus Newcomb, Sawyer Skinner (neighbor), Sheriff and Missus Marlow, deputies Abrams and Burke, leather-man Adelbert Abbott, mom and dad, sisters Cindy Sue and Anna Mae, bank president Goddard and Missus Abernathy, Pastor and Missus Peabody and the five butcher shop customers with their wives.

Once home, the couple started preparing dinner of bacon, pancakes and coffee since there were few vittles in the larder. After supper, Bryce and Allie found themselves on the parlor sofa. Bryce said, "I told you when you were awake that I would never leave you again. Do you recall?"

"Oh yes, but that means your bounty hunting year will end prematurely. How will your uncle feel about this?"

"It's only a couple of months early, and besides, his purpose was to build a retirement account, and I assure you this has been thoroughly accomplished."

"Before you revealed this news, I knew that I could no longer stay away from you. They say that separation grows fondness of the heart—well separation has torn me apart. I had decided to join you as a bounty hunter. I was lucky to find an old gunfighter, the one and only Eustache Backus, and he trained me with all three firearms, and taught me some basic self-defense hand to hand combat. I practice shooting twice a day and I can assure you that I am now proficient. So I was going to put the law down, when you left, I would join you or follow you. It was a situation where it was easier 'to ask forgiveness than to ask permission.' But you beat me to the punch."

Bryce looked at her and said, "you've changed since my last visit."

"Yes, two ways. When you stirred the pot during our intimacy, I think you woke up my ovaries. I am taller, leaner, lost some weight, my breasts are fuller, and I've grown some.........well you'll notice later. My attitude has changed, I want to be with you and will do anything to make that happen."

Bryce simply reacted by taking Allie in his arms and shower her with passionate kisses. Both reacted quickly and fondling started. When things were approaching loss of control, Allie stood up and pulled Bryce to her bedroom. After closing the door, she said, our bedroom will be our private domain. Standing in front of Bryce she dropped her dress to the floor, pulled open her chemise and lowered her underwear. Standing nude in front of him she said, "take a good look, this is the best you're going to get with me in my prime."

Bryce couldn't stop staring and finally responded by, "my God, you are voluptuous." Without a word, he undressed, with his manhood already responding, he said, "let there never be shame in sharing our bodies. I want you; I want us to pleasure ourselves, but let's not consummate our union till after the wedding."

Allie smiled, took his hand and pulled him to the bed. Their first sexual pleasure was a pure reaction to pent-up lust. They quickly reached their simultaneous peak and release. The rest of the night was spent exploring their bodies and reaching their nirvana several more times. After a few hours of sleep, the sunlight woke them up. They looked at each other and without a word expressed complete contentment. Allie was first to get up to rush to the privy. Eventually they were both in the kitchen cooking beans, eggs and coffee. When they sat down to eat, Bryce commented, "this is a necessary replenishing breakfast to restore our spent energy stores." Allie mussitated, "but what a way to spend down all that energy, heh?"

***

After breakfast, Bryce was shown the business ledger. It was clear that since chopped corn was used to feed the hogs, the profit margin was quickly expanding. The highest expense was still buying bagged grain and Bryce knew that this was the expense that needed to be nearly eliminated.

When they heard Eustache arrive with a full load of chopped corn, they went to the barn where Alva and Alec were already at work. The Duo watched the three men feed the hogs with wheelbarrows. Five full size hogs were separated. Alva explained that the three of them would be butchering all five for the five butcher shops in town. Bryce said, "I want to watch. I read the textbook you gave me, but I am still a visual learner. I need to see how it's done and see if changes could make the process more efficient."

Bryce was taking mental notes and found several things that could be changed. The three men could butcher a 250-pound hog in 30 minutes. The carcass was split in two halves, the heart and liver packed for transport. The blood was processed when hot by Alec adding all the ingredients to make blood sausage. The mixture would then congeal and would be ready for cooking at the butcher shop. Three hours after the slaughter started, Alec was on his way with ten half-carcasses, hearts, liver and blood sausage. Eustache was on his way to town also, but with the offal to the rendering plant.

Walking back to the house, Bryce said how much are you paid for these five hogs. "The butcher shops pay us $40 per full carcass, $6 for the liver, heart and blood sausage—each week. Our expense now without bagged grain is $10.50 a week for Eustache labor and corn, Alva gets $7 a week plus room, board, and all personal expenses. Alec gets $2 per day for butchering. That's approximately $20 a week. Figure another $5 for miscellaneous expenses. That comes to $46 minus $25 equals a rough profit of $21 a week or $1100 a year." "That is a good living for you—but not for an entire family which is why we will grow the business." "Agree, and I especially like the family part, heh."

By the time they reached the porch, two riders were seen arriving from town—Red and Uncle Joe. Allie looked at Bryce and said, "Boy, they are a sight, I wonder what brings them here?" "When I sent them a telegram inviting them to the wedding, I also mentioned that we could benefit from some security—till this issue with Ayers is settled."

With the two riders setting down, Bryce said, "Allie, this is Uncle Joe, and this is Red Sky. Gentlemen, this is my fiancé, Allie Adkins. Introductions completed, the visitors were invited in the house for refreshments and a detailed explanation why security was needed for a week. Bryce explained that he was going to visit Herschel Ayers in the morning with Sheriff Marlow. He would make this man an offer he could not refuse. In case he had already planned some revenge, the Duo would stay with Allie until his return from Ayers office. Plus, he would ask Uncle Joe and Red to stay in the house and guard it and the farm until they returned from their honeymoon.

Allie invited them for supper but realized she was short of meat. Uncle Joe laughed and added, "hell, we thought we'd have to eat pork, so we brought four beef steaks." Great, well, we have plenty of coffee and vegetables. What vegetable would you like Uncle Joe, "oven baked potato with butter!" "Can do, how about you Red?" "Boiled beets with butter if you have some." "Can do as well. For dessert, I have left over bread and will make a bread pudding."

Waiting for supper, the Trio was talking about their capers over the past months. It was a cordial discussion. Bryce started talking about the pig farm and most of their questions were answered by Allie. As the potatoes and beets were cooked, Allie announced that the four steaks were going on the stove. The three men moved to the kitchen table and Uncle Joe kept the one serious issue on hold till after supper.

It was a great meal except for the rare to raw steak that Red was relishing. After dessert and several pots of coffee, everyone pitched in to clean the dishes. When everyone moved to the parlor, Uncle Joe began talking. "Marshal Balinger in Dallas is aware of our traveling to Abilene for your wedding. He needs to know if this means that we are all retiring from our profession. If that is so, he will inform the wire to avoid unnecessary requests."

"Uncle Joe, do you have enough funds to support you in retirement?"

"Hell, I'll never live long enough to spend it all."

"What about you Red?" I was a bit short, but this pigheaded uncle of yours just gave me $20,000, so I'm good now. My family is eager to get me back."

"Well, when Allie was in a coma, I promised God and myself that I would never leave Allie alone—ever again."

Allie then joined the discussion. "I'm not marrying this man to keep him from doing what he wants or needs to do—the only difference is that I am going with him, and instead of the Trio of misfits, it's going to be the Quad with a woman."

Uncle Joe and Red were expressing chortles, guffaws and slaps on their thighs. "Whoa, a woman with a gun."

Bryce added, "well it appears that during my absence, Allie was trained by an old gunfighter. I suspect she can shoot rings around you two, but we'll need a demonstration to be certain. Just to remind you, she killed one of her attackers before she was buffaloed from the back!"

"Ok, it looks like retirement may be around the bend. Let's put the final decision a month off. I'll telegram Marshal Balinger to put us temporarily out of commission, and we'll give him a final answer in a month. Red is going back to his reservation, and I'm going to start looking for a house in the center of town, close to the hospital and a doctor. Goodnight for now, and we'll be here at pre-dawn to make sure that nothing happens to you Allie."

***

At dawn Bryce was in town to pick up Sheriff Marlow. His second stop was the undertaker. Bryce walked in with a saddlebag, placed a tool in the bag and the undertaker said, "your specimen has been kept on ice and is still fresh. I'll bring it in a sealed bag that you can tie to your saddle horn."

Riding to a specific address, Bryce noted the business sign, Ayers Meat Packing. The two men walked to the building and were given directions to the boss's office. As agreed, Sheriff Marlow stayed in the waiting area as Bryce stepped in with the sealed bag and a tool in the back of his belt. Stepping right up to the main desk, the occupant had not even lifted his eyes off the paper he was writing and said, "what do you want?" Bryce reacted and suddenly a 4-pound hammer came flying out of his back belt. Thru a full arc, it landed smack in the middle of Ayers' writing hand. Bone, blood, and tissues exploded in every direction including Ayers' face. The man screamed, Ah---aah, and groaned as he looked at his smashed hand with fingers dangling by a thread of skin."

"Ayers was crying and groaning but managed to say, "Why?" as blood was covering his papers.

"The next time you have someone enter your office to do some business, you need to lift your face up and ask them how you can help them. You are one arrogant snob. Now this is why I'm here. Without any warning he put his hand in the sealed bag. Out came flying a man's head that he smacked on the desk directly in front of Ayers. Ayers automatically pushed his wheeled chair backwards, but abruptly stopped against the wall as his head tipped backwards and hit the wall. Bryce grabbed the chair and brought it back to the desk where the two heads were mere inches apart. The decapitated one was oozing a foul putrid liquid all over the desk and papers, and Ayers was gagging and dry retching. "Now that I have your attention, I am marrying Allie Adkins in two days, and I am a vengeful bounty hunter to boot. If you ever come close to my fiancé or send the likes of someone resembling this turd, your head will be separated, but while you are alive. The days of being high handed, and riding rough shod over another human being, are gone. This is the 1900's and what gives you the right to threaten my fiancé just because she said no to you."

Bryce paused and allowed Ayers to sit back so he would stop retching. "Now, it seems to me that a word to the wise should be sufficient, but I know that people like you don't heed to a legitimate warning, so I'm going to add two options."

The first is straight forward, you liquidate this business or sell it and get the hell out of town. To guarantee that you are out of town in one week, I will send an Indian madman who will put you down and cut off your testicles while you are watching. The other choice is prison. Sheriff Marlow is in your outer office and he will arrest you for ordering an aggravated assault and attempted murder. You'll find yourself in Huntsville within a week. Which will it be?"

"I'm leaving. The many pig farmers in the area are not sending me any hogs for processing because the Adkins girl was holding back. Without the supply of her hogs, I'm bankrupt anyways. A big meat packing and processing plant, Noble Meats, in Dallas wants my equipment and the shop and warehouse will be easy real estate to sell."

***

Riding away, Sheriff Marlow was satisfied with Ayers' decision to leave town. He pointed out that at a trial, an astute lawyer could possibly get him acquitted. This way, the likes of a shyster, would be out of his town.

Bryce arrived home at dinner time. Allie said, "are we free of that man?" "I think so, but to be sure, I'll send Red over in ten days to be sure. Now what is on the agenda for the next two days?"

"This afternoon, we meet with our neighbor, Sawyer Skinner, who has a business proposition for us. Tomorrow morning we go to town to buy your suit and my wedding dress. Your mom is meeting me at Harriman's Garment Store, and your dad is helping you get your suit. Tomorrow afternoon, I bring you up to snuff on how the crossbreeding program is going plus reviewing some management procedures. Then the next day is our wedding and reception." Bryce added with a smile, "And then our four-day honeymoon at the Abilene General Hotel."

***

CHAPTER 9

The Wedding

During dinner, Bryce asked Allie if she had any idea why Sawyer Skinner wanted a meeting. She said, "all he gave for a reason was that he was getting old." "Oh, well he may be wanting to retire. I had mentioned some time ago, that if he ever wanted to retire, that I would want to purchase his ranch. If that is the case, how much of the ranch should we purchase?" "Well if we want to expand, then we need the land and buildings." "That means that we need to pay his price to get it all." "Remember, I have $5,000 in my bank account and would be willing to spend it all on our future." "Allie, you'll soon find out that money will never hold us back from expanding the business— but that can wait till after the wedding."

Sawyer Skinner arrived on schedule. As he set down, he said, "Joe Sullivan handed me your wedding invitation yesterday and that is why I'm here today. I am 60 years old and really feel my age. I've been a widower for 5 years and I've been managing the ranch alone. I'm losing interest in the day to day activities and I've decided to retire. The ranch is for sale and you have expressed an interest in purchasing it."

"That is true, but we are interested in the land, buildings, and their contents—not the cattle or cattle cutting horses."

"Well that's not a problem. I can sell my cattle to the buyers at the railroad yard, and the cutting horses/saddles will go at a premium on the auction block. You can have the three harness geldings with tack. So, I'm interested in making a deal."

"Great, can you go over what real estate we're talking about?"

"I have two sections or 1,280 acres of very fertile land with one river, two streams, and two spring fed ponds. The buildings include the ranch house with two bedrooms and one office—all furniture as is. The bunkhouse holds 12 bunks, the cookie shack includes the dining area and kitchen. The barn has a full loft and has 15 horse stalls. The attached carriage house holds a buckboard, buggy, and two large utility wagons. The windmill water pump supplies running water in the house and barn. I will also include the full loft of quality hay and three hundred pounds of oats."

Allie was thinking and finally suggested, "can you break down the value of each item in dollar values and add an amount to make it the complete package."

"Sure. The 1,280 acres are worth $1,920 at $1.50 an acre. The ranch house/furniture = $500. The water system = $200. The work geldings and wagons = $300. The bunkhouse/cookshack = $200. The barn/hay/oats = $200. That comes to roughly $3,000. As a complete package, I would dare say it might be worth another $1,000—max. That $1,000 package value is negotiable."

Allie interjected, "so you would sell everything but your personal items, cattle, and cutting horses for $4,000?" "Yes, Ma'am."

Allie looked at Bryce for the nod of approval, but instead she got a clear negative head sign. Bryce came back, "Mister Skinner, Allie and I are not going to start our life with the notion that we are out to swindle our neighbors. Your ranch as listed is worth a lot more to us. It is adjacent to our farm, has well maintained buildings, and with a fifty-year-old fermented manure pile. We would only add a drive thru implement shed and an oats storage bin to establish a crop farm."

Bryce whispered an amount to Allie, and she nodded yes. "We would add another $1,000 for good will and will make you an offer of $5,000. If you accept it, I will give you a deposit of $1,000, we'll make a promissory bill of sale, and then will schedule the final transaction at the town clerk's office after our honeymoon."

"I would be a fool not to accept. You are very generous. I will gladly pass that sentiment once I retire in town."

"You know, many a new retiree gets bored after some time. It's not healthy to not have enough to do. If you ever get into that predicament, we will be hiring to establish a crop farm and we can always use men to drive implements, wagons and steam powered equipment."

Allie prepared a duplicate 'bill of sale' in ink as Bryce wrote out a $1,000 bank draft. Signed by all as Alva and Eustache signed as witnesses to their signatures. After Sawyer left, Allie said, "you are shelling out some money and we aren't yet married."

Bryce grabbed Allie and said, "if you're considering absconding, I will put you in manacles and you can skip the wedding dress. We are getting married day after tomorrow—and that's not negotiable."

That night they talked for hours till bedtime. Again, the couple continued to explore their bodies while pleasuring themselves. How they managed to get some sleep time was not clear, but they didn't care. After a necessary replenishing breakfast, they arrived at Harrriman's Garment Center to find mom and dad sitting on the boardwalk rocking chairs. After an hour, Bryce had chosen a well adorned classic western dark grey striped dress suit with a red wool vest and a light grey flat-top cowboy hat. He even included brand new cowboy boots to match the elegance of the outfit. With a second vest to match the suit, his dad pointed out that this suit would be used, in the big city of Dallas, when having business meetings. As they were preparing to leave, Bryce paid his bill of $32.50 when his dad came back from checking on the ladies. "Allie is just trying her second dress with four to go. Looks like you have a two hour wait. I guess I'll open up the shop." "And I've got errands to run."

Bryce's first stop was the local newspaper. He placed an ad looking for a college trained agronomist with five years of field experience in a private crop enterprise or as a county agent. The job description included starting a crop farm for feeding hogs. Salary would include a private home on the premises, and wages to be agreed upon. When he was done writing out the ad, the head printer looked at Bryce and said, "Sir, there is no one in this town that fits this need. May I suggest that we send this clip to our parent newspaper in Dallas where there is an agricultural college."

"Excellent idea, but still publish it here as well. I want the townsfolk to see the ad, and get the notion that we will be expanding. Actually, only in our local paper, add a footnote that we will be looking for homesteading crop workers and have them send their names to the newspaper. After the honeymoon, we'll write a second article about when and where the interviews would be held."

Bryce paid the $3.10 fee for both ads and they walked over to the railroad yard. After meeting with the station manager, he started, "my farm is about a quarter of a mile away, across the town road, and I want to have a side rail to my farm for holding refer cars and dry boxcars."

"That can be done, it will involve a switching system to access the side rail, a road crossing for wagon wheels, and rails up to your farm. I would estimate that this would cost you $4,000 but the final price has to be set by our business office after the site has been inspected by our engineer. In order to start the process we would need a 10% deposit of $400. If you choose not to do the project after the business office comes to a final cost, we will refund $300 of your deposit."

"Very well, here is the bank draft, let's fill out the application and get the process started. To me, this is a great deal."

His next stop was Tate's Hardware. After introductions were made Bryce said, "I'm starting a crop farm and will need some 'rideable' implements to include, large manure spreader, plow and disc/finish harrows, seeder, phosphate/lime spreader, oats binder and thresher, winnower, corn chopper, plant residue grinder/chopper. There may be others, but get me a fixed price on these items and a delivery date to the Adkins pig farm—the name which will soon be changed. We will be back sometime in the next week."

With his errands done, he picked up Allie with her packages that he added with his, in the buggy's rear flat bed. Bryce was heading to Bessie's for a noon dinner when Allie said they had to go the parsonage to meet with Pastor Peabody. They needed to go thru the expected proceedings as a dry run before tomorrow. After the practice, they did make it to Bessie's Diner. Bessie wanted them to try the two dishes she was planning to prepare for their reception—chicken and dumplings, or meatloaf and mashed potatoes with tomato sauce. They each got a half serving of each and were pleased with the taste. They whole heartedly approved of each dish. These would be accompanied with several vegetables, rolls, relishes, coffee and a wedding cake dessert. The diner was closing after the breakfast crowd. By 10 o'clock, the staff would be decorating the diner and the cooks would be preparing and cooking the two entrees. Before leaving the diner, Bryce asked Bessie to plan on 70 meals since their 35 guests would all want seconds. The final cost for 70 meals/wedding cake, and beer or lemonade for 35 guests was $85.

After dinner, the couple went home. After changing in work overalls and galoshes, the dynamic Duo headed to the barn. Allie began, "I was eager to show you the early results of cross breeding. We now have several first litters of crossbred piglets. Let's begin with the white Yorkshire (erect ears) gilt bred to a red Duroc boar (droopy ears). First of all the piglets were 2 lbs. heavier than pure bred Yorkshire piglets. Note how the red color has persisted in the hybrids. The ears are half erect to signify a 50-50 inheritance. Now compare these piglets with this pen of purebred Yorkshire born a week before the crossbreeds. The crossbreeds are larger, more alert, and lively. They are aggressive feeders, both nursing and eating gruel milk starter with water. Now look in this pen, these piglets are also crossbreeds, but have black areas and some are totally black. These are the hybrids of the black Hampshire (erect ears) and the white Landrace (droopy ears). They mimic the size and activity of the other crossbreeds (Duroc and Yorkshire). Again the 50-50 inheritance is easily seen by the mid position of the ears."

"Again, remind me of the crossbreeding advantage."

"They grow faster on less feed, efficient absorption of nutrition, reproductive efficiency and ease, docile personality, improved cleanliness, meat that is leaner with more tenderness and flavor."

Bryce added, "In other words, less expenses to produce more lean meat that is more tender and more flavorful. I can't imagine that any meat packer or distributor would not pay more for these carcasses!"

"That is correct. Now the other good news. These red and black one-year-old boars were active males. They were mating every other day and we had to keep them at that schedule because the vet said that if we over mated them, they would start producing small litters. Whether that was true, I don't know, but we didn't want to risk it. So most of our crossbreed litters are 8 to 10 lively piglets. There were very few stillborn."

"As I recall, you purchased 2 Duroc and 2 Hampshire colored boars. How many females did you have to breed?"

"Um-huh-um-well I had been hoarding the female piglets for a year and ended up with 50 selected lively gilts and 10 mature sows. In the next 30 days, all sixty females were bred since each boar was mating and impregnating a sow or gilt every other day—or 15 per month times 4 boars equaled 60, um-huh-um-heh?"

Bryce took a hold of Allie's neck and said, "If you keep this up, they are going to call you the 'insemination queen.' Those poor boars will never be the same."

"Nonsense, they are looking at the workers and wondering what happened to the supply of females."

"Well if the piglets start weaning at 4-6 weeks, the sows will come into heat anywhere from 6-8 weeks and we can resume gradually to breed the next batch of 1st generation hybrids."

"And to continue mixing the genes, we'll breed a droopy ear white with a colored droopy ear and an erect white with a colored erect ear. After that we will eventually enter the next generations. The hybrid first generation will eventually be ready to breed and then we'll take a hybrid with a red hide(50-50 red and white) and breed them with a black Hampshire boar, and vice versa with the other 1st generation hybrid. Now that is when it can get confusing, but with ear tags, we'll be able to keep the generation ledger clear by ear tag number— certainly not by an allegory pictorial." "Yes, I'm sure you can get the gene pool well documented using ear tags to create a commercial family tree."

Now, in case you did not think ahead, how many hogs will we have to market in just 20 weeks…(60 sows X 10 piglets)……that's potentially 600 hogs, of which 400 will likely be castrated barrows going to market and maybe a couple hundred gilts also going to market. Do you think your five butchers in town can handle 600 full size hogs?"

"Why of course not. That's why it's up to you dear husband-to-be. Your job, should you accept it, is to find a way to feed these piglets and to find a profitable market for them. I have every bit of faith that you will succeed." Alva was standing nearby and started laughing out loud as he added, "and I wouldn't doddle because the 20 weeks to market maturity will come quick."

***

That evening, they realized that by noon tomorrow they would be wed. It was a temptation to pre-consummate their vows, but Bryce finally said, "we found each other, we committed to each other and found the beautiful route to intimacy. So let's enjoy each other tonight and tomorrow night we'll consummate according to tradition. Then we'll have a lifetime of sharing the ultimate intimacy."

Come morning, their replenishing breakfast was interrupted by three aggressive females—Sally, Cindy Sue and Anna Mae. Bryce was told he had 30 minutes to take a bath, shave and get out of the house with his suit in a bag. He was told to change at his dad's house and go directly from there to the church with his dad. The bride had to bathe, dress, get her hair placed, find something old, new, and blue, fit her veil, tie her flowers in a bouquet and get a manicure. Fortunately, except for bathing, the three gals did most of the work.

Bryce finally got dressed after delaying it as long as he could. As on cue, he entered the side door and walked to the front of the church with his dad as witness and best man. Standing there, he could see all of their invited guests and knew that Uncle Joe and Red were outside providing security. Suddenly, the organ blasted the wedding song, "here comes the bride," and all guests stood up. Everyone saw Alva Bassett's proud smile as he walked Allie in the church. By the time they got to Bryce, Alva had a tear running down his cheek. It was then that Bryce had missed the fact that Allie was more than a boss to him. He made a mental note to correct his mistake in the near future.

The ceremony was short, the rings were shared, the I do's done without stammering, and the married couple's kiss was the end of the ceremony. The newlyweds walked down the aisle holding hands and guiding the guests to an outside gathering. Fortunately, Uncle Joe guided everyone to Bessie's Diner as the buggies lined up and the guests proceeded to the reception. Bryce and Allie were first to arrive, set up by the door, and welcomed all their guests individually.

Afterwards, liquid refreshments were served, lemonade or punch for the ladies, some with alcohol, and beer for the men. After some pleasant visits, Allie saw Azra Albright whisper something in Bryce's ear and Bryce simply nodded yes. Allie would later ask what that was all about. Bryce finally got to meet the five butchers and their wives. The visiting continued when Sheriff Marlow came up to Bryce and whispered something. Bryce went straight to the diner's front door and had the sighting of his life. There stood Victoria Vaughan with her husband Calhoun standing behind her. Sheriff Marlow then said, "these two with their four bodyguards were found wandering the street looking for a wedding reception when they walked right into Uncle Joe. They are here to crash your party."

Bryce looked at Victoria and said, "what are you doing here and why?" "We have a nephew in town by the name of Ralph Vaughan. He sent us a message that you were getting married, that your uncle was looking for a retirement home and

Red had gone back to his family. You three men risked your lives to save me. That is nothing we will ever forget, so we decided to deliver your wedding present in person. So first, could we meet your chosen wife?"

"Oh, my apology, Allie these are the Calhoun's that I mentioned to you—the kidnapping caper." "Oh my, so happy to meet you, please join us for refreshments and dinner."

Uncle Joe announced that dinner was ready. After Pastor Peabody gave the blessing, dinner was started. Of course, the tradition of hitting a glass with a knife started immediately. Since the recipients seemed too eager to kiss, the guests decided to hold off. The dinner was a success and Bessie was proud to see that, although close, they didn't run out of food. After a delayed dessert for fresh coffee, Bryce made a short speech thanking the guests for attending their special day.

After dinner, the guests were still milling around and waiting for the newlyweds to leave when Bryce went up to the Vaughan's and said something to them as they answered, "whenever you're ready." As they said goodbyes and stepped outside, a brand-new fancy carriage was parked in front of the diner. A sign on the carriage said, "congratulations, from Victoria and Calhoun." Uncle Joe was holding the reins of the two white geldings. Like the king and queen, they were delivered to the Abilene General Hotel for their secluded sojourn.

***

The registration formality was quickly completed, and the receptionist rang the bell for the bellhop. A pleasant young man greeted the newlyweds, took their luggage and escorted them to the hydraulic elevator to the fourth-floor suites. Entering the honeymoon suite, Bryce gave the bellhop a dollar. Before leaving, the bellhop explained that whatever they wanted in food, drink, or housekeeping services could be accessed thru the bell system. As it was explained, by pulling this white cord three times, an attendant would arrive to take their order and send the appropriate personnel with their goods or services.

Allie was barely hearing the bellhop as Bryce was wrapping his arm around her lower back, and his hand was roaming around her bum. When the bellhop finally left, Allie jumped in Bryce's arms. It was an uncontrollable sequence of disrobing each other till they finally were standing nude. Bryce was randy at Allie's assistance and finally they laid down on the bed. Allie felt some resistance as Bryce made his entry. Naturally thrashing, kissing and thrusting led to simultaneous shuddering, spasm and ejaculation. Their first nirvana lasted only seconds, but it felt like an eternity to a couple who was experiencing their first ultimate consummating intimacy.

It was Allie who first caught her breath and could speak. "Gosh, it felt like you possessed me as I took your soul and gave you mine. This ultimate union will last forever."

Bryce answered, "now that we got past all that wonderful first-time experience, let's go again but this time let's stay, as long as we can, on the edge of the dam before we go down the waterfall."

After several times, visiting the dam's apogee, Allie finally said, "husband, you've been in full tumescence since you undressed me, are you going to be like that all night?"

"Well, it appears my tally-wagger will stay a tally-WACKER till you get dressed!" "Well, in that case, I'm not dressing till noon dinner tomorrow!" "So be it, boy we really will need a replenishing dinner by then, assuming we can walk to the restaurant." "I prefer to be totally spent and we'll pull the bellhop cord to make the bellhop 'hop up,' heh?" "Well, if we're that spent, we'll probably be content, but we're not there yet, so come here you wicked wife."

***

By noon, they were dressed in their robes as their first meal arrived. Beef tenderloin steaks, mashed potatoes, gravy on the side, squash, a string bean casserole, sour dough dinner rolls with butter, coffee and a dessert called cheesecake with a sweet berry sauce.

After finishing their replenishing meal, they started talking about their house and what they wanted to add to make it more modern and user friendly. Over a second pot of coffee, Allie started, "a woman needs more room to prepare meals and do laundry, I would like to expand the present all-purpose kitchen."

"Done, we'll build a scullery with utility sinks and cabinets, it will be separated from a laundry room. We'll buy a new manually operated agitator washing machine with rollers to ring out the clothes. That expansion goes along with a windmill pump and underground water lines for indoor plumbing of cold and hot water to the kitchen, scullery, and water closets. That also means a hot water tank to clean dishes, do laundry, and take a hot bath. Since we are talking about expanding the house, we need three more bedrooms, so we'll add a second floor and a second water closet. Your present bedroom will become our office. The parlor and dining room will stay the same, and I want to keep the kitchen table for everyday use. We'll also add two more coal heat stoves in the upstairs bedrooms or hall. Last of all, by adding a second floor, we'll end up with a new shingled roof—which we need anyways."

Allie was a bit surprised as she said, "heck, I just wanted more room in the kitchen. Bryce, we can't afford this expense, we have several expensive items needed in the barn before we can modernize the house."

"That does it, my dear wife, that's the second time you refer to the cost of things. It's 3 o'clock and the town clerk is open. We'll transfer our titles on the deeds and then we'll go to the 1st National Bank to add you to my account and the Benefactor Fund."

While the newlyweds were dressing Allie asked what the Benefactor Fund was all about, and Bryce said he would let President Abernathy explain everything to her.

The deed changes at the town clerk's office was done and new deeds would be ready the same time tomorrow. Arriving at the bank was a revelation that Allie was not ready for. Bryce said hello to President Abernathy and then said, "I would like to transfer $5,000 to my Benefactor Fund, add my wife to that account, still keep Azra Albright on the account and then explain to Allie what this fund's purpose is." The President started, "........................... and that's it."

Allie signed all the forms and listened to President Abernathy's explanation how Azra Albright was distributing the funds. Allie simply smiled and squeezed her husband's hand. Moving along, there were several forms for Allie to sign as Missus Bryce Sullivan. President Abernathy said, "and this is the last form that certifies what your new account balance will be after the $5,000 transfer. Allie bent down to look at the balance, turned white as a sheet, claimed there must be a mistake, and seemed frozen in "shock and awe."

"No Missus Sullivan, there is no error, you are the joint owner of an account with a balance of $96,492.53. So please sign on the line to finish the paperwork. Allie signed and appeared frozen in place. Bryce broke her trance and said, "and from now on, never hesitate to get the material things in life that can make our lives easier and more comfortable. This money won't make us happy, but we can see to that. Let the money bring us some luxuries and we'll use it to build the future by expanding and modernizing our farm."

They left the bank and walked the boardwalk in silence. Finally, Allie spoke up, "do you have any other secrets that I don't know about?"

"Yes, I have several secret projects on how to expand and modernize our business, which I will present to you in degrees of 'need to know.' We'll talk about that tomorrow morning. Now we need to eat. We need the energy before we return to our private time."

After a light supper of chicken pot pie, rolls with butter and coffee, they then returned to their private room. They spent an intimate evening when Allie brought a light side and said, "are you trying to fill the three bedrooms all at once. The way you are ravaging me, I'm beginning to think that I'm going to end up with triplets." Bryce cracked up and added, "I didn't know that furious and passionate love making could lead to multiple births. If so, do you wish me to turn down the heat?"

"Heck no, I'll take my chances. And I see, you're ready again!"

Despite making love repeatedly, they both fell asleep by midnight and both got a full night sleep. In the morning after a hot bath, they dressed and headed downstairs for breakfast. After enjoying hot cakes with corn syrup, home fries, scrambled eggs and coffee, they ordered a second pot of coffee and Bryce started. "What are the immediate changes we need to make to keep the farm going?"

Allie said, "Three things: first, we'll have at least 500 newborn piglets to make room for. We need to expand the barn ASAP. Secondly, we need to find crops to feed and grow all those hogs for the next 20 weeks. Eustache's corn won't be enough and he's already chopping corn that is not yet mature. We can't make money if we buy bagged grain. We need to find and feed chopped corn, soybeans, barley and or sorghum, ASAP. Third, we need to start looking for a meat packer/distributor of our carcasses, also ASAP, since the 20 weeks will be here before we know it."

"I agree, I already have the wheels in motion, and if you don't mind mixing our honeymoon with a few meetings, we can address the first and second issues, sooner than later, while still in town. The third problem will have to be addressed when we take a trip to Dallas."

The newlyweds went for a walk and stopped at "Wainwright's Construction Company. Walking in, a 40-year-old man came to greet them, "hello, I'm Carl Wainwright, how may I help you?" Allie jumped in and threw out, "we want to triple the size of our 7,500 square foot (50X150) barn, add a scullery to our kitchen, dig a well/windmill and install internal plumbing to the house and barn, add a hot water tank, add a second floor to the house for three bedrooms and a second water closet, and shingle the new roof." Bryce added, "plus we need a modern slaughterhouse to process hog carcasses with a hydraulic lift, a scalding pit and a septic system for blood and liquid waste."

Carl and three of his workers stood in total wonder as Carl spoke, "folks, that could cost you 5,000-7,000 dollars!" Allie came back, "heck, we've got more money than that, can you start today?" "No, but I can start tomorrow with ten workers and in a week can add five more to the project—and that's my total staff."

"Great, here is a 1st National bank draft for $7,000 to get you started."

Carl took the draft, looked at Allie and Bryce, and politely asked, "who are you?" Allie said, "the daughter of a pig farmer, and born and raised in town." "Oh, of course, I know you Miss Adkins." "And who are you sir?" "Bryce Sullivan, retired bounty hunter and son of Jim and Sally Sullivan." "Of course, the gun shop." Allie adds, "and we are the newlyweds, Mister and Missus Bryce Sullivan." "Great news, so please step to the planning table and let's set up some basic specifications for the improvements and new buildings."

Allie started listing the barn basics: concrete floor with gutters for waste, plenty of screened windows for light and ventilation, a low building without a loft, piped water to all the pens with auto feed valves, cedar roof shingles, and ceiling vents for air circulation/ventilation."

Carl added, "All standard. What bothers me is the danger with a 22,500 square foot building. Fire can wipe your building and your entire stock. I strongly recommend two new 50X150 buildings at least 50 yards apart—one here, and one here."

Bryce saw the advantage, "Yes, wise move, plus we'll want a large center aisle with doors at both ends to be able to drive a horse driven wagon in the center aisle to feed chopped crops to the hogs, and avoid using wheelbarrows. Actually, plan to modify the existing barn so we can do the same thing at feeding time."

Allie added, "we'll work on laying out the pens and other service areas at a later date, when we have more time to think it out. Now, we are still on our honeymoon, so when you get to the farm, take the time to inform my three workers, Alva, Alec, and Eustache, of our plans."

"We'll be hauling gravel, water, and cement for a week to get the floor and gutters laid out and built to your specs. We won't be getting in their way."

Their next stop was the railroad manager. "Come in Mister Sullivan, I've had our engineer survey the area between your farm and the existing line. The business office has sent an estimate and a tentative contract should you accept our offer. For the switching station, line, road crossing for wagons and a side rail for holding boxcars, the total cost will be $3,722."

"Great, give the man a bank draft and we'll have a refrigerated boxcar next to our slaughterhouse. I'll explain this later, heh? When will this be started?"
"In a week as soon as the switch, rails etc. arrive."

Their last business stop was at the local newspaper. The editor said that only one man responded to the add and seemed qualified with a college degree and seven years' experience. His name was Maitland Winslow from Dallas and his address was included. Also eleven local homesteaders had responded to the "work wanted ad" and all had experience planting and harvesting crops with horse driven implements.

"Great, I'll send a telegram to this Maitland Winslow and set up an interview. Plus, would you add a notice in your next edition that we will be conducting interviews at the farmhouse in four days."

At the telegraph office he sent off the note to M. Winslow requesting a response ASAP. He also sent the messenger to Sawyer Skinner's ranch requesting a meeting at the town clerk's office today at 1PM.

Afterwards, the newlyweds headed to their hotel room, skipping the noon dinner meal, for more pressing private time. The lovers were still in their fondling stage when there was a knock at the door. Bryce got up but realizing his physical state of arousal, he suggested that Allie was better prepared to handle whoever was at the door. Allie saw the problem and said, "wow, that certainly looks more majestic when you're standing up, hey, hey?"

"Well, whose fault is that, hey, hey, hey?" Putting her robe on, she thought, *well my good work is to my benefit, hey, hey, hey.* As she walked over to answer the door, a bellman handed her a yellow telegram which she read out loud. It basically said that Maitland Winslow would arrive in the morning on the overnight express. The bellman was asked to send back a reply for him to make his way to the Abilene General Hotel no earlier than 9AM, and they would meet with him in the hotel's restaurant for breakfast.

The remainder of the afternoon was spent in their room, again for more private time. By supper time, on their way to the hotel restaurant,they decided to visit the concierge and see what was available for evening city tours. They quickly decided to visit a slaughterhouse and meat packing house—a tour only provided after work hours. They had a quick supper of beef stew with all the side fixings and were ready when the carriage arrived to bring them to McCafferty's Meat Packing.

Arriving at the slaughterhouse, the guide explained the different stations: killing station with 22 rifle, hydraulic lift, blood collecting vat, scalding tub, shaving station, evisceration and organ removal, offal collection, halving hydraulic saw, work-tables, work sinks, hanging tract for transfer to processing plant. The Duo was busy taking notes but realized that they would need to send Carl himself to take measurements and notes to duplicate this slaughterhouse.

The visit to the packing plant was enlightening. This plant was selecting the different cuts of meat, and processing them for commercial distribution. Their preserving methods included curing bacon and other cuts, smoking and wrapping, cooking and sealing in a brine solution. Bryce noted that this plant was still using old fashion methods of preserving meat. He knew that they would have to go to Dallas to find a modern processing plant that would accept refrigerated carcasses in large volumes. Yet, they could use McCafferty's plant to send live hogs or carcasses while their barns, slaughterhouse, and side rail were under construction. Before the end of the tour, the guide pointed out that this plant was now the only beef and pork processing plant in town as their only competitor had closed its doors. The newlyweds simply smiled and boarded the carriage back to their hotel.

After a pleasant intimate evening, the newlyweds finally got their first full eight hours of sleep as they headed down to the restaurant for a replenishing breakfast and a business interview.

***

They informed the Maître D' that they were meeting a Maitland Winslow. They were escorted to a waiting young couple. After introductions were completed, Allie said, "we see you are with child, how far along are you and how do you feel?"

"I'm six months along and I feel great."

Bryce interjected, "let's order and then you can tell us your background while we wait for our meals."

Once the waiter left with their orders, Maitland started. "After high school, I went to the Dallas Agricultural College and majored in crop farming. After college I worked 7 years for a large grain company planting crops, harvesting them, and making grain."

Allie interrupted them and said, "sounds great, but why are you leaving Dallas and a good job?"

"Because, we don't want to raise our children in a big city, and we need to distance ourselves from the tentacles of my father's business."

"Which is?"

"Winslow Agricultural Implements. My dad wants me to take over the business, but I'm not ready to do that."

"Oh my, I'm waiting on a bid for ten implements from your father." As the meals arrived, the interview was put on hold.

Afterwards, Bryce started, "guess it's our turn to tell you what we are after. We now have 600 growing piglets that will be ready for the meat market in 20 weeks. We are presently feeding them with corn silage, but that supply is running out. So, your immediate job would be to find a crop and buy it by the acre. Then have your men harvest it by chopping and haul it by wagon to the farm."

"The second thing is to take charge of the cultivating, planting, harvesting and feeding of the hogs. We are purchasing today two sections of fertile land, bunkhouse, barn and ranch house adjacent to our farm. To accomplish this, order any implements you'll need at Tate's Hardware. In two days, we are holding interviews for crop farm workers and would like you to be the lead interviewer."

"So, am I to understand that you want me to grow crops to feed your hogs by chopping corn, soybeans, barley and sorghum. Do you want any grain?"

"Oops, I forgot. Of course, we need oats for the horses and as pig feed and we absolutely need the straw for bedding. Otherwise, it's chop and feed."

Allie asked, "is this a project you are comfortable with?"

"Absolutely Ma'am. This is my training and for seven years this is exactly what I've been doing."

"When would you be available to start?"

"Today, I've already worked my two weeks' notice and have had my exit interview."

"What was your salary and benefits?"

"$65 a month and no benefits except Sundays off."

"Waaah, that's ridiculous. We will offer you $100 a month, your own house for housing, free meals if you both eat at the bunkhouse cookie shack. After the baby is born, we'll arrange for the cook to send your meals to the house. All my field workers will have Sunday's off. You'll have a riding horse at your disposal and a harnessed horse for the buggy as well. BUT, the entire crop business is on your shoulder. What do you say?"

Maitland looked totally puzzled, as he looked at his wife for a nod. Cynthia simply blurted out, "he'll gladly take it, this is an opportunity of a lifetime. And I don't care what the house looks like, we'll make it our home."

Allie looked at her and said, "I've been in the house and it's quite nice. We are signing the papers at 1PM today, and afterwards, we'll show you the house and other buildings, as well as sampling the soil."

Maitland stood, offered his hand, and said, "thank you, we have a deal."

As they entered the town clerk's office Sawyer Skinner was already there waiting for them. The clerk handed Allie her new deed to include her husband. The paperwork for the sale of Sawyer's property was processed with all the necessary signatures. Allie gave Sawyer the balance bank draft of $4,000 and hands were shaken.

Afterwards Sawyer said that his herd will be driven to the railroad stock yard for sale and he would be out of the house by tonight. He had rented an apartment in town till he found a house to buy. Bryce told Sawyer that they were bringing a couple to see the house, buildings and sample the soil. Sawyer smiled and said, "thank goodness that I had a cleaning service spend four days cleaning the house and the bunkhouse. Bring them over and I'll give them a tour."

Bryce and Allie rented a double seat buggy and rode over to the Skinner ranch by 3 PM. Sawyer was waiting with lemonade and coffee as they toured the house. Allie was impressed. She saw a well maintained three-bedroom single floor house. The kitchen was extra- large with a separated laundry room. The house was fully furnished with a firewood cooking stove and several coal heating stoves. Cynthia had a tear on her cheek and finally asked, "is this really going to be our included housing. It is perfect. It's on site for Maitland's work and Allie added, "and it's only a half mile to my house."

The party then checked the bunkhouse, cook shack, barn and the three gelding horses, buggy and large utility wagons. Totally satisfied, Maitland agreed to go to Tate's Hardware and order the ten implements on bid and to add anything else that was needed. He would then visit several liveries to buy heavy duty work horses like Percherons or Belgians for plowing and chopping crops. The work geldings should be able to handle the remainder of the workload. Sampling the soil, Maitland said, "low on clay, low on sand, minimal rocks, this is a rich loam that will hold moisture nicely—ideal crop growing land."

Before they returned to town, the party traveled the half mile to the pig farm. They visited the house, but it was the barn that gave Maitland a better idea of why there was pressure to proceed with haste. On the ride back to town, Bryce asked, "if you place your order today, how long will it take for delivery?" "My dad has all these implements in the warehouse. When he sees my name on your order, you'll see the implements arriving in town in three days."

Arriving in town, Allie suggested they make a list of everyone's responsibilities for the next weeks:

Set up Ag. bank account for Maitland to use=Bryce

Order implements=Maitland.

Hire crop workers=Maitland and the Sullivans.

Find corn or soybean crops for sale=E. Backus and Maitland.

Set up a payroll and ledger for crop business=Cynthia volunteered.

Move in Skinner's ranch house—the Winslows tomorrow.

The Winslows were given a room in the Abilene General Hotel and the two couples obtained theatre tickets for a comedy play after an elegant supper in the hotel's own restaurant—all on the Sullivans' tab.

After a great evening and much social contact, it was clear that Bryce and Maitland were getting along, and the gals were forming a bond that would last a lifetime.

***

CHAPTER 10

Expansion Woes

The next morning after their replenishing breakfast, Allie looked at Bryce and said, "We've had the honeymoon of a lifetime, but I think it's time to get back to our business. We've got things to do and a couple dozen carpenters at work—we need to be there."

"I agree, but I didn't want to be the one to suggest it. Before we go back, let's get some housewarming presents for the Winslows. We can drop them off on our way home. What would you like to give to Cynthia?"

"With diapers on the way, she needs to hide that washer board and use a washing machine like the one we just bought for the new scullery."

"Great, I'm buying them two holstered pistols, Smith & Wesson Model 2 in 32 for Cynthia and

Model 3 in 44 for Maitland. They need to practice and be comfortable handling them in this violent land."

"Let's do it, we'll rent a buckboard to bring our luggage and the washing machine. Let's pack and go, I'm eager to see what the carpenters have accomplished."

On the way out of town, Bryce sent a telegram to Marshal Balinger requesting information on meat packers and distributors. The last minute, Allie saw a sign maker and suggested we need to make a business sign for both locations.

"Ok, what have you got in mind?"

"How about, 'Sullivan Pork Meats' and 'Sullivan Crops.'" "Are you sure you don't want 'Adkins Pork Meats' and 'Sullivan Crops?'"

"No, we are going to grow this business together, and I'm now a Sullivan. I want both businesses to be known as a Sullivan enterprise."

Arriving at the Skinner ranch, Cynthia started crying when she saw the washing machine in her laundry room. Maitland kept looking at the two new pistols and finally said, "you've given us so much already, how do we repay you?' "By going to work and find a crop to buy." "Well as soon as Eustache gets here, we're off to find one or more."

Arriving home, it was total mayhem. Four men were working on the house. The roof had been torn off and the second floor was going up. The scullery was already finished. Three men were digging a well with some massive contraption, and several men were making concrete for the second barn. Wagons were arriving with gravel as the others were mixing cement, gravel, and water. Four men were already putting up walls for the first barn.

Standing there in total awe, Carl came over to greet them. "High folks, things are going well. Tonight, I'm going on a tour to McCafferty's Slaughterhouse. I will take measurements and take careful notes. We plan to start working on the concrete floor for that building tomorrow."

Allie said, "we'll start working on the inside floor plan for the pens today." Bryce added, "When you're done here, next door at the Skinner ranch, we're going to need a bin to store bags of oats and bales of straw, and a drive thru implement shed for a dozen implements."

After a quick dinner of cold roast beef sandwiches and coffee, they designed the barn floor plans, then the telegraph messenger arrived with a message from Marshal Balinger. Bryce read out loud in a letter format without the telegraph 'short lines and stops,' "the city's largest and modern meat packer and distributor only accepted carcasses since they did not have a slaughterhouse. They provided refer boxcars as long as they could be filled within two days. The city had many independent slaughterhouses that contracted with the distributor. The name was Noble Meats and would be glad to meet with us ASAP."

Allie had trouble hearing Bryce with all the nail pounding on their first-floor ceiling. Allie suggested, "we are not needed here at the moment, while they add our second floor. What do you say we make reservations and head to Dallas to set up an account with Noble Meats?" "Great idea let's pack our luggage and get out of here. It will be interesting to see what we're up against in the big city's meat district. Besides, Maitland needs a few days on his own, and we'll stop on our way to the train and tell him the interviews to hire crop workers are now in his hands."

***

The five-hour trip to Dallas gave Bryce the opportunity to expose Allie to two new ideas, refrigerated 'refer' boxcars and canning meat. He handed her the booklet on refrigeration and half an hour later they were discussing the matter. Bryce reviewed the subject. "Today, refrigerated box cars can hold forty hogs (80 half carcasses). They cool by a mechanical compressor that is steam driven. This allows gaseous contraction that cools the air to 35-40° F. This will require a large team to slaughter forty hogs in two days, to send the refer back to Dallas asap."

Allie thought, "I agree, this will be the only way to handle large amounts of market ready hogs at the same time."

The next book Bryce handed to Allie, he prefaced it with, "this is what will bring our business into the 20th century and make us rich."

Allie took the book, read the cover and exclaimed, "Canning Meat in Tin Cans" by Calhoun and Victoria Vaughan! "Are you for real?"

"Most definitely, read it and we'll discuss it afterwards before we get to Dallas. It will take you a couple of hours, so wake me when you're done. Nap time," as he sat back with his hat over his face.

Out of a deep sleep, Allie was poking Bryce in the ribs, "wake up husband, you are a 'friggin' genius. Let's talk about canning meat."

"I see you're impressed with the Vaughan's book, heh? Well let's start. Meat processors are now preserving meat by curing, brining or smoking. We're not going to get involved with that. We are going to can our pork in tin cans. Canning meat preserves it at ROOM TEMPERATURES FOR YEARS. Can you imagine the business implication?"

Allie added, "yes I can, what I really like about canning is that, over years, the can's contents maintain organoleptic quality because the cans are hermetically sealed, and the contents sterilized by heat. Bryce thought, *hermetically sealed means airtight; and organoleptic quality means to maintain taste, smell, color, and feel of fresh meat.*

Allie asked, "can we review the canning steps?" "Sure, they are:

- Fully cook the meat to 160° F.
- Pack meat in cans.
- Add liquid (brine, water, syrup, gelatin) to replace most of the air out of the can.
- Pass the filled cans in a boiling water bath to expand the food and drive out the remaining air.
- Seal the can by crimping the cover on.
- Sterilize the sealed can in a pressure canner for 45 minutes under 15 psi of pressure.
- Allow cans to cool which allows contraction of its contents and produces a partial vacuum.

"Great, seems clear-cut but I'm certain that it will be a detailed process. Now, can you explain to me the crimping of the cover and how high psi can speed up the sterilization time."

"The cover has an edge curl, and the body of the can has a flange. With a sealing compound on the cover's curled edge, the crimping step spreads the sealing compound between the layers of steel providing a hermetically sealed product once the two edges are crimped together."

"Now pressure canning. Sterilizing canned goods at room pressures means the water boils at 212° F, and the process takes 90 Minutes. Now, let's compare:

PSI	Degrees F	Cooking time
0	212	90 minutes
10	240	60 minutes
15	250	45 minutes"

"Home pressure canning is done at 10 psi and commercial canning is done at 15 psi." The high heat kills organisms that can spoil meat and deactivates enzymes that digest and decompose meat."

"Now for equipment, the commercial canner has six bolts to hold the cover in place, and without any gaskets. The pressure is controlled by a 15-pound weight that jiggles when the pressure goes over 15 psi. Some have a dial that measures psi. The pressures are maintained by the heat of the cook stove. Most, however, come with both systems on the cover. They are perfectly safe. Just remember, the steam has to hit the entire metal, so wire stacks allow several can layers by allowing the steam to do its work."

"Well, I'm wholeheartedly convinced. When do we visit the Vaughan factory, get a tour, set up an account and order our tin cans?"

"Well, after our business in Dallas, since we are already halfway to Wichita Falls, I suggest we take the train and head north."

***

Arriving in Dallas, the Duo took a taxi to a hotel located within walking distance to Noble Meats. They took a room, had a bath, enjoyed some intimate time, and then walked downstairs for supper. That evening, they attended a musical rendition of a popular ragtime band with Western singers. In the morning they walked to Noble Meats, and with an appointment, they were escorted to Silvio Noble's office.

"Mister Noble stood up, shook hands and said, "what can I do for you folks?" Allie responded as she sat down, "buy our hogs!" "Well let me tell you what I can provide. I only accept half carcasses as long as they pass a cleanliness inspection. For a half carcass weighing at least 70 pounds, I pay $22. I don't accept any internal organs. In order to send you a refer boxcar, you need to slaughter 40 hogs in 48 hours. My employee will keep the steam powered compressor operating for that time, but he takes off after 48 hours as he is scheduled. For every hog missing, we charge you a fine of $5."

"We can abide by that. Now what do you know about crossbreed hogs?"

"I know a lot about the advantages, but I can't get them. Why?"

"Because in 16 weeks we're going to have at least 400 crossbred barrow hogs. Half will be a hybrid of red Duroc and white Yorkshire and the other half will be a hybrid of black Hampshire and white Landrace."

"Whoa, for crossbreeds like that I'll pay $27 for a half carcass weighing 70 pounds."

"What if they weigh 80 pounds or more?"

"$29. Do you have access to the railroad?"

"We have a side rail next to the barn."

"Can you handle slaughtering 40 hogs in 48 hours."

"We will be by that time."

"Well, let's sign a contract. I will take any crossbreeds you can send me. Whenever you have a boxcar load ready, telegraph me and I will send you a refer within 24 hours. Keep crossing the genetic pool at every generation to increase the beneficial inheritance. I'm eager to see your stock in four months. If the second-generation barrows are showing more meat changes, I'll up the price $2 for 70-80 pounders, and add $2 more for a half carcass over 80 lbs. I'm serious about paying for the quality I get."

"The last thing, we are planning to start canning some pork meat that will last a long time at room temperature. Are you interested in distributing this product all over Texas?"

"For a fee, of course. We'll be talking about this again, since, as a processing plant, I'm looking into doing this as well."

The Duo left with a sense of accomplishment and a contract in hand. They went back to the railroad office and bought a ticket for Wichita

Falls. A telegram was sent directly to the Vaughan factory office, bypassing the local telegraph office, requesting a business meeting with the owners, Calhoun and Victoria. The telegrapher said, "you might as well wait here, since the telegraph room in the factory is next to Mister Vaughan's office. You should be getting your answer shortly—as the clacking started. The answer said, "nice to hear from you, we'll be here, just come straight to the factory, if you need lodging, stay at the Vaughan Grand Hotel, signed Calhoun."

Arriving in Wichita Falls at 9PM, the travelers took a taxi to the designated hotel. After requesting a room, he signed the register. The receptionist nonchalantly looked at the name and just about fell off his highchair. "Yes Sir, we were told you might arrive anytime. I have Mister Vaughan's private suite ready for you." "That's not necessary, any room with a bed and a water closet will do." "Oh no, that won't do. If I don't give you the suite, I'll be unemployed by morning. Please Sir and Ma'am, accept the penthouse? The bell hop will bring your luggage and escort you to your suite."

In the morning, after a fabulous replenishing breakfast in the hotel's restaurant, the Duo took a taxi to the Vaughan factory. The building was a massive five story structure with a railroad side rail to its receiving and sending area. Walking in, the Vaughan's office was near the front door. As they entered the reception area, a prim and proper lady asked who they were and whether they had an appointment. When she heard the word Sullivan, she looked up and said, "are you that bounty hunter that saved Victoria, I mean Missus Vaughan?" Bryce wasn't answering so Allie responded, "Yes he is!" To Bryce's surprise, she stood up, walked around her desk and hugged Bryce with the soft words, "Thank you. The Vaughan's are waiting for you. Please follow me."

The Vaughan's jumped up, hugged their guests and were finally introduced to the woman of the day, Allie. Calhoun added, "you must be a powerful person to have sucked up the best bounty hunting savior Texas ever had. So we congratulate you."

Victoria then asked, "what are you doing here, some 300 miles from home." Bryce asked them to sit down as he went thru a lengthy story that finished with......" and we want to start canning our pork meat, and start a new method of preserving meat without refrigeration.

Victoria added, "well you're at the right place. We're going to give you the tour from A to Z. Follow us." As they were walking, Victoria started, "the tin cans today are made of steel from Illinois, Ohio and California. The steel is rolled into thin sheets that are cleared of rust by pickling the steel in acid. Then a thin layer of tin is added, and the result are sheets called 'tinplate.'"

Allie interrupted and asked, "what actually is tin and where is it found?"

"Tin is a white/silver soft metal easy to melt and spread. It comes from China, South America and Indonesia. It is often mixed with other metals to form an alloy such as pewter housewares, sodder, lead for bullets, motor parts, or spread, as mentioned, as a coating over sheet metal for making tin cans. This tinning of steel prevents rust and oxidation, absolute deterrents to preserving food."

Entering the first division of the plant, Calhoun takes over. "I will now walk you thru the different steps in making a tin can. The tinsmith takes a sheet of tinplate, places in under a predesigned hammer, applies a heavy hydraulic pressure, as the tinsmith proceeds, the hammer instantly generates a one piece can with a bottom as part of the sides of the can." The tinsmith demonstrated several in a row.

"Moving on, this next station cuts the tops of the sides into a uniform height." The worker demonstrated the fine metal saw that produced a perfect cut all around.

"This next station cuts a top to fit the size of the can. The top is cut by a heavy hammer with a cutting edge that cuts the top just like a cookie cutter."

"And this is the magic room divided in two sections. The first is where the top has its edge rolled and a sealing compound is applied to the rolled edge. The other section applies a flange to the cans top edge. The Duo watched all three workers perform their portion of this stage. Before leaving, Calhoun took the can, placed the cover on and placed it in a press. By manually operating the handle, in seconds he crimped the cover to the flange's side and said, "voila. This type of can will be in use for the next 100 years!"

Allie asked, "what can sizes is your factory producing?" Victoria answered, "we presently make three sizes:

- #2 can. This will hold 1lb-4oz of meat or 2 1/2 cups of liquid. This is the perfect size for a family of three or four.
- #5 can. This will hold 3 lbs. of meat or 6 cups of liquid. This is what we call the 'large family size.'
- #10 can. This holds 6 lb-6 oz of meat or 12 cups of liquid which is also 3 quarts. This is the banquet size portion, or the multiple guest size portion."

Calhoun continued, "let me now show you the three major food processing tools. The first is the crimping tool which I've already demonstrated. The second is a must if you're going to can meats. This is a meat grinder. Let me demonstrate by adding a mix of differing sizes of meat chunks." The machine started and the meat came out in strands.

By passing it a second time, it came out perfectly ground up.

Allie could not believe her eyes, "wow, we need one of them!

Ground up pork will be a big seller in sealed cans."

"The last item is the commercial canner. Ours is without gaskets, has six to nine bolts to secure the lid, has a dial and a 15- pound jiggling weight, and comes in two sizes—commercial and magnum. The commercial holds six #10 cans, and the magnum holds twelve in two layers separated by a wire cage. If you use these two for smaller cans, there is a wire cage for each layer as explained in our textbook."

Allie asked, "what does each of these three tools sell for?" "These are innovative tools that are priced at $200 each."

Bryce added, "we'll take two grinders, two crimpers, four commercial canners and four magnum canners." Calhoun added, 'what about the size and number of cans. How many would you want on your first order?" "A standard order would be 1300 #2's, 900 #5's, and 300#10's. But tripple the 'standard' for the first order to build up an inventory. In any event, in the future, what would our lag time be for future orders?"

"We have a large inventory and any size order would take a week to get you a boxcar at your plant—freight is based on the boxcar."

Allie added, "what about labels? We would like each can with a label that says, 'Sullivan Meats' and a sub label to show the contents such as ham, tenderloin, roasts or ground pork etc."

Victoria added, "technology as it is today, we do not have a method of labeling a tin can that can withstand the cleaning power of steam. What our customers are doing is to see the local printing shop and order labels that are printed in water resistant ink, and the label has a self-adhesive back side. That way you can easily have labels for every cut of meat in each can. Only apply the label after the can is out of the canner, has dried, and cooled."

Bryce said, "to summarize, there are three avenues that have to be financially settled. The first is the three tools which comes to $2,400 for twelve tools. Then there is the cost of the can order."

Calhoun said, "an order of 1300 #2 at 5 cents each is $65, 900 #5 at 10 cents each is $90, and

300 #10 at 20 cents each is another $60. So a standard order will cost you $215, a double $430 plus shipping."

Bryce was doing the math and said, that comes to $3,045. Broken down, $2400 for the tools of the trade, and $645 for a tripple 'standard' order. In the future, as you hinted, it could be necessary to make each order the size to fill that boxcar to minimize shipping costs, heh?"

Victoria had a closing statement. "Before you write that draft, canning meat is an art in itself which requires precise cooking and processing methods to guarantee a safe product. We have a three-day program, taught by our section managers, that will make a commercial canner out of anybody. This would be a life-long investment for your employees. The charge is $300 per group of three with as many as five per group for $100 per student. Your meals and lodging are extra."

Allie added, "I'm adding $300 to the bank draft. I'll be coming with two workers, as soon as I select them. If I bring more than two, we'll pay for them later."

After signing all the contractual agreements, the Duo left with a railroad crate holding two meat grinders, eight canners, and two crimpers with adjustable heads for different size cans.

With their business completed in Wichita Falls, the duo decided to take the midnight express to Dallas. Their goal was to spend the day ordering specialty tables, sinks, vats, butcher knives, rubber gloves, shelving, drying racks, cabinets, etc. for both the slaughterhouse and canning shop.

The train ride allowed them to sleep the entire trip. Arriving in Dallas, the Duo went to Uncle Joe's favorite office spot, Sam's Diner. They ordered a full breakfast and plenty of coffee. Afterwards, they asked several store owners where they could order parts for a commercial specialty kitchen. When they defined it better and said, a slaughterhouse and cannery, they were universally directed to Webster's Commercial Kitchens.

Walking into Websters, an attendant greeted them, "I'm Silas Webster, how may I help?"

"Allie said, "we need to furnish a slaughterhouse and a cannery.""

"Very well, shall we start with the slaughterhouse!" Stepping into a separated area of the showroom, Mister Webster started, "what is the size of the building and do you have indoor plumbing with an outside septic system?" "30X70 and yes, we have both."

"So you're going to need sinks, counter tops, knives, aprons, butcher blocks, meat hooks and saws." "Why yes, that should cover it!"

"Now the cannery, the size is? "According to Mister Vaughan, it will be 40X90."

"I see, you are buying his equipment and canners! That is very important to know before you purchase anything. So let us begin. The gold standard for sinks are the copper sinks. They are durable, not affected by foods, water, acids and or steam. They come in three sizes, small for hand washing, medium for general use and large which are deep utility sinks." "We'll take three of each."

Counter tops in a slaughterhouse should be nonporous or polished stone. This allows wiping them clean. These are polished stones that are 24-inch deep and come in 4, 6, and 8 footers." "We'll take two of each." "Countertops in a cannery need to be able to handle water and hot canners. We recommend polished engineered quartz that come in the same sizes as stone." "We'll take three of each."

You need cooking stoves in the cannery. You can always have coal fired kitchen stoves outside in a lean-to, but you'll be converting to natural gas within a month since the pipeline from Dallas to Austin is passing thru Abilene. Now, Mister Vaughan has designed a table-top gas stove made of steel with two circular burners, one small inside the large one, to guarantee even heat to the canner's bases." "We have four commercial and four magnum canners, so we'll need eight stoves."

"Aprons, you'll need some basic cotton and some sealed canvas." "Fine, we'll take two dozen of each."

"Knives, you'll need two types in both buildings. 10-inch butcher knives and 5-inch boning knives. These knives have a synthetic handle with a finger-stop that prevents you from slipping your hand on the cutting edge." "Fine, we'll take two dozen of each."

"Meat hooks, our hooks are made of an alloy that won't rust. You need ceiling hooks with a roller for a track, manual hand hooks, and several manual hand saws. The newest thing is the hydraulic saw for halving carcasses." "We'll take two dozen track hooks, a dozen manual hooks, four manual hand saws, and two hydraulic saws."

Allie added, what about cabinets?" "We don't sell cabinets, have you carpenter build simple shelves, and add doors to keep things clean."

Allie said, "Ok, then add these items, and we'll pay you with a bank draft from the 1st National Bank in Abilene."

"Ma'am, did you say you are going to pay for the items before you receive them in Abilene?"

"Of course, you don't know us from a hole in the ground, and we live 150 miles from here. You're not crooked, are you?"

"No Ma'am, I'm an honest businessman. Ask my uncle, Marshal Balinger!"

"Go ahead and prepare a bill as we walk around to see if we need anything else." "Very good."

"This is the invoice, sinks=$550, countertops=$550/, tabletop stoves=$300, aprons=\$30, knives=\$80, multiple hooks=\$100, 2 hydraulic saws=\$200, shipping=\$50. Comes to \$1,860."

"Hold up, we want this box of rubber gloves for handling meat before canning. The price for 1,000 pairs is \$320, and that changes the total to \$2,180."

***

Arriving back home, Alva told them that they needed to meet with Carl about building issues, Maitland with crop issues and Eustache with personal issues. Since Carl was standing next to Alva, it was assumed that he was first in line.

Carl started, "let's go over the scullery. We have inside plumbing to the sinks and washing machine. The hot water tank and coal bin are in an attached shed that opens to the laundry room. We now have cold water to the horse barn and all three hog barns. The slaughterhouse will also have hot and cold water. As you can see, the two new barns are built. We added an office and a tool closet to each of your designs. Your house's 2nd floor is also done, and you now have two water closets with bathtubs.

Your slaughterhouse will be done in a few days. So, is there any more work you want us to do?"

"Yes, the slaughterhouse will need cabinets; and there are sinks, countertops, and hydraulic saws to install. Afterwards, we'll need two more buildings, a drive thru shed at Sullivan Crops, and a 40X90 cannery/factory with a lean-to on each side. One open side for cooking stoves and an enclosed side for supplies and finished products. It will also need the installation of gas table-top stoves, sinks, countertops, cabinets and several hydraulic tools of the trade. This building should be along the side rail to ship products, and close to the slaughterhouse."

"My second team of five men is already working on your drive thru shed, so as soon as the slaughterhouse is completed, we'll start on the cannery."

"How are we doing money wise?" "My accountant is adding labor and supplies every day. He says that you're still ahead with left over credit, so we'll settle after the job is done."

The next meeting was with Maitland, "I spent all day interviewing potential crop workers. I ended up hiring a wrangler, a cook, a combined mechanic/ blacksmith and ten field workers. I ordered all the implements on your list and added a baler to package the straw. The drive thru shed is half done. With Eustache's help we purchased two large crops of corn and two soybean crops—all in different stages of maturity. We moved the two choppers and work horses at a corn and a soybean site so we can alternate the feeding choices. By the time these four crops are harvested, our cultivated land will be ready to take over."

"What is this about two corn choppers?"

"You inherited a corn chopper, plow, two harrows, a large wagon, a manure spreader, and a team of Percheron work horses. The donor will become evident later today. We have already planted 50 acres of corn in three rotations and we are ready to plant 50 acres of soybeans. The workers are a mixed bunch, half arrive for the day and go home at night to their families, the young single men live in the bunkhouse. Everyone is working well together. All workers get three meals a day, including the men going home at night if they want the supper meal. All in all, I'm pleased with the way things are going. It saddens me to lose Eustache, he's a very good and trustworthy worker."

"Why is Eustache leaving?"

"If you don't have any other status issues, I'll let Eustache explain it to you, he's waiting on the porch to speak with you."

Eustache entered with his wife, Imogene. Bryce and Allie were obviously disturbed since the appearance was that this was a goodbye in the makings. Eustache started, "two years ago I was given some $1,500 with which I started planting a crop. I now know it was you who took me out of poverty, plus I made a profit selling my corn to you this year. So, I've returned your generosity by bring back the team of Percherons and all the cultivating implements. Working with Alva and Alec has been a pleasant revelation—these are good men to work with. I like animals and I like working with hogs. My two kids are gone, my daughter married a local rancher, and my son is in the Colorado gold fields. So, being alone on the homestead—well to make a long story short, I would like to work full time in the barns taking care of your hogs. Imogene is also somewhat bored left alone at home, and we're hoping to find work for her, here on the farm."

Bryce and Allie looked at each other and smiled. Bryce went first, "Eustache, we'd be proud to have you on board permanently. We'll pay you $2 a day with three meals included." Allie then took over, "Imogene, we'll be building a cannery and start sending our pork in tin cans. Would you consider working in the cannery. You could come to work every day with your husband and also partake in the three meals."

Imogene was totally surprised, was holding her hands to her face and said, "yes, yes, yes, I'd love to."

"Great, here is a book on canning for you to read, once we find a second person, the three of us will be going to Wichita Falls to take a three-day course on canning, with paid lodging, meals and wages."

"Oh, you have a worker, the mechanic/ blacksmith whose wife is my best friend. She has been canning for years and her kids are all gone as well, I bet she would be interested in this job."

"Great, ask her to come for an interview?"

***

After the meetings, the duo walked around to inspect the barns and the slaughterhouse. With nothing to add, they went to the house for a cup of coffee. While enjoying their brew, several hoofbeats were heard coming down the access road. Bryce looked in the window and said, "Oh no, it's Sheriff Marlow, Uncle Joe and Red—this is not good."

Sitting in the parlor with a gill of coffee in their hands, Uncle Joe decided to get an answer to an issue that was nagging at him. "Now Allie why did you give me a half-cup of coffee like they do in the diners, and follow it with a dab of cold water?"

Allie smile and said, "a gill is a half-cup. In this case, the coffee pot just came off the stove, the coffee is still boiling in your cup. Your cup is metal and if I had filled it to the brim, you wouldn't have been able to hold by the metal handle or by the upper half of the cup's metal. Now with the top half of your cup being empty, it gives you room to add cold water to the coffee which makes it cool down, and the grounds are pushed to the bottom of the cup by some strange law of physics. Plus, when you blow on the coffee, your cool breath sits in the cup instead of blowing off the top—more efficient that way, heh!"

"Wow, now that was a complete answer to a simple question, yup I get it!"

Then Sheriff Marlow got down to business. "In the past week, we have had five young women disappear, the last one was last night, and she was Ralph Vaughan's pregnant wife. Two of the gals were single, two were young mothers with babies and one was Mrs. Vaughan who is only ten weeks along."

"Now, Ralph's uncle is the renowned philanthropist from Wichita Falls, who is very upset at the second kidnapping in his family, and is offering a $50,000 reward for the return of the five ladies and capture of these evil kidnappers—who want to make a quick buck out of other people's misery."

Bryce finally said, "but what does this have anything to do with us?"

"Because we need a young appealing woman, who can defend herself, to be a planted hostage."

Bryce came back, "well it's going to be a cold day in hell before I put my wife on the chopping block." Allie added, "Bryce, let's hear what their plan will be to save our local women."

With a pause, Sheriff Marlow continued, "I have a confidential informant who just reported to me that he heard two men discussing how this establishment was able to keep women of the night. Apparently, they come from Dallas and actually hire out voluntarily to outlying communities. For every soiled dove they receive, they are expected to replace them with new victims that they sell at private auctions."

Bryce asked, "which saloon was this?"

"The Watering Oasis and Cribs."

"Now Joe has a plan, and I'll let him explain it." "Since I'm not known in town, I will take up a card game and lose all my cash of $100. I'll appear totally distraught, and if everything goes to plan, someone will offer me a quick money scheme. Let's say I have to bring a kidnapped victim to them; I get $200 and I disappear. Now the victim will need to be gagged and act like she was drugged, but armed with a Bulldog in the false bottom of her reticule. Then Red will take over. As an Apache, we've seen him run as fast as a trotting horse, plus you can never see him the way he disappears like a ghost. Red is certain he can follow a buckboard to the hideout holding the ladies—heck it may even be in an unused building right in town."

Uncle Joe then adds, "once the lair is found, we bust the door down with a driving ram, and enter with guns a blazing. We shoot to kill and it's all over. So tonight I lose at poker, tomorrow night I arrive with a hostage, and we end it that night."

"So, the person in the most danger is Allie—I don't think so."

Allie took over, "Bryce please reconsider, these are innocent women, mothers and mothers to be. If I was one of the victims, would you do nothing? Besides, think of all the good that money will bring in the Benefactor Fund. I know I can handle myself and stay safe, please?"

Bryce paused, looked at Red and asked, "are you sure you won't lose them?" Red stood with his arms crossed and simply nodded his head up and down. Bryce came back and said, "under one condition, that we save a kidnapper, we need to know who the organizer of human trafficking is in town or this will happen again!"

That night, Uncle Joe was in the Oasis playing cards, it was five- card-draw—two up, three down. There were four players, and it was a low stake game. With added drinks, the stakes started to climb to the point there usually was $20 in the pot. To give his ability some credence, he won a bit more than he lost, so as the night moved along, he intentionally started to lose. Within five hands he was cleaned out. Uncle Joe made sure that his emotions came thru. He looked so upset that the table winner gave him a dollar to buy some drinks before leaving.

Standing at the bar, a stranger came by with some sympathetic small talk. "I commiserate with you, it's a terrible feeling to be broke. Now I know a way you can make $200 for an hour's work." Stepping outside, Uncle Joe got all the details and the meeting location with his package wrapped up.

The next day, Allie was sewing a false bottom to her reticule that ripped open with snaps. To make her capable of shooting her Bulldog thru the base of the reticule, thereby avoiding lost time to pull the pistol totally out of her purse, Bryce made her shoot several times blindly thru an old reticule's base.

More time was spent replacing the base than actual shooting time. Eventually, she was able to shoot different spots on a man size target at five feet.

The last details involved making plans on how to attack the kidnappers knowing they would have six hostages to hide behind. Bryce said, "Uncle Joe, after they take Allie, you leave them and go get the buckboard loaded with a 6X6-inch 8-foot beam. We'll use the ram to bust open the door. This all depended on Red being able to locate the hideout. It also depended on Bryce being able to follow Red, and Uncle Joe to follow Bryce. Once inside, Bryce knew that his fast draw and speed shooting would be the thing that would save the hostages and especially his wife.

The time came, Allie was bound up, gagged, and shown how to act drugged. Uncle Joe arrived at the meeting time and place. The same man was pleased at the specimen and gave Joe the $200. Joe bolted away as Allie was tied to the bottom of the buckboard and a tarp was thrown over her. The kidnapper took off at a very slow trot, which was the accepted fast speed in town. Red and his followers had no trouble staying on the buckboard, and to everyone's surprise, it made its way to an abandoned warehouse on the edge of town.

Watching from afar, Allie was dragged out of the buckboard, her hands were untied. and mouth ungagged. After unlocking the front door, she was pushed in and the door locked. The Trio stopped a block away from the warehouse, all three men grabbed the beam and ran to the warehouse, they never changed their pace and rammed the beam at the estimated lock site. The door exploded with a violent and loud crash as the door came apart.

Bryce rushed in as he saw, in slow motion, three men who were lifting their pistols to a hostage. Bryce went into action before Uncle Joe and Red had even crossed the threshold. A triple Bru...p. up.pup was heard as three outlaws crumpled to the floor with a hole between their eyes. Some of the ladies were covered with brain, bone, hair, and blood but all were alive and unhurt.

Meanwhile, Allie was situated at Bryce's back, and he had not yet seen her. Little did he know that the fourth outlaw had a gun at Allie's neck. Suddenly, the outlaw moved his pistol and pointed it a Bryce's back. She saw the outlaw apply his thumb to the hammer to pull the hammer back. Allie had moments to respond. She shoved her right hand in her reticule, pulled the fake bottom up, grabbed her pistol and pulled the trigger as she pointed the reticule at the outlaw's feet. The gunshot blew out the wood reticule base which smacked in the outlaw's crotch, but the bullet hit the top of his foot. The outlaw collapsed to the floor, his pistol went off as it hit the floor, and Allie felt a burn to her right thigh. Like a pouncing cat on a mouse, Bryce was at Allie's side trying to decide where all the blood was coming from. Allie finally said, it's just a superficial cut. So, don't tear off my dress, this is not the time and place, just to bandage it, heh."

Reality to the situation finally set in as they saw the outlaw holding his crotch with one hand and his foot with the other hand. This time, Bryce pounced on the outlaw, grabbed him by the collar, stood him up and said, "you think you're hurting now, wait till I get done with you. You're going to tell me who your ringleader is, or you won't make it to sunup alive. Now let's get you to the local jail."

Red had to almost carry this animal with a bad foot. Once he was thrown on the cell cot, Red, without warning, grabbed the outlaw's hand and after a few twists manage to break four fingers. The outlaw had his mouth open, kept looking at his mangled fingers and finally let go the delayed whoop/scream that caused Doc Newcomb to startle as he was bandaging Allie's thigh.

Doc Newcomb then entered the cell to tend to the kidnapper's injuries. The outlaw said to check his crotch first, Doc Newcomb simply added that there was nothing to do for his 'bluing jewels." He then splinted the broken fingers and cleaned out the bullet hole of boot leather pieces, and then poured carbolic acid in the hole. Uncle Joe then added, "that poor boy hasn't stopped screaming since Allie plugged him. Can you imagine his condition after Bryce gets to him."

Bryce said, "I want to know who you are working for?" "Never!" Bryce went to work. As the awl hit a black juicy molar, the outlaw acted as if lightning had hit him in the head. His body stiffened, the eyes popped out of his sockets, his bladder exploded, and every muscle started jumping like grasshoppers. When Bryce started jiggling the awl, his body went into some type of spasm where all four extremities flexed inward like a convulsion. Bryce couldn't help but notice the effect on the four watching his work. Uncle Joe was holding his chest and dancing around on one foot, Red was standing on his toes and puckering his lips, and Allie, who had never seen the awl at work, was white as a sheet, grinding her teeth and holding on to the door frame for dear life. Sheriff Marlow had his eyes closed and was holding his hands on his ears.

Bryce pulled the awl out and said, "now that was fun, wasn't it?" The outlaw seemed to be in another world, and was staring at Bryce with a total look of shock and awe. Bryce even wondered if the outlaw had died during the ordeal, but then the room's silence was broken with a delayed, "AaaRRR-EeeEE." "That's funny, I don't recognize the name, now open wide," as Bryce forced his lower jaw open and shoved the awl home. This time Bryce heard a vaguely familiar name…Heeersh—Iire. Pulling out the awl, the outlaw yelled, "Herschel Ayers, now get this animal off me."

This time, instead of the original Trio, it was the new Quad in total shock and awe. Being totally disgusted, Bryce said, "that man is like a bad penny, he just keeps coming up. I thought the threat to cut out his cojones or amputate his head would be sufficient, but now we're going to do a lot more, we're going to send him to prison for life."

Arriving at the Ayers' residence, Red had dressed in full Indian regalia with a tomahawk in hand, several feathers in his hair and a face full of red and black war paint. Red knocked and stood in the doorway. Ayers himself opened the door, and as he saw the Indian, knew he was going to die. Like a scapegoat, he was frozen, could not scream or move a muscle. Bryce stepped in front of Red, pulled back a round punch and placed it directly on Ayers' nose. Ayers went down hard, put his hands on his crotch to prevent from being castrated by this savage, but Bryce was not done. He grabbed him by the collar, lifted him off the floor, and pummeled him several times till he was on the edge of losing consciousness. Afterwards, Uncle Joe and the sheriff each grabbed a foot and literally dragged him thru the mud and horse manure to jail. There he was stripped of his clothing, as a belly gun fell out of his back, and then was left in his union suit.

The kidnapped women came to see the two men in jail, and realized that someone had provided a bit of justice with a bandaged foot, hand, and a busted face. They thanked the Quad for their bravery and left. Sheriff Marlow said he would arrange for the reward and place it in their accounts.

That night, Bryce pointed out that in normal circumstances, he would never have missed a gun at his back. Now as a family man with a business, he was losing his edge, and it was time to retire. Allie joked, "that may be the correct path, but if we were the 'Quad,' instead of the 'Trio,' we might............................but I guess not, heh!"

***

CHAPTER 11

The Cannery

The Duo worked closely with the construction company. The concrete floor was extended to 45X125 and a center ridge pole was supported by center poles. The ceiling had a high pitch with large vents at the peak that could be opened by pulling on ropes at floor level. These panels allowed steam to escape. There were also many double-hung windows throughout the walls to help with ventilation.

The building ends had large panel doors that allowed wagons to enter and run the entire shop to deliver supplies or pick up finished products. Outside, along both sides of the 125-foot building, were full length lean-tos. On one side of the shop, three walls were left open to allow coal fired ovens or cook stoves to dissipate its heat. On the other side, the lean-to was closed on all four walls, had a wood floor, access doors, shelves that would hold supplies and finished products.

All the production activity occurred against the walls of the long shop. The first station (wall A- on right as you entered) had a sink and a large quartz countertop. This is where the meat cuts were selected before cooking them. On the opposite wall (wall B- left as you came in) was an insulated and refrigerated room kept at 38 degrees by a steam powered plant activating a compressor/contraction unit similar to the one used in boxcar refers, but much smaller. The carcass halves were hung there till used.

The next station went outside to cook the selected portions. Next in line on both walls were the cooling stations for the cooked pork. There, the cuts were fitted in the tin cans and the containers filled with the chosen liquid for that cut of meat. After going into a boiling water bath, the tin can cover was crimped and hermetically sealed.

The next station would be the high pressure/ high heat canning station with the special circular steel gas stoves that fit either the commercial or magnum canner. The next station would be the cooling station. All these stations were interspersed with sinks, countertops, and doors to either the storage lean-to or the cooking lean-to. Shelves with cabinet doors were everywhere on both walls.

The last station was the labeling station and packing in boxes that contained 15 #2 cans or 8 # 5 cans or 4 # 10 cams. Then the products were brought to a waiting boxcar or stored in the north side lean-to away from the sun.

The layout was tentative and once the production started, it was clear that changes would likely be made.

It was at this point that a telegram arrived informing them that the Vaughan factory had now shipped their triple tin can order, and it would be time to send the workers for a canning course. Allie said, "yesterday Imogene and I interviewed her friend Samantha Ellsworth. She is a very dynamic 45-year-old woman. Has a captivating voice of a leader. I hired her on the spot."

Allie added, "Imogene had already shared Vaughan's book on canning and we could tell she was enthused to be involved with an innovative way of preserving food at room temperature. We are ready to go to Wichita Falls and taking the hands-on course. Of course, both new gals are in heaven, since neither has ever been on a train, stayed in big hotels or eaten in fancy restaurants. They have been sewing some new dresses to be presentable. We are all looking forward to this trip. I will make reservations and depart as soon as I get a confirmation for the three of us."

Bryce hated to let Allie and the gals leave. It was a ten-hour train ride to Wichita. Remembering his promise to never leave Allie, he decided to hire an old and retired friend of his dad. The man, Spence Jameson, was 55 years old, could handle himself in a fight and was good with a pistol. The deal was for him to be on the train to and from Wichita Falls, watch and follow the gals to work and back—with the remainder of the time as free time. Spence was paid an expense free train trip with room and board plus $150 fee for Bryce's peace of mind.

The night before the morning train, the Duo made love and then they had a talk. Bryce started, "carry your Bulldog in your shoulder reticule at all times and encourage Imogene and Samantha to always have their derringer in their pocket. As soon as you know which cut of meat you will learn to select, send me a factory telegram before you head to your hotel so I can get labels made. Anytime a new item or tool comes up, send a telegram to Websters and order it or notify me and I'll order it at Tate's Hardware. If anything changes in the factory set up, let me know right away. Otherwise I'll see you in five days. While you're gone, I will supervise the slaughter and the first shipment, by refer car of 40 crossbred hogs to Noble Meats in Dallas".

***

Bryce had hired one of the five butchers in town, who had just retired, to work whenever they were loading a refer. Plus, he had hired several homesteaders with experience butchering their own beef and pork. So when the refer arrived, he had Eustache, Alex, the retired butcher and five homesteaders who quickly adapted to the routine. The first day started at 8AM and finished at 5PM with twenty butchered barrows. The side carcass weights were over 80 pounds and would yield the bonus fees. The second day, they finished at 4PM because they were learning to all work together. The refer was on its way as soon as the last hog carcass was hung up. The engine brought it to Abilene where it was switched tracks and headed to Dallas by midnight. That meant that it would be in Noble's receiving station by opening time.

The process was scheduled to be repeated. It quickly became clear that a refer had to arrive in Dallas on Wednesdays or Fridays in order to receive and unload the carcasses into their refrigerated rooms and avoiding the plant's closing on Saturday and Sundays. For now, it meant that they had to slaughter on either Monday or Wednesday.

Bryce did an inventory with Alva and decided that 40 hogs slaughtered each week would be adequate for now. But soon, they might need to temporarily slaughter hogs twice a week to cut down on an early surplus from the first generation's crossbreeding. This would require more men to work the slaughterhouse. And besides, as soon as he could find a replacement for Eustache, he would be transferred back to the barns to help Alva feed, clean and generally care for the hogs.

***

The gal's train ride was moving along nicely when they were interrupted by a smiling and talkative ladies-man. When his presence was becoming a bother, Allie politely asked him to return to his seat. The man answered, "hey little lady, maybe you're not interested, but your friends might be." "Sir, we are all very well married women and I assure you we are not interested in whatever you have in mind. Now, step back to your seat or I'm going to punch you in the nuts, and you'll spend the next hour on the floor holding your jewels and dry heaving for everyone to enjoy."

"Well, you win for now, but I'll get even."

Spence was watching from nearby, heard the conversation and decided not to intervene since the philanderer backed down. He thought, *a man like that will not stand for humiliation, it's only a matter of time before he gets his revenge. Allie is now in real danger; Bryce was right to send me along.*

Later, Imogene had to go to the privy. As she got up, the philanderer followed her and stood in line. Allie didn't like the scene and decided also to get in line. The philanderer suddenly turned around, shoved his hand under Allie's dress and started to pull down her underwear panties. Allie reacted, put her hand in her reticule, and pointed at the man's foot. Because of the passenger car's swaying, she ended up shooting the man in the big toe, literally pulverizing the boot and his big toe into shreds. The philanderer fell to the floor, screaming as if dying, as Imogene stuck her head out of the privy in total surprise.

Arriving on the scene, the conductor said, "what is going on here, Ma'am?"

"This pervert assaulted me. He put his hand under my skirt, and was grabbing my private parts, so I tried to shoot him in the foot, but I missed and took his toe off instead." "Well, good job Ma'am. Addressing the scoundrel, he said, "get up and you're going in the locked security car. We'll let Marshal Balinger take care of you in Dallas."

Arriving in Dallas, it was a one-hour layover to change trains. Marshal Balinger came over to meet the wife of the famous bounty hunter. "Nice to meet the lady who retired Bryce. Now if you file a complaint of sexual assault, he gets 30 days in my jail. That also means that you have to appear in court in two days." "I can't do that; I'm going to Wichita Falls for a three-day course." "Well, in that case, I have to release him in 48 hours." "Ok, so be it, at least that absent big toe will remind him forever of his nefarious activity."

Spence again had seen the sexual attack and the shooting. He thought, *if I tell the marshal that I witnessed the entire event, then I would have to lose my anonymity and expose myself to a trial. My job is to stay close to Allie in case I am needed. So I must stay quiet.*

The second leg to Wichita Falls was uneventful. During the five hours in route, the three gals discussed Vaughan's book on canning.

It was dark when they arrived in Wichita Falls. To their surprise, Calhoun had arranged for a taxi to take them to their hotel. Registering, Imogene and Samantha took one room and Allie had the other. Since the restaurant closed at 10PM, they elected to leave their luggage in the room and head immediately to the restaurant for a late supper. Allie could tell that the gals were totally overwhelmed with everything, a taxi, fancy stuffed furniture, drapes, nylon sheets, wallpaper, water closets with a bathtub, hot water, waiters in suits, soft music at supper, and an unreadable menu of strange dishes.

Allie realized they did not know what to order when she said, "I'm ordering the meatloaf." "Which one is that?" "Number eleven, spiced ground sirloin with caramelized onions au jus with twice baked potatoes—which means meatloaf with over cooked onions and brown gravy with baked potatoes that have been opened and the potato is mixed with cheese and re-baked. Just like home, heh?"

The next morning, after a quick breakfast, the gals took a taxi to the Vaughan factory. After meeting with several managers, they started their first day. "Today we are going to show you how to take the cuts of meat out of a side of pork, how to fully cook and then fit them in three tin can sizes, #2, #5, and #10."

The butcher showed them the shoulder roast, tenderloin roast, back roast with bone, pork chops, pork steaks, eye of the round, how to divide the ham, and how to use the other parts to make stew meat and ground pork.

Cooking raw pork in a coal fired oven required +-30 minutes per pound at 350⁰ F. To guarantee reaching this goal, the internal ambient oven temperature could be checked with an oven thermometer. Even more accurate was a meat thermometer. Pork needed to be cooked till the internal meat temperature reached 160° F. This heat level guaranteed protection against trichinosis, roundworm, tapeworm, and meat spoiling germs— as it produced cooked meat ready for canning.

After the noon dinner in the factory cafeteria, the pork was cooked and had already cooled down. The gals were shown how to fill the different tin cans with all the cuts of meat, including ground pork. Wearing rubber gloves to minimize contamination, they got very proficient in filling the cans in an organized fashion. Once the cans were all filled, the canned meats would be left overnight in the refrigerator and processed tomorrow.

A taxi brought the gals to their hotel where they had a fine relaxing supper followed by a hot bath and some special reading prepared for tomorrow's class.

The next day the same routine. Up at dawn, perform usual ablutions, eat breakfast, taxi to the factory and day 2 of the course.

"Today, we are going to show you how to cover the canned meat with a liquid to replace the air. Then we will run them in a boiling water bath to finish removing any remnants of trapped air. Incidentally, you will need these vats used to make a boiling water bath. They were designed by Mister Vaughan and you can get them at Websters in Dallas."

"Now for the choice of liquid to expel the air and fill the can, we now recommend a gelatin for pork meat. Gelatin in a boiling state is liquid but, when at room temperature, it is a tasty solid. The exception to gelatin is ground pork where water is probably the best meat sealer. This is the gelatin recipe, and the ingredients can be found in any store."

After the boiling water vat, the full cans were placed on the counter to be sealed. The covers were applied with the crimping press. All three gals got to use the press repeatedly, and learned how to change the conversion kits for the three can sizes.

The remainder of the day was spent filling the canners. The commercial canner was used for #2 and #5 cans whereas the magnum canner was used for either #5 or #10 cams. One inch of water was added, then wire racks kept the tin cans above the water level and separated the layers of cans for the steam to come in contact with every inch of the cans. The high heat of 250° F at 15 psi. sterilized the meat. All organisms that could spoil meat were killed and the enzymes that degraded meat were inactivated.

With four canners loaded the manager said, "now watch and listen to the vent as the heat is applied under the closed canner. When the air is expelled from the canner and steam starts coming out of the vent, then it's the time to add the 15 psi. weight to the vent. Once the jiggle starts and or the dial says 15 psi, start timing your 45 minutes. We strongly recommend that you use these minute timers that go up to 90 minutes although 45 minutes is enough to sterilize the contents at 15psi. Tomorrow morning, when the cans have cooled, you can apply your label. Just remember that as the cans cool, the meat and liquid contracts as it cools and creates a vacuum which also preserves the meat. When the can is open, you'll all hear the 'whoosh' of air being sucked back in the can. That tells you that the meat was preserved and is good to eat."

At the end of their day, Allie went to the inhouse telegraph and ordered the many boiling water vats for all three can sizes and notified Mister Webster that they would pick them up in a few days on their way home. She also telegraphed Bryce with the message to order at Tate's Hardware the following things: meat thermometers, oven thermometers, two fine-tooth manual hand saws for meat and bones, potholders, and labels for 'each cut of meat.' As an example the labels should say:

SULLIVAN MEATS
CROSSBRED PORK MEAT
HAM
June 1899

At the closing of the day, the gals wondered what the instructors could teach them beyond what they already learned. When the managers were asked, they said, "tomorrow you will begin your day with a fresh supply of recently cooked cuts of meat. You will start by filling the cans with meat, fill them with liquid gelatin, put them thru a water bath, crimp the cover in place, put them thru the high pressure canner, and do it several times till you are certain of your skills and we are certain that your canned meats are sterilized, hermetically sealed and organoleptic. This will be your final exam and we'll give you your training certificate."

The gals called a taxi and were on their way home. This time, Allie spotted a man, following them on horseback, who seemed familiar. She said nothing but was suddenly startle by a masked man who jumped in front of the horse pulling the taxi. He yelled out, "this is a robbery, put your hands up or you're dead." The driver and the three gals had no choice—up went their hands. The robber took the driver's cash, took the gal's three reticules and then looked at Allie as he said, "this is payback, you bitch." In slow motion, Allie knew he was going to shoot her as she recognized him as the toeless miscreant. Allie closed her eyes, said goodbye to Bryce and heard a loud shot from afar. Opening her eyes, the outlaw's pistol had fallen to the ground, the front of his shirt was red with blood, his face mask was turning red from red foam, and like a fallen tree, simply keeled backward like a stiff in rigor mortis.

Everyone turned around and saw Spence sitting tall in the saddle with his pistol still smoking. Allie said, "don't I know you? Wait, I know who you are. You're a friend of my father-in-law, aren't you?"

"Yes Ma'am." "Are you here because of my protective husband?"

"Yes Ma'am. I wish you had not recognized me. I was supposed to remain anonymous. Now Mr. Sullivan might be upset I was found."

"You think so, maybe not. I'm alive thanks to you. That deranged animal was about to kill me. So, after clearing the shooting with the local law, please join us at our hotel's restaurant for supper at 7PM. The taxi driver will be your witness and if the lawman needs to talk to us bring him to our hotel before supper."

The ladies all enjoyed their last pre-supper hot bath and then packed for their upcoming rain ride to Abilene. Supper was a delightful event with Spence present. Everyone enjoyed their best filet mignon steak with all the fixings and desserts. Afterwards, the gals were heading upstairs to their rooms when they saw Spence follow them to their floor. To their surprise, his room was located between the gals' two rooms—also arranged by Bryce.

After Allie entered her room, she placed the shim under the door to supplement the door lock and then laid three rat traps along the window-sill—all of Bryce's ideas. The next morning, the gals met with Spence for breakfast and as they were eating heard a man yell out in obvious pain. Allie knew that a thief had tried to enter her room but had encountered some angry rat traps.

Their last day of training was the hardest day. It was one thing to know what to do, but something else doing it. It took a lot of energy, but at the end of the day, they knew they could do the job. Allie knew that several employees would be needed to handle the volume they were expecting. Imogene and Samantha would have their own production line. Imogene would have wall A, and Samantha would have wall B. Allie would spend many days training new workers. She envisioned working the cannery on a full-time basis and Bryce would have the responsibility of the slaughterhouse, providing carcasses to the cannery, carcasses to the refer boxcars, and arranging shipment to Nobel Meats of processed canned meats. Maitland would be in charge of the crops and feeding the hogs. Alva would be in charge of the barns with Eustache his foreman. Allie could see that the number of piglets turning to growing hogs would soon be a major enterprise and Alva/Eustache would soon need a helping hand.

***

The next day at 11AM, the overnight train arrived in Abilene. Waiting on the platform was Bryce, Eustache and Wayne Ellsworth. Hugs and kisses later, the three couples were on their way home. The Duo was only satisfied after two rounds of lovemaking. Afterwards, they made some fresh coffee and sat down to share their past week.

Bryce went first and reviewed the events. The hogs were being well fed with alternating feeds of chopped corn or soybeans. The gardens had been tripled in size and replanted with the popular vegetables—carrots, beets, squash, pickles, potatoes, turnip, string beans, pumpkins. A separate 30-acre patch was being planted with sugar beets.

A second vegetable grinder was in place, and most important, the crop boys were now in charge of the vegetable gardens, planting, cultivating, harvesting the ready vegetables, and grinding/feeding them to the animals. That meant that Alva and Eustache were free to care for the hogs from birth to market.

Bryce then covered how the slaughter and shipping of hog carcasses was going, and reviewed the finishing touches to the cannery.

Allie went over every detail of their three-day instruction. Afterwards, she said, "we are ready to start canning. So what is our next step."

Bryce looked at her and said, "we need more workers. Alva and Eustache need three workers, Alec needs at least four more men, and you'll need at least four gals to start with. So, I need to find a dozen workers plus a cook and a man to serve your factory to do the heavy work. So, tomorrow morning, I'll talk to the men at breakfast and ask if any of the young men's mothers or the married men's wives would like to work in the cannery. For interested ladies, you'll be conducting interviews all day tomorrow. Then I'm going to town to find 10-12 men."

Bryce arrived in the business district and saw several men in Union uniforms sitting on the boardwalk next to the 1ˢᵗ National Bank. Bryce stepped up to them and addressed a soldier with sergeants' stripes. "What are you men doing here instead of the nearby saloons?'

"We are not heavy drinkers and we're desperately looking for work with a wage. Sitting here exposes us to potential employers."

"How come you're still in uniforms?"

"We were career men, but now that the Indians are subdued, we got mustered out two weeks ago."

"Well sarge!" "Bill Caruthers." "I'm looking for full time workers, can you collect me 20 or more men and meet at the town hall in two hours?" "Of course, heck I know that many that mustered out with me—if you don't mind ex-soldiers." "Veterans are fine with me."

For two hours, Bryce checked on his orders at Tate's Hardware and the printing shop. He then stopped at Wainwrights and arranged to have the small bunkhouse at the farm expanded, to include a private room and office for Alva, several more bunks and a cook shack.

Walking in the town hall, Bryce counted over two dozen men—all in Union uniforms. Bryce welcomed them and started. "I'm looking for a dozen men and a cook. First of all, as I describe the job, if this is something not to your liking, it's best to leave now. This is not cow poking on a cattle ranch"—three men got up and left. "There is no drinking on the job till the day is done"—two more got up and left. "I need men to either work in a hog slaughterhouse or take care of hogs in three modern barns"—five men got up and left. Bryce counted and saw 14 heads still present.

"I need a cook." Fingers were pointing when Bill said "Sam was one of the company cooks." Sam got up and said, "I'd be happy to take the job."

"Rarely, you may have to work on weekends"— one man got up and left.

Bryce then said, "looks like the rest of you are hired. Now to discuss pay and benefits. First of all, you all go to Albright's Mercantile and pick up, at no cost, three pairs of work britches, three shirts, five pairs of socks, two pairs of gloves, five sets of union suits, a pair of leather work boots, and a pair of rubber barn boots or galoshes. Keep your military hats. The pay includes room and board seven days a week. The pay is $1.50 a day Monday thru Friday. After 30 days, if you work out and stay with us, your pay goes up to $2 a day which starts at 8AM to 5PM, five days a week, with a half hour off for the noon dinner. If you work Saturday or Sunday, your pay is time and a half. If you work on Sunday, you get paid time to go to church. Your horses can stay in the pasture or we'll stable your horses in the barn if necessary. If you get hurt on the job, we'll pay your medical bills. Any questions?"

"When do we start?"

"Tomorrow, but you'll have to camp out for a week till the bunkhouse is expanded and a cook shack is added. Sam, you can start today so you can direct how you want the cook shack designed, and you can start shopping for vittles which is part of your job. If you need an assistant, we'll get you one since you'll be feeding workers three times a day, from the barn, slaughterhouse and cannery." "Approximately, how many heads is that to feed per meal?" "Could be as many as 30." "Yep, I'll need some help, how about a worker's wife?" "Good idea, we'll work on that."

The next day Carl Wainwright was on the job, Sam arrived with his belongings and moved in the bunkhouse. Allie started interviews early and by eleven came to see Bryce. "Eight local women who either have sons or a husband working here have applied. I like them all, what do I do?"

"The cook needs a helper, find one who will do that job and hire the others for the cannery. Until we get our first shipment of tin cans, you can start training them along with Imogene and Samantha's help."

"What do I offer them for pay and benefits"

"Same as we are offering the other workers. EXCEPT no housing, we don't want women in the bunkhouse. As a complimentary gesture, the wrangler will corral their horses in the morning and at night will saddle or harness their horses. But no housing."

Allie look puzzled and finally spoke, "are you sure you want to offer women equal pay. Aren't the men going to object."

"When it comes to money, conjugal supremacy becomes hogwash. Boy, that was a pun wasn't it? Anyways, it is happening over in the big cities, where women are making equal pay, especially in the sewing and cloth mills. Besides, that way, we'll never have trouble hiring help. We need to treat employees as people who work for us and make us money, they are not to be treated as a commodity that follows old ways."

"Speaking of being socially correct, I think it's time to take my allegory off barn #1's entrance." "I'm not following you, what is an allegory?" "It's that pictorial display of a sow having piglets, that grow into bigger hogs till they get to be huge, then are turned into half carcasses and finally into a ham. I did it when I was 13, and dad liked it and put it on the barn where it stands today." "Oh, maybe you're right!"

Things were rolling along well, the buildings were done, the employees were all trained, the sows were dropping litters like clockwork, the crops were being harvested while others were growing, the shipments to Nobel Meats were on a fixed schedule and the farm was still processing 40 hogs per week. Finally, the first shipment of standard tin cans arrived. Now the status of sending half carcasses to Noble Meats would change. The new priority would be to ship canned pork meats, and only the extra carcasses would be sent as such.

It was with time on their hands that Bryce knew he had to talk to Alva. One day he went to the barn and found Alva in the #3 barn's office. "Well Alva, how do you like your own room and office in the bunkhouse extension?" "Great, but why the special treatment. I'm just an employee?"

"Alva, I know better! You are someone special."

"What do you mean?"

"The first time we met, I immediately saw the resemblance. Then when I saw the tear on your cheek as you handed Allie to me in church, I knew that my suspicions were correct. I know you are Allie's biological father."

"Oh my God, what do we do now. I've spent the past 19 years hiding the truth and now.....how do I face it?"

"Alva, I think I know you a bit, so there has to be more to the story than what it appears. Tell me the whole story, please!"

"Well alright, you're right, there is a lot more. This was all Mister Adkins idea. You see, Doc Newcomb told Allie's father that he was sterile and would never father any children. One day, he came to see me and after explaining the sterility issue, he begged me to impregnate his wife. I refused but after a month of pushing me and convincing me that, this would be the greatest gift, he could give Missus Adkins, I finally consented. When Doc Newcomb told the Missus that she was fertile, Mister Adkins left to go on business for four days. During that time, I visited the consenting Missus four times. After the last time, she thanked me and made it very clear that if she became pregnant, only her husband and Doc Newcomb would ever know. To make the long story short, two months later, Doc Newcomb announced the Missus was pregnant. Mister Adkins came to tell me, and I knew he would want me to leave the farm. Instead, the man hugged me, started to cry and told me that I would have a job for life on the farm, and could enjoy seeing their child grow up. I was totally shocked at the possibility, but after a short time, I realized that I wanted to stay and see my offspring grow up. I hope you don't find the truth vulgar or upsetting?"

"Alva, that's the most uplifting story I've ever heard. Now, the only thing left is for you to tell Allie."

"WHAT, ARE YOU NUTS?"

"Alva, stop to think how Allie has treated you. This is no 'dumb broad.' I think she already knows. Why did she ask you to walk her down the aisle at her wedding. Think back on other milestones in her life, were you involved?"

Alva pondered, "no, it can't be. I didn't tell and I know Doc Newcomb didn't either. You're wrong!"

"Alva, trust me, let's go see Allie."

Stepping into the house, Bryce said, "Allie, Alva has something to discuss with you."

Allie stepped forward and without warning, kissed Alva on the cheek and said, "Alva, I know you are my biological father."

Alva started blubbering, trying to talk thru his tears and his tremulous lips. Finally got the words out, "how did you know and how long." "I suspected it since I was a teenager. It was the way you walked, talked, smiled, and those eyes like mine. But I was given the proof recently. On my father's death bed, he told me the entire story in every detail. He also asked that I take care of you forever—no matter what you needed. So, there it is, and things will continue the same between us, heh?"

Alva broke the ice by saying, "yes boss!"

Allie turned around and added, "now what about you husband, how did you know?"

"Well, uh, you see it's like this, after we have relations, you seem to really relax and then you talk in your sleep."

"Well the way you've been servicing me, you must know all my secrets by now."

"Well, certainly more than I need to know"—with a proud grin, he walked away to leave father and daughter alone for a while.

***

Days later after supper, Allie said, "the gals asked me today why we weren't canning bacon, and I couldn't answer them. Why not and what are you doing with the pork bellies." "The pork bellies need to be cured thru a multi-step process and then need to be smoked. We are not in the curing or smoking business—we are in the meat canning business! The pork bellies are wholesaled for curing and smoking to three sites: McCafferty's Meat Packing in town, Noble Meats in Dallas and our five local butchers."

"Any surplus carcasses not used in canning is sent to Noble Meats along with some pork bellies. Plus, our five local butchers still get their one full pork each week and can take as many extra pork bellies as they wish. The price they pay us is the same as Noble Meats and McCafferty's—but they pick up their own since we simply don't have the time to deliver them."

And so, after settling the distribution conundrum, the Duo now knew that the first shipment of tin cans would start the wheels in motion and Allie was ready for the challenge.

***

CHAPTER 12

Present and Future

Maitland had requested a meeting with the Duo. Sitting in the house office, he started, "my workers have now achieved a status quo. We now have 50 acres for hay, 600 acres under cultivation, and several crops planted in rotation to include corn, soybeans, barley, sorghum, oats, sugar-beets plus a forty-acre vegetable garden."

Allie added, "what does status quo mean?"

"We are at a comfortable equilibrium. At the present size of a dozen field workers and supporting staff, the size of gardens, planted acreage, and the implements we have, we can feed 900 hogs in three barns twice a day. If you want to add a fourth barn, we'll need to increase everything and everyone by 25-30%."

Bryce asked, "are we buying bagged grains for feed?"

"Yes, but the absolute minimum. We buy milk starter to supplement a large litter or a sow with inadequate milk. We also purchase a transitional feed for 'weaning' piglets, and of course, we need a 'finishing' feed high in protein, vitamins and minerals."

"Are we producing any grains?"

"Yes, one. We are producing oats as a byproduct of straw. Ironically, we can't go without bedding straw and we can use the oats as a supplement for working horses and all hogs like oats as feed."

"How much are we spending on commercial phosphate?"

"Very little, we use it only on the 50 acres that produce several crops of hay for the horses. One yearly application is manure and the 2nd and 3rd crops are supplemented with phosphate. This gives us enough hay to feed our remuda year-round."

"How are we doing in finding a supply of manure?"

"We have six manure piles under contract to include chicken, hog, horse, and even one dairy.

These are all within three miles and with the two industrial size manure spreaders, we can fertilize the fields as we go."

"Great, I'm pleased that you are at a status quo. As it is now, you can continue to feed the 900 hogs we have in three barns. If we expand further, the supporting crop enterprise will need to follow suit."

"Yes."

*****

Things changed drastically when the first supply of tin cans arrived. A partial boxcar load for the first shipment filled half of the storage lean-to. Allie then added, "we're ready to start, so have the slaughterhouse load our refrigerated room asap so we'll start cutting up the meat and start cooking."

Days later Bryce was doing some more planning for the future. A meeting with Alva was in the cards. "Alva, how many hogs are we now shipping"

"Each week we ship a refer load of 40 hogs to Noble, plus the five locally to butchers. Our projections look like we'll end up with 2300 hogs to market in the next 12 months. Now each sow is producing an average of +-18 piglets per year.

So 125 sows are just barely keeping up with the required minimum, and everything will change once we start canning our own meat. The Noble deliveries will drastically drop."

Alva continued, "now we are chucker-block-full, with the 40 sows per barn, and the growing hogs don't have enough room. The veterinarian is afraid that the growing hogs will start getting sick from the congestion. I think we now need to expand each of the three barns."

"No argument with you. I'll notify Carl Wainwright today and start expanding each barn. How much do we expand?"

"Fifty feet in length with the same width."

"Done, now for the reason I came to see you. If we wanted to expand our business by 25% what would it take?"

"A fourth barn and three more full time workers."

"Agree, last question, where are we in the crossbreeding plan."

"We just added three more purebred lines for crossbreeding. Our original white Landrace and Yorkshire boars were getting too big or old for breeding and we replaced them with four purebred young hogs: a Chesterwhite sow and a boar, and two other boars—a black Berkshire and a black Spotted Gloucestershire. These three boars will add to the genetic pool and the Chesterwhite sow will help maintain the while hide line. The original red Duroc and black Hampshire are still very active breeding the original and the hybrid sows."

"How do you keep all the hybrid generations classified and documented, and prevent accidental inbreeding?"

"I don't, Allie does it with the ear tags. She has a family tree created for every generation. Her diagrams are a work of art. Check them out some time."

***

The next meeting he had was with Allie. "How are things going? "We are doing fine. I have a smart bunch of hard-working women. The only problem area is our man helper. There is too much for him to do with bringing in the supplies, helping us move the heavy canners, and transferring the finished product to the storage holding area. He's not complaining but we'll need to give him a helper, before we start loading boxcars for shipping to Noble Meats."

"Is there anything I can help you with?"

"Yes, we need to know how many cans we can put in each railroad crate."

"I'll go to the railroad yard and find out what the deal is, and I'll get back to you."

"Before I forget, I wanted to let you know that we are going thru eight half carcasses a day or that will be 20 full hogs a week. That means this will disrupt your carcasses being shipped by refer."

"Not a problem, we'll call for a refer when we need one. I strongly suspect we'll have a better profit margin with canned meats instead of shipping carcasses. By the way, what is our profit margin with shipping carcasses?"

"My 12-month projections show 2300 hogs with a $10 profit per hog—or $23,000 per year. Now with shipping canned meat, I agree that it should be higher, but time will tell."

Bryce went to the railroad yard and met with the manager.

"Welcome Mr. Sullivan, and how can I help you?"

"We are converting a big portion of our meat business from shipping refrigerated carcasses, to shipping tin cans packed with pork meat. We will still be using refers, but not as many. Now, I need to know how many tin cans we can put in a standard railroad crate."

"A standard crate is 3X3 feet and 2feet high=to 18 cubic feet but only 9 square feet of floor space. We have some larger and smaller. The size is not the issue. The weight is. Our mechanical loaders limit the weight to 300 pounds. So start with the standard crate and you can change it if necessary. Also, remember that shipping crates is not the same as shipping a full refer of carcasses. You pay by the weight and the size of crate, and you can ship one crate or as many as you want. Of course, the best deal is a full boxcar but at 9 square feet per crate, it would take 55 crates to fill a 'single layer' boxcar—not very practical."

"Got it, that means that we need one of those mechanical loaders, how much are they?" "$50 each and well worth the price." "I'll take two." "We'll include them when you call for a boxcar."

As soon as Bryce got home, he went to Allie's office in the cannery and did the computation. Speaking to himself, he said, "A #2 can holds 1lb. 4oz. So, 250 cans weigh 300 lbs. The #5 can holds 3 lbs. so that means 100 cans. The #10 can holds 6 lbs. so 50 cans hold 300 lbs. Calling Allie over he said, "each crate is limited to 300 lbs. So that means, 250 #2 cans per crate, 100 #5 cans per crate, and 50 #10 cans per crate. Plus, your helpers will have two manual lifts to handle the 300- pound crates."

"Can we mix the three cans in the same crate?" "No, the bottoms won't match, and you'll have bottoms sitting on edge tops—not good!"

Allie thought about this and finally said, "seems like a heavy load for our men to handle. I think we should cut the number of cans in half and only have our men handle 150 pounds at a time with the mechanical lifting wagons, plus with less layers of cans, that lessens the chance of crushing the bottom cans." "Huuum, I think you're right."

"Now, I have two questions. If we were to expand the business 25%, would we have to enlarge the factory?" "No, we still have room to spare, but we'd have to hire 3 new workers."

"Ok, good. The second question is the proverbial saying 'never to put all our eggs in the same basket.' With the system we now have with our canned meat and carcasses going to Noble Meats, what would happen to us if Mister Noble dropped dead, or the company went bankrupt."

Allie was somewhat taken back and finally said, "I guess like the proverbial saying goes, 'we'd be screwed blue and tattooed'—whatever that means, heh?"

"Presently Noble Meats' distribution area is the state of Texas. Don't you want to eventually go national"

"Yes, but without a doubt, right now we are prepared to send our first shipment to Noble Meats. The idea of a backup system is very appealing, but I'm too busy to help you with this. So what do you propose?"

"Well, as long as we agree, the best time to look into this is when we aren't pressured from an acute situation. I have several ideas that involve starting an account with another meat processor, or another canned meat distributor, or direct sales of our product to a large retailer. Let me work on this and we'll talk again."

That same day, he rode to town to send this telegram"

TO: Calhoun and Veronica Vaughan
Wichita Falls, Texas
FROM: Bryce Sullivan
Abilene, Texas
NEED   TO   ADD   A   SECOND
DISTRIBUTOR – STOP
CANNED   MEAT   MARKET   FRAGILE
—STOP
WHAT   DO   YOU   THINK   OF
SEARS - ROEBUCK–STOP

Bryce knew that the message went directly to Vaughan's factory and Calhoun or Veronica would respond shortly. Waiting in the telegraph office, the clacker started singing. The yellow message said:

GREAT IDEA—STOP
OLD CLASSMATE NOW HIGH VP AT SEARS—STOP

WAIT FOR MORE INFO—STOP
Signed Victoria

The next day, the telegraph messenger brought a telegram:

FROM: CALHOUN VAUGHAN
WICHITA FALLS, TEXAS
TO: BRYCE SULLIVAN
ABILENE, TEXAS
OLD CLASSMATE ALSO OLD BOYFRIEND-HAH'—STOP
SEARS REP WILL ARRIVE WITHIN 30 DAYS—STOP
TO SEE OPERATION AND TASTE PRODUCT—STOP
PS OLD BOYFRIEND STILL HOPEFUL-HAH HAH--STOP

***

Over the next weeks, things reached an equilibrium that matched Maitland's interpretation of the status quo. Bryce's expansion ideas were put on the back burner, but not far from the fire if the need arose. Bryce was observing all four locations, the barns, the slaughterhouse, the cannery, and the crop farm for signs of inefficiency and waste of time and money. He managed to find a few errors, but with good managers in each section, there was little to correct.

Yet, the biggest deficiency was keeping up with supplies and replacement parts. As an example, one day he found the crop farm was at a full stop. All the workers were weeding in the garden. Apparently, no one had thought of getting oil and grease and Maitland wouldn't let any of the implements out of the shed till a worker arrived with the supplies. Other examples, a broken water valve in one barn, and the workers had to haul water by the bucket. The slaughterhouse was on hold since no one had picked up the barrels for the offal. The one that frosted Bryce is when the farm ran out of coal because no one ordered it when the bin was empty—of course, without a steam powered cooling system, the cannery's refrigerator stayed empty till coal arrived. With these examples, Bryce set up to rectify the problem.

Bryce asked Allie, "how much time are you spending making the payroll, and keeping the books?" "At least 10 hours a week, and it is all spent in the evening when we could spend more time together." "That does it, we need an accountant, a crossbreeding planner, and a procurement person to maintain an inventory and order supplies."

The next day, Bryce was at the local newspaper to place an ad. The editor looked at the written ad and read it to verify Bryce's unique penmanship. He read, "Wanted, college trained accountant to do 30 employee payroll, handle debits, credits and accounts receivable, maintain inventory of supplies and parts in three buildings(barns, slaughterhouse and cannery) document each generation of cross bred hogs by family tree and procure supplies as needed."

The editor looked at Bryce and said, "Mister Sullivan, do you know my brother-in-law Bert Craymore, he's the head teller at the 1st National Bank. He needs to change jobs since he is not earning a livable wage with a wife and two kids. Instead of placing the ad, would you take this ad and show it to Bert at the bank, and see what he says. He is a reliable and trustworthy individual, and you would do well by him."

Bryce saw the potential, and walked straight to the bank. Bert was on break and Bryce was escorted to the breakroom. "Hello Mister Sullivan, what can I do for you?" Hello Bert, "would you read this ad I'm about to place in the newspaper." Bert read it, his eyes lit up and said, "Wow, what a real job, gosh offer me more than $40 a month and I'm your man!"

"Is that what your salary is?" "Yes sir, and I cannot support my family with that wage without benefits."

They discussed the job in detail and Bryce was certain that Bert would do well on the farm. So Bryce asked, "do you have any other work clothes?" "No." Do you have a horse to travel to work?" "No, can't afford one, or feed one on this salary." "Do your kids and your wife need new clothes?" "Sad to admit it, but yes." "Is your larder full?" "We can only afford basics by the week." "Enough. I would like you to work for us."

"This is what I can offer you. A monthly salary of $80. If you work weekends at the barns, slaughterhouse or cannery, you'll make an extra $4 a day. I will build you a one-horse barn/carriage house at your home, and include a harnessed horse and buggy to come to work, pick up supplies on your way home and to use for personal and family use."

You will be added to the business account, be able to deal with all our suppliers and creditors, and will be able to issue bank drafts in the business' name."

"When do I start?"

"Tomorrow, the bank owes you nothing, so don't work out a notice. Quit today and then go to Buster's Livery and buy yourself a good horse and buggy. Then go to Albright's Mercantile, buy yourself a western hat, work boots, gloves, work pants and shirts, new dresses for your wife, clothes, toys and candy for the kids, some well needed vittles, and pay off your credit at the store. This bank draft is your bonus for signing up with Sullivan Meats. It does come with a promise to stay with us a minimum of 18 months."

"Excuse me, but there must be a mistake, this draft is for $600."

"Bert, you need to be free of financial woes to be able to function at maximum ability. Plus, we want you to enjoy your work. Your office will be shared with mine, and I'll arrange to have a business entrance built off the front porch. See you tomorrow."

When Bryce got back on the farm, Alva presented an issue. "We are running out of straw. I've been saving our supply by only applying the straw where the hogs sleep, but now the pens are beginning to smell of urine. I think we need to buy some sawdust." "Done, send Eustache to the horse barn, we're going to visit some timber mills this afternoon."

There were three mills within hauling distance. Each mill produced 75 % rough construction lumber and 25% planed/finished boards. Because each mill only had one conveyor belt, the floors were swept and all sawdust was mixed with wood shavings, soft or hardwood, and swept into the conveyor belt. The mixed pile of sawdust, shavings, soft wood, and hard wood was stored in a rain protected elevated shed. Loading was easily done by driving under the shed and opening a panel that allowed free flowing sawdust/shavings. This mixed product was ideal for keeping hog pens dry and easy to clean. By the time Bryce left he had purchased the rights to unlimited access, and arranged a payment system by the load after depositing a $200 credit at each mill.

***

The remainder of the month ran smoothly. Every unit got into a comfortable rhythm and productivity was at its maximum. The reality was that the barns and the slaughterhouse were there to provide the 25 hogs now needed weekly to keep the cannery at full production. The refers were used only when there was a 40-hog surplus.

One fine day, Alva found Bryce helping out in the slaughterhouse. "Bryce, this is Mister Greg Munson from Sears and Roebuck. "Well hello, we've been expecting you for a month but didn't know you were arriving today." "That is perfect, since I wanted to see your operations while in every-day use." "Fine, then let's start in the barns."

"We have three barns that hold 350 hogs each in every stage of development from breed-able stock and newborn piglets to marketable hogs. At the other end, we have the enlarged pen for growing stock heading to market. As you noticed, the air is fresh, and the pens are clean and dry." Greg's first words were, "I cannot believe that there is no stink in the barn, and how do you get pigs to poop in the same corner?" "If you offer pigs a clean pen, they will keep it as clean as humans."

Checking out the slaughterhouse, Bryce wondered if the man would even be interested in looking around. Bryce was mistaken, Greg wanted to see an entire hog from the gunshot to the sides being pushed into the cannery refrigerator. After seeing every step, Greg said, "this is a very clean operation, I'm impressed even down to the way you load the offal to the rendering plant." His last inspection was walking into the cannery refrigerator with a thermometer. He came out saying, "why did I know that I didn't need to check the temperature—a perfect 38° F."

Allie did the cannery tour, not knowing why this man was here from Illinois, also not aware he was from Sears and Roebuck. Allie was a natural. She kept the tour interesting and informative. Greg was very curious and asked many questions. Bryce couldn't believe that the two were still chatting about canning some two hours later. Finally, Bryce asked if Greg wanted to taste a sample of their canned pork products. "Yes, I would definitely appreciate that. The Duo started turning the can openers, and the first 'whoosh' startled Greg. When he was explained what it meant, he simply said, "that's a classic advertising twist."

With a sample of each meat cut open, Greg started tasting, all the Duo heard was, "uuum, delicious, fresh, so tender, tasty, wow, the best, lips smacking, I love that gelatin, and, as much as I know, I cannot believe you can keep this fresh taste for years at room temperature. Oh heck, you have a winning product. Let's make a deal."

Allie looked at the guest and finally said, "and who are you, sir?"

"I'm the approval inspector from Sears & Roebuck. I want your product and it will be in our next catalog that will be out in six weeks. Allie simply looked at Bryce and whispered, "you're a genius. again!" Sitting down to do the contract, Greg asked what they were paid for each product in each of the three can sets. Greg wrote down the amounts and guaranteed that the business office would guarantee the same price. If the product sold well, they would up the price they would pay the supplier. In any event, because the duo did not pay the meat distributor a fee, they would be making that extra 10% automatically.

Greg then ordered 2000 cans of mixed cuts and mixed can size. Before leaving he paid for the 2000 cans with a bank draft. The duo said they would start working on the order immediately. The order would be on the train in five days and be ready on their shelves way before the new catalog would be out. Greg added, "I'll hand in the ad for the grocery section as soon as I get to the factory and we'll be advertising your Sullivan Pork Meats specializing in canned crossbreed pork meat. As soon as the catalog is out, I'll personally send you your copy. Check your ad out on pages 279-285 (the canned foods section)."

***

The cannery had just shipped a large order of 500 canned meats to Noble Meats and so their holding shed was very low on canned products. The Duo decided to make an announcement at the morning breakfast meetings, "for the next four weeks, anyone who volunteered to work Saturdays or Sundays in the slaughterhouse or the cannery, they would earn $4 for a ten-hour day. The volunteers were plentiful and by four weeks, the storage lean-to held 3000 canned products ready for shipping. Plus Sears' first order had been sent on schedule. Bryce said, "we now have a respectable inventory of products that we can use if and when Sears places a second order. Plus, barn workers, field workers, and horse handlers now know they can find a job in the specialized areas of the slaughterhouse or cannery. When it's push time, everyone can help and make the extra income."

The cannery continued increasing the inventory and was hoarding its product from Noble Meats until they could establish Sears' demands. When they got to 6,000 canned units, they resumed shipping to Noble Meats and Silvio Noble finally stopped pestering them.

It was a month later that the Duo received the new catalog edition. It had a full page of Sullivan canned meats with the different products listed, the can size with the weight of the contents, and the prices. The ad clearly stated that this was crossbred pork meat that could be stored at room temperature for one year. Ten days later the duo received an emergency telegram.

ORIGINAL ORDER SELLING OUT—STOP LACK OF HOME REFRIGERATION PROMOTING SALES—STOP SEND 5,000 MIXED UNITS ASAP—STOP TELEGRAPH VOUCHER WILL COVER ORDER—STOP

The carcass and canned meat orders to Noble Meats stopped—much to Mister Noble's chagrin. The cannery was now processing six full hogs daily. To everyone's surprise, Sears sent a telegram informing the cannery that the #1 seller was ground pork (the cheapest), ham was the second (economically priced) and stew meat was the third (also economically priced. All the other cuts were equally popular.

Knowing these facts, Bryce asked Allie how they were processing ground pork. "After all the other cuts have been selected, we are cooking all the left-over meat, which has been doubly ground, to a meat temperature of 160° F. Then we add salt according to the can size and cover the ground meat with water, not gelatin like all the other cuts of meat, and put it thru the boiling water bath to rid the air out of the meat. Then we crimp the cover on and put the cans thru the 15-pound pressure canner. The result is that the fat comes to the top of the meat and a layer of water accumulates on top of the fat. I know, because we've opened cans after they've cooled."

"Before I forget what is gelatin and why do we use it with all the other cuts of meat?"

"Gelatin is a mix of broken and complete proteins extracted from collagen which are the structural proteins found in skin, bones and connective tissue of animals, mostly cows and pigs. Heated up it is liquid and when it cools it is almost solid. We use it in our canned meats because it absorbs meat juices and provides form and structure to meats that would otherwise fall apart. In ground meat, it is a problem, so we use water instead."

"Alright, now what dishes do people make with ground pork?"

"Pork patties, meatloaf, meatballs, turkey stuffing, meat pies, soup and by adding the spices they make sausage."

"BINGO—SAUSAGE. So, our customers add spices and make sausage, but not in natural casings. They make hand molded patties and cook them in the frying pan. We could make sausage in natural casings and sell them as canned sausages."

"You mean, with natural casings, we can make bangers—meaning, the natural casing can burst open if it is exposed to high heat in the frying pan. Now if the spiced meat is precooked like ground pork, it can be heated at lower heat and not burst, or go bang, heh?"

"Truth be known, I've been working on this with Alec for about a month. To be clear, a pig's small intestine can be as long as 60 feet. Now if you cut it up in four-foot sections, it is manageable. The intestine is flushed clean and then the internal mucosa lining has to removed. That has been the drawback to making natural casing sausage. Today we have a machine with rollers that break up the lining which can now be flushed out thru the water faucet, with the sections being +- 4 feet. Of course, we now have two of these machines' courtesy of Webster's in Dallas. Alec has been training his workers and we have two full barrels of intestines soaking in a super saturated brine solution for preserving the casings till we're ready to use them."

"When we are ready to use them, we place sections in warm 90° F water to soften the casing and rinse off the brine. Then by using, a wooden dowel that goes from ¼ inch at the tip to ¾ inch at the base, the natural casings are stretched to the base of the dowel. Then they are transferred to the tip of the manual grinder with an adapter for filling the natural casings. As the still warm meat enters the adapter, you choose the desired length of each link by twisting the link twice and continue filling the next link. Voila, you have sausage links that you can now place in the chosen tin can and then you process them just like any cut of meat with gelatin."

"Wow, where did you get all this information?"

"In this book, 'how to make and pressure-can link sausages!'"

"Humm, well done, I'm convinced. Where do we start"

"By creating our own original recipe using a combination of any of the following spices: Dried sage, salt, pepper, dried marjoram, brown sugar, ground cloves, thyme, rosemary and nutmeg"

"Ok, I have an idea. I have ten women and two cooks working here and each one has their favorite recipe handed over the years. I will take their family recipes, plus my mom's, and make four original recipes. I will prepare four dishes of finished cooked breakfast sausages, invite all our 28 employees for a taste test and cast one vote for their choice, to see which recipe will become our original pork breakfast sausage."

Two days later was taste day held before the noon dinner. After the last worker cast his vote, Alva was the judge who counted the votes. "The result is 23 votes for #3 and the remainder five votes were scattered about."

The next day, Bert Craymore collected a gallon of each spice and the cannery started producing bangers sealed in gelatin. As soon as they had 250 cans ready, they prepared a special crate for immediate shipping to Greg Munson at Sears. It was received in time to be included in their special new item flyers.

And so with all their canned products now in the system, the Sullivan's embarked on their first full year of production. During that timeframe, several milestones and changes occurred.

First, Mister Noble got tired of asking for deliveries by telegrams. One day he showed up unannounced and corralled the Duo in listening to him. "I know you went with Sears because you didn't want all your eggs in the Noble basket. Well, there is nothing sure about big business, even Sears can go belly up. Now my business has been serving Texas for 75 years, and when I'm gone, my sons will take over and continue our good work. Now let's say Sears dumps you next month, do you think I will take you back? Of course, I would. But that should demand some degree of business respect."

"We agree with you, but with the present demands Sears is putting on us, we can't produce more than we are now—unless we build a fourth barn and expand our workers by 30% and our equipment by the same percentage."

"Is that all it will take, here, take this $3,000 bank draft and do it. I want some crossbred carcasses and some canned pork meat."

Allie gave Bryce the silent nod and Bryce said, "take your bank draft. Give us 30 days and you'll have more crossbred pork meat than you can process or distribute."

Thanks to Bert Craymore who kept the system going at top efficiency by preventing down time. Bryce found himself the man to hold his finger in the dyke by working any job when a worker was ill. At the end of the year, Bert and Allie were working the books for days on end. They were preparing an end of year report to share with the workers at a special dinner. When Bryce was invited to see the bottom line, Allie teased him into guessing what he thought would be their profit for the year and what would be new next year.

"If all the bills are paid, the workers payroll done, a replacement and building account fully funded, our product liability insurance paid up thru Lloyds of London, it would be nice if we had a profit of $25,000 assuming we have no debt. As far as what could be new, I'm not planning anything."

"Well, you are off a bit, our absolute profit is $41,329. As far as what will be new, you're going to be a dad in six months."

Bryce's jaw fell, his eyebrows curled up, a smile came on his face as he grabbed Allie, put her across his lap and gave her a gentle spank on her bum. "That my dear, is for pulling my leg." Meanwhile, Bert was turning red when Allie said, "I'd say we did more than pulling your leg, heh." Bert said, "TMI-TMI-TMI-I think I will now take my exit."

At the yearly meeting, Bryce took the lead. "We had a good year and because our new accountant did not steal us blind, we made a profit. Actually, we made a big profit, more than any businessman deserves to make. So, Allie and I believe in the trickledown effect. When we make a profit, you all get a bonus." Whistles, guffaws, and applaud followed.

Allie continues, "to our six managers, Alva, Eustache, Maitland, Samantha, Imogene and Alec--$300 in US currency. OMG's were freely floating about the room. To our new accountant and procurer who kept honest books, often times in the late hours at home, and kept the system going, another $300. To every worker who worked every day and on weekends when we asked you to work, $200 for each and every one of you. The cookshack exploded with hollers of total disbelief.

That night, in the privacy of their bedroom, Bryce looked at Allie and said, "with you, it's been the ride of a lifetime. Finding you, falling in love, becoming intimate, marrying, building an extensive enterprise, seems nothing compared to the prospects of becoming parents. It's all a bit surreal isn't it?" Allie thought, *not quite, from the time I was a snot nose kid and you were the popular 10th grader who never knew I existed, I knew this day would come,* as she snuggled and agreed with a sly smile.

***

The End